PRAISE FOR *THE BEST WE COULD HOPE FOR*

"Writing with grace and intelligence, Kraus explores the complex intersection of memory and loyalty in a sweeping story about a broken family and the women who knit together the remains. Perfect for book clubs."

—Sarah Pekkanen, #1 *New York Times* bestselling author of *House of Glass*

"From a beloved writer comes a unique, deeply moving story told with heart, depth, and humor about the women we are, the women we come from, and the way we heal."

—Rebecca Serle, *New York Times* bestselling author of *In Five Years* and *Expiration Dates*

"So heartbreaking and so good I couldn't stop reading—even when I needed to catch a train or make dinner. Like Ann Patchett, Kraus gets at the heart of how people can disconnect from their truest selves, and how, if they're lucky, they can find their way back."

—Caroline Leavitt, *New York Times* bestselling author of *Pictures of You* and *Days of Wonder*

"For anyone who grew up with *Kramer vs. Kramer* and MTV, Kraus perfectly captures the ache and stretch of adolescence, the grief and rage of middle age, and the loss and doubt that form the drumbeat beneath it all. Consistently surprising in all the best ways, this book is a beacon!"

—Catherine Newman, author of *We All Want Impossible Things* and *Sandwich*

The Best
We Could
Hope For

The Best We Could Hope For

A Novel

Nicola Kraus

Little
a

Published by Little A, New York

www.apub.com

Amazon, the Amazon logo, and Little A are trademarks of Amazon.com, Inc., or its affiliates.

ISBN-13: 9781662522642 (hardcover)
ISBN-13: 9781662522659 (paperback)
ISBN-13: 9781662522635 (digital)

Cover images: © Tom Kelley Archive / Getty; © pics five / Shutterstock

Printed in the United States of America

First edition

For Emma, always

Vivid memories produce widespread activation in the brain . . . a pattern that is virtually identical whether the "memory" is based on experience or not. There is, it seems, no mechanism in the mind or the brain for ensuring the truth . . . of our recollections.

—*Oliver Sacks*

The Celtic Christians believed that there were mystical spaces, called "thin places," where the veil between the holy and the human is traversed. A place in which the physical and spiritual worlds are knit together, and if we are so attuned, we can transcend the ordinary for a glimpse of the infinite.

—*Jean-Paul Bédard*

PROLOGUE

In my life—in my allotted time—I bought, used, organized all the prosaic things: food processors, foil, thread, wood polish, baking soda—and yards of wrapping paper. I was also lucky enough to engage with the extraordinary, saw Tuscan sunsets and the Mona Lisa and, frankly, yes, it was a bit . . . small. Not like The Winged Victory. I loved that statue. The impossible wings. A woman in flight. Every visit my breath caught as it rounded into view—for whatever that's worth—

What is it worth?

I did all the pedestrian things, the expected things. I dined out and joined clubs and bought sweaters—bought one, in fact, the day before. I participated. I voted and gardened and tried to stay abreast. I raised people, I tipped people, I loved people. And yet—yet—none of it staved it off.

It's just so . . . circumscribed. We pick things, and they become the things we picked. A moment's impulse, or a decision that must be made, a group of men, always men, standing around, waiting, with barely concealed impatience, for you to select a grout color or sign a name to the birth certificate, to point at one thing or another, and then one day you discover you had a vegetable-tiled kitchen for over twenty years. You were that person. And you'll never know what any other option might have felt like—who you might have been. Maybe an Alpine pioneer—maybe a businesswoman—maybe someone who picked up the phone and said, what? "I'm sorry—I love you—I miss you—"

But you didn't. That isn't what you chose.

And now my daughter is sitting with all my choices, and she has no idea what to do with them. How many beige cardigans did one woman need, *she thinks.* And who *was* this woman? *She cleans and sorts and tries to make sense of it all—and other times she sits on the floor of my room and she cannot move.*

She cannot move.

If I had not—if he had not—if she had not—but I did and he did and she did—and our parents did—and their parents did—back and back to the first drought, the first failed crop, the first spike of rage taken out on someone smaller, weaker, more vulnerable nearby who learns a new option—a new choice. And so, it goes. She cannot move.

But she will.

She will peel back the coverlet and empty the drawers and sift the jewelry—she will make the calls and find the Realtor and disperse my choices, all the while asking why, why, why—*and I will be revealed to be everywhere and nowhere.*

I was not supposed to be here.

PART I

1

December 1943
Cherry Hill, Maryland

Y ou're fine." Margaret snaps the words at her daughter in the cold, still air. Air pregnant with snow. "Please stand up." Even at four years old, Jayne knows as she collects herself from the frozen ground, lip quivering, that the *please* is not for her benefit. It's a guard against the ladies gathered, the ones tacking red and green bunting to the fronts of their display tables, the ones who will judge her fuss. Who will judge her mother. "Honestly, those boys," Margaret says with studied polite exasperation, also for effect. As though the boys in question, who just ran through the holiday bazaar knocking over chairs, spilling toolboxes, stealing Linzer cookies, and upending their half sister were not, in fact, her own.

The women give polite smiles in return, even though Jayne can tell that they think the Linden boys, twelve and thirteen already, ought to know better, ought to have been taught better. Jayne watches her mother turn away, tuck her boiled-wool cape a little closer around her. In the safekeeping of their three-story home, as she knits in the evenings, Margaret is always talking about their judgment, the townsfolk. That's what she calls them: *the townsfolk.* As though she hadn't grown up nestled under their chins, the soot from their bakery oven under her nails.

Jayne looks down at the broken angel in her hand and hiccups a small sob. She spent so many hours on it—wanting to *contribute*, as her mother exhorted. And now it's in pieces.

"There, there," Margaret says brusquely, wiping her calloused fingers roughly across Jayne's cheek to dry her tears. She takes the severed paper wings and crushed pipe-cleaner halo and shoves the whole mess in her pocket. "Where's your sister?"

Jayne extends a mittened hand from under her velvet cuff in the direction of the fir tree erected at the square's center. They catch sight of little Bunny watching the older children hang strings of popcorn. The children whose coats do not have velvet cuffs.

"Keep an eye on her," Margaret instructs. "I have a lot of work to do."

Jayne knows that, as Joseph Linden's wife and therefore head of the Ladies Auxiliary, her mother always has a lot of work to do. The young mothers whose husbands are overseas need extras, as she calls them. She coordinates the donation of outgrown shoes, organizes the days of vegetable canning, the distribution. She's not a war widow herself, but after losing her first husband in a roofing accident, she understands being left in the lurch.

Margaret returns to the unsolicited work of straightening another woman's holly-berry tablecloth, repositioning a tower of fruitcakes. "There." She moves on to a table of jams manned by two young widows all in black. At home Jayne has watched her mutter, sewing needle momentarily clamped between her teeth, *Oh, to have been one of them when the boys were small—to have had commiseration and compassion, a pension, an actual pension.* Jayne can hear Margaret clear the jealousy from her throat. "Jaynie, *now.*"

Jayne nods solemnly and walks toward her sister, understanding that there is no justice forthcoming. That her half brothers, already significantly taller and broader than her father even in the special shoe that levels his gait, can wreak whatever havoc they like. Her wrist smarting, she weaves carefully between the men carrying tables, wondering if she will still be allowed a ginger cookie later, now that her contribution is no more than trash, now that there is nothing to reward.

She approaches the spot where they will gather after the fair to sing carols and Father Houlihan will lead the service and they will have to *behave*. Michael and Luke have already been exempted.

"Bunny," Jayne calls, and her little sister turns. The two-year-old has something in her mouth, her rosy left cheek swollen, drool bubbling over her bottom lip.

"Bunny, what do you have?" Jayne demands.

Bunny's green eyes widen, and she tries to purse her mouth closed, but there's no room, and she begins to laugh, exposing a giant half-masticated caramel balanced on her tongue.

Jayne is furious. "Where did you get that?"

"It's a treat." She cannot pronounce her *r*'s yet. It comes out as *tweet*. "That's not fair."

Giggles shaking her, Bunny struggles to hold on to the candy, finally spitting it into her mitten like a torpedo. Bunny raises the candy back to her mouth, bites off half, and then holds out the other fuzz-speckled half to her sister.

"I don't want that," Jayne rebuffs, tears of frustration welling. "I want my own."

Bunny shrugs and pops the rest in her distended cheeks, now evenly chipmunked on each side, stretching out her dimples.

"Bunny, you tell me *right now. Who* gave that to you?"

But Bunny just shakes her head, pin curls wobbling before she says solemnly in her small voice, "Jaynie, it's a secret."

2

September 1957
Cambridge, Massachusetts

After years of lobbying to be sent away to school, for her father to make the investment, the first weeks at Radcliffe are exhilarating. Even as Jayne tries to find where she belongs. Coming from rural Maryland, she lacks the vernacular of the girls from the elite finishing schools—she's never been to Europe, never done a "crossing," her mother does not make "shopping trips to the city." Her clothes don't have department store tags because Margaret makes most of them on her Swing-Needle Singer Automatic.

Yet Jayne still finds herself invited, included, asked along—to the library, the ice-cream shop, the dining hall. And when asked where she's from, what her father does, she finds she can choose. She can paint a picture where perhaps this man, who does own much of what is now a burgeoning suburb of Baltimore, stands tall beneath a fedora, a handsome face in shadow. Perhaps her mother eagerly awaits his return in the evening, cocktail in hand, and perhaps they all gather in the sitting room and play cards.

She references Michael and Luke, her significantly older brothers, as though suggesting these strapping men have good jobs, might visit one weekend, might want to date a girl on her hall. When in fact they moved out west years ago after one too many run-ins with the local law enforcement. She isn't lying so much as simply nodding along with the other girls' childhoods as if she understands.

Then, one afternoon in late October, when the air has turned blustery and the red bricks are mirrored in the leaves, there's a call for her.

"What do you mean she's *gone*?" Jayne asks her mother, gripping the residence hall's communal phone, which smells permanently of cigarettes and Pond's.

Margaret relays the facts briskly. "When I went to wake her for school last Wednesday, she wasn't there."

"Last Wednesday! Have you called the police?" Jayne's knees feel rubbery.

"There's no need. She left, Jaynie. Left of her own accord. And either she will come to her senses and return or she won't."

An uncomfortable heat fills Jayne's face. Is fainting even permissible? She clutches the receiver with both hands like it can keep her upright; rumors, her mother has told her often enough, aren't a dress or a hairdo that can be altered later to flatter. They're a scar on your face that there's no living down.

"I don't understand, Mama. Gone *where*? And *why*? She's only sixteen—why on earth would she leave?"

But Margaret Linden has no satisfactory answer. Not then, not ever.

~

As the months wear on, having been given strict instructions—"We'll manage."—Jayne finds she somehow does. Manages to cry quietly, and only in the shower behind the thick oak door. Manages to make her face and assemble her outfits and listen—just enough—to acquit herself in class and make friends and double date. She even manages to go home, to tolerate the place where Bunny isn't, and her parents, who won't discuss it.

"Jayne," her mother castigates her upon finding her forlorn at the sight of Bunny's Christmas stocking languishing at the bottom of a carton. "Why do you insist on carrying on?"

"Because it's my fault," she tries to explain.

"What is?"

Jayne looks at her mother's face, settled into a lattice of scorn, vertical lines between brows, thin mouth compressed permanently into an angry horizontal. And now she's unable to enumerate why exactly. "All of it."

Margaret scoffs, moves on with looking for her bifocals. The ones that don't just enable needlepoint one minute and a sharp eye on Jayne's posture the next, but how Margaret Linden views the world. Looking up and out to the surrounding hills and the town beyond, she sees clearly, distinguishing briskly between those who truly deserve aid from the Auxiliary and those who just made poor choices. But looking down into the folds of their home, her perspicacity dissipates.

"Your sister made a choice, Jaynie. Don't ever forget that."

~

At the beginning of Jayne's sophomore year, the first letter arrives, postmarked Georgia. It waits, sheepishly, on the marble table with everyone else's pedestrian mail, dime-store cards from girlfriends at other Seven Sisters schools, telegrams from beaux seeking pick-up confirmations, and brown-paper-wrapped packages from home containing reports of younger siblings who are where they're supposed to be, doing what they're supposed to do.

And sitting among those bright and boisterous voices is Bunny.

> Jaynie, I'm so sorry,
> I know you must hate me. It's impossible to put any of this into words so it could make sense to you. It was bearable while you were home—

Bearable? She'd never been hit like their brothers. Or grilled at dinner as though applying for a job. Bunny had always been their father's blatant favorite. She wasn't even forced to wear Jayne's hand-me-downs—their father wouldn't hear of it. She had new ice skates and pearl earrings—*real* pearls. Yes, their mother was . . . exacting, but that was surely *bearable.*

> But those last few weeks there alone with them.
> I just couldn't. I needed to find a place where I could
> just be.

Jayne doesn't understand. Everyone hates being a teenager. Everyone can't wait to get away. Why couldn't Bunny have just been patient?

Bunny goes on to explain that, at first, she thought she could follow Luke and Michael out west, but once she found their unopened letters in Margaret's hope chest, and looked up Jackson Hole on the map, she abandoned that prospect. Then she remembered a man she'd met at the Horned Owl who made produce runs from farms in the south to their suburb of Baltimore—

Jayne pauses at this, lowering the pages to her wool skirt. *The Horned Owl?* That Bunny had spent her summer evenings not on the Broadkill boardwalk with the other kids but at a bar is a surprise to Jayne. But she had been on the boardwalk. And Bunny had not. Where had Jayne thought she was? Why hadn't she paid more attention?

> So, I'm in Georgia, on a farm here run by two
> couples along Christian principles, as they see them,
> meaning blacks and whites working beside each other
> and paid equally. It's really a marvelous thing, Jaynie.
> We've attracted a little attention in town, but nothing
> to worry about. I hope you're well and enjoying school
> and that you can find a way to understand that I had

to go. I am sending you my love. Please write and tell me how you are.

Yours, Bunny

The paper in her hands notifies Jayne that she's trembling, flooded with relief and rage in equal measure. The selfishness. The raw, audacious selfishness. *Did she not think we'd be worried?*

Clutching the envelope, she trips down the stairs to the phone, the one that no longer smells like anything now that Jayne is also cloaked in Pall Malls and Jean Naté. *Bunny has an address.* This can all be over.

"Connecting you now," the operator says.

"Hello?" Margaret's voice comes down the line, pushing itself through cables and wires with its plump truculence.

"It's me, Jaynie."

"Jaynie, is everything all right?" Jayne can picture her mother's look of alarm at the cost of the call.

"Yes. I—I've had a letter," Jayne says urgently, "from Bunny."

There's a pause. Jayne waits, heart drumming, glancing up and down the worn Oriental carpet, the numerous nicks in the baseboard.

"Barbara is dead, Jayne."

"No, Mama," she rushes breathlessly, "I've just had a letter. She's in Georgia!"

Another silence. Another crinkle down the line, like wax paper being carefully unwrapped, and Jayne imagines that whoever is connecting the call is eating a sandwich.

"Barbara is gone." Margaret speaks the words carefully, and Jayne pictures the ferocity of her mother's gaze. "This has been a very hard year for your father and me, and it's better if we don't all have to go through this again. I can't have her turning back up here and then running off. I trust this is the last we'll speak of this?"

"Of course," Jayne says, thinking, *What? No, wait.*

"Let me know when you've decided your Thanksgiving plans. If I need to cook for three." There is never any suggestion of their visiting.

"Okay, yes. I'll, uh, I'll let you know." As she replaces the receiver, any lingering indignation leaves abruptly, like a guest who's suddenly realized he's too drunk.

She returns to her room, with its crimson pennants hanging from a ribbon she tacked to the wall, thinking, *Penance.* Sitting at her battered desk, she takes out a sheet of stationery. And then she finds herself struggling to communicate with someone with whom she shared a room for sixteen years, their nightly baths, sometimes a single brass bed, nose to nose, their combined breath a gently souring cloud hovering between them. She knows the feel of Bunny's skin, how it changed from the pale softness of childhood to the scab-kneed, tan shell of adolescence. That when it's her time of the month, she needs to lie down with a compress until the pain passes. But she says none of this. Instead, she begs Bunny to come home, stay in touch, stay safe, all the while thinking, *I miss you, I miss you, I miss you.*

In return, long letters on tissue-thin paper arrive, defiant in their exuberance as they detail a life agrarian in its mission, wholesome in its outlook. But the manic quality of Bunny's descriptions always gives Jayne pause, and when the disillusion comes—as it inevitably does when over a thousand people choose to live together because they cannot function elsewhere, ultimately afterbirthing friction, frailty, and abuse—Jayne loses Bunny a second time.

3

January 1960
Cambridge, Massachusetts

Without question, change is underfoot. Like the news reports of the first moving sidewalk recently installed in the Dallas airport, it feels as though everyone can just stand still and a current will carry them along into the future. But while the boys are free to graduate and move to their chosen destinations, for the women there is no further schooling, no moving anywhere but home—without a husband. So Jayne observes the less academic girls on her hall, the ones who put unabashed effort into the pursuit, and tries to decipher their taxonomy of husband potential.

When boys take her out, she's been advised to listen for family names, childhoods on New York City's Upper East Side, in Main Line or Greenwich, good boarding schools, and second homes on the rocky Maine shoreline or east end of Long Island. She's to listen for job prospects and plans for graduate entrance exams. Yet, despite their guidance, she doesn't know if she wants any of that. What she does know is that her mother once worked at the bakery, knows that for a widow with two small boys, need and gratitude must have factored somewhere in the equation of her second marriage. Knows that what she doesn't want is the perceptible distance her mother's shoulders rise when her father's car pulls into the drive.

~

The weather is miserable on the night of the English department mixer, and as she shakes the snow off her duffle coat and removes her galoshes, Jayne isn't sure why she isn't home writing her paper on Brunelleschi. But before she's even off the bench, a senior is at her elbow, remembering her name, asking if he can get her a drink. Tall, strong chinned, and bound for Yale Law in the fall, he wears his confidence as comfortably as his collegiate sweater.

"Yes, thank you," she says. They cross the threadbare carpet of the department's small reception room, and he asks how her winter break was.

"Very nice," she says, reflexively touching her curls, ensuring they survived the blustery walk across campus. "My mother still chairs the annual—"

"Mine, too. Mine, too," he cuts in. "My mother got us tickets for *Little Mary Sunshine*." He rolls his eyes. "What a bore. Every year we all have to traipse to the 21 Club and then out to a show."

She smiles but doesn't know what to say, never knows what to say when confronted by a boy trying to seem sophisticated, jaded by a world she can't wait to see.

"Webb!" a deep voice booms. "You shouldn't be here."

Jayne turns to find a boy whose face is unfamiliar. It's an unusual face, a pugnacious face, a bone structure that looks like it's been broken, but why? Is it the off-kilter nose? The slightly asymmetrical cheekbones?

He pokes her escort in his barrel chest. "You still owe me a thousand words on the inauguration."

Webb hangs his head. "Rodger, this is Jayne Linden, of the Cherry Hill Lindens." Jayne flushes with embarrassment. Who on earth has ever referred to her like that? "Jayne, this is Rodger Donoghue—"

"Junior editor of the *Crimson*, howdyado?" He barely glances at her as they shake hands. "Well?"

"All right, all right!" Webb holds up his hands. "Jayne, a rain check?"

She smiles demurely. "Of course. No hard feelings."

Webb departs sideways through the crowd, and Jayne is suddenly stranded with this boy, his uncombed hair, and ink-stained fingers. The large, deep-set eyes whose eyebrows have a picket fence of scars.

"Hungry?" he asks, like she's a teammate, like she's a guy.

She nods, and he maneuvers her to some chicken-liver mousse, thoughtlessly placed by the radiator.

"Are you in the department?" he asks, smashing a gob of the brown stuff on a cracker. It breaks halfway to his mouth, smearing a trail down the front of his corduroy jacket. "Dammit."

Jayne passes him her napkin. On closer inspection this does not look like the first snack to have made contact. "That jacket needs to be washed and pressed," she says.

He doesn't look up. "Did you read about the lunch counter protest in Greensboro?" he asks, running the napkin ineffectively over the smear.

She flushes again. "Of course I did."

Now he raises his head and fixes her with a stare. "Well, a lot of people need a lot of things, and my jacket does just fine at what a jacket's supposed to do."

She knows she's been insulted—patronized, even. But she can't help it . . . she laughs.

"What's so funny?" he asks.

"I'm just so *proud* of it, is all. Can you imagine if it got up one morning and wanted to make your toast? Or drive you to the library? But no, it's doing what it's supposed to do."

Rodger smiles then. And she gets the impression that it's something he doesn't allow himself too often.

"And yes," she says, "I do follow the news, I do read your paper. And no, I am not in the English department. Art history. Which is embarrassingly useless, and I'm sure confirms everything you think about us Radcliffe girls. But did you know that Radcliffe has awarded

17

more than seven hundred and fifty PhDs so far? My roommate, Ruth, she's going to stay and get one in something called biomechanics."

"So, I should be talking to Ruth?"

"I'll go get her from the lab."

"No, don't," he says quickly. "Let's go get a grilled cheese somewhere. You like grilled cheese?" he asks as an afterthought.

They venture back out into the snow, which seems to be coming at them from all directions, and she takes his arm, though her shoes are sturdier than his, and soon it's unclear who's holding up whom.

In the warmth of Charlie's Kitchen, she relaxes into the odd and unexpected encounter with this boy, who seems happy for her company and yet utterly without agenda. "It's all theoretical to them," he says, dipping half his sandwich in ketchup. "Which is fine. I'm not some Bolshevik down-with-the-rich type who thinks you can't care about anything if you play tennis. These guys are smart, and they're connected, and if I can convince them to go in an exciting direction"—here he smiles at himself, mocking his influence—"they can change the world. But still, sometimes I have to remind them that they don't know what a gallon of milk costs because they've never bought a gallon of milk in their lives."

"One dollar," Jayne offers. "It used to be ninety-three cents, but the market just raised it."

"Cheers," he says, tapping her sandwich with his.

How has she never had a conversation remotely close to this in three years? She wants to turn her cuff inside out, show him the irregular stitching where Margaret mis-measured.

He continues eating, looking over the crust directly into her eyes, making her feel as though he might be the first person since Bunny to really see her. See her beyond what men always see—the incandescent blonde hair, round blue eyes, high cheekbones, the upturned nose that must have been her father's birthright had he not been born with such a severe and disfiguring cleft palate.

"Still," he says, finishing some internal line of thought, "you don't strike me as a scholarship girl." He reaches across the shared plate of fries and touches her hand, tilting it in the light like a geologist. "You don't work in the dining hall."

Jayne thinks for a moment, decides to answer. "My parents have a funny . . . *arrangement*, I guess is the best word for it."

He waits for her to continue, so she looks up into the glass shade overhead, searching for the words in its pattern of fruit and garlands.

"My father likes things to be . . . nice," she says at last, bringing her gaze down as she finds her footing, repeating her mother. "He's worked very, very hard for what we have, and it's important to him that we do things. Belong to things." She adds, "The things other people do and belong to. Like we have a house on the shore, even though neither of them likes the beach. But just because the other men . . . The ones from bigger banks and bigger companies, they go to Delaware in the summers, so we go to Delaware in the summers."

"And your mother?"

Jayne has never been asked about her parents before. Because everyone has always assumed that her parents are like their parents. "That's not her background. I think it all makes her uncomfortable. She doesn't play bridge. She doesn't host. She does do a lot of charity work; that's how she interacts with our town. Which is less a town and more an outer ring of Baltimore at this point." She looks squarely at him. "Honestly, it's as though they live in two different worlds, and I move between them. I'm the ambassador. I go to the grocer . . ."

"And you go to Radcliffe."

"Exactly. You?"

He shovels in the rest of his sandwich, seemingly bored by the anomaly of himself already. "Youngest of eight. Pennsylvania coal country. Dad was a grammar school teacher. Yet all my brothers ended up in the mines."

"Lucky you," she says.

"Lucky me."

He smiles that sly, sideways smile, and her focus narrows to his lips, to a tiny scar in the corner of his mouth that she suddenly wants to touch with the tip of her tongue.

"What are you going to do when you get out of this place?" he asks.

"Well, I'm torn. I've always wanted to start a Bolshevik revolution. Lock up everyone who plays tennis. But I'm also looking for museum work. While I apply to PhD programs."

They look at each other for another minute, variants of an unexpected future unwinding behind each of their eyes, before he gestures with his chin toward the window. "It's stopped. Do you want to go for a walk? There'll be snowball fights in the yard."

And Jayne, who is afraid of any kind of impact—who flinches at a flung pillow and avoids sports, unexpected movements, and loud noises—suddenly can think of nothing she'd like better.

4

During the first disorienting weeks of marriage after graduation, Jayne discovers that she loves Rodger so much it frightens her. Even before the duckling imprint of orgasm. Although it's an enormous relief, after endlessly batting away and negotiating hands in the backs of cars, trading inches of skin and access and contact and gratification like a diplomat, to be able to allow him in. And then he reaches down between her legs and touches her with the calloused tip of his index finger and rubs there until she collapses in like a soufflé and detonates out like a dandelion all at once.

While Rodger completes a very brusque orientation at his new job, she's shown three walk-ups in Morningside Heights, just steps to the Columbia campus, where Rodger will be starting his master's in the night school while working a starting position at the *Times* during the day. Each apartment has high ceilings, inlaid floors bordered by an unsettling Victorian swastika pattern, and original fireplaces, which Jayne inspects while the broker watches like a dog with a mangled squirrel in its jaws, waiting for a hearty pat on the head.

Jayne opens the 1940s stoves, just like her mother's; examines the tiny iceboxes, which smell of the lives that came before; inspects the cracked bathtubs ringed with mildew. "Could we . . . ?" Jayne starts to ask, voice rising on the last syllable.

"Yes?" the broker replies briskly, mouth compressing instantly and relegating Jayne to a new category: silly woman.

"It's just that none of these—I was picturing . . . you know. Something like nothing we have back home."

"You want a post-war," the broker says flatly.

"Yes!" Jayne agrees effusively, because it sounds right. "A post-war."

"Those are on the East Side."

"All right."

"Your husband's work and classes are on the West Side."

"Is that far?"

The broker simply exhales her opprobrium and says, "We'll start again tomorrow."

On the second day, Jayne loves everything about the apartments they see—the doormen, the elevators, the parquet floors, the new kitchens, flowing layouts, and picture windows. She feels like she's in a spread for *Life* magazine: The Home of the Future.

"I'll take it," she says of the last one, restraining herself from twirling, knowing that she's squinting, that Rodger's salary and whatever she'll be making at the New-York Historical Society won't cover this.

The woman uncrosses her arms and relaxes her face behind her cat-eye glasses. "Mrs. Donoghue, can I just say, I have been helping the wives of your husband's future classmates find apartments all summer. And the summer before this. And the summer before that. They're all on the Upper West Side. In walk-ups. They make a community. They cook each other dinner and watch each other's kids. Look, I make more if you take this place, but—don't you want to fit in?"

It's all she has to say.

Rodger signs the lease for the railroad apartment on West Eighty-Third the following morning.

~

What do they expect of that first year? The romance of struggle, of entering a world surely waiting for them? Rodger graduated standing tall on the shoulders of his own literary reputation—within the paper, the department, the university. And engaged to one of the most beautiful women on campus, no less. It was the fruition of an impossible dream. And it blunted his guard.

Before Thanksgiving even arrives, he drops out of the master's program, sick with envy of the guys from wealthy families who can afford more schooling without a paycheck. Who can get *better* before it counts.

"How was work?" Jayne asks brightly, ferrying one of her new culinary experiments to the tiny table by the window adjacent to the air shaft.

He does not look up, does not take in her expectant face, the effort she's made to put herself back together after a day at the museum, the smoothed hair, the fresh blouse. He scowls at the roast, the side salad on a separate plate.

"I don't have time for this," he says. "I have to deliver my reporting by tomorrow."

She serves him new potatoes from the green glass bowl gifted by her sorority sisters. "Something exciting?" she asks, imitating her mother as he unexpectedly imitates her father.

"No, Jayne." His fork clatters to the plate. "It is not exciting. It's about the city increasing the fines for littering."

"Well," she says, unsure how to proceed. Unsure of this newly hostile person she's talking to. "That sounds like it could affect a lot of people?"

"Jayne. Even if it wasn't a total bullshit assignment, I will turn it in, and my editor will completely rewrite it because, apparently, of all the *Crimson* editors they've ever hired, I'm the least talented."

"Oh, Rog, no, you know that's not true."

"Do I?" He jumps up and goes to the satchel left by the door, extracting drafts ringed with red wax pencil, fanning them in Jayne's face.

"You knew," she begins, scrambling as he drops hard in his chair, "you knew there would be an adjustment period, learning their style—"

"You don't understand." He brings the pages to his chest, slumping around his violated prose. "I'm just not cutting it. My family's right— who the hell do I think I am?"

She gets up and kneels so he can see her, hand on his thigh. "You are Rodger Donoghue, and you are brilliant, and you will survive whatever hazing this is."

He places a hand on her face, meets her eyes. After a moment he says, "Oh, Jayne. You need that to be true."

Then he stands, leaving the meal—and her—behind.

~

As 1962 arrives and departs and Rodger finds his footing, Jayne tries to cultivate a life in the city, inviting former classmates to lunch, accepting their invitations to dinners at those East Side starter apartments she envied, dragging Rodger along when he can leave work. She understands now what those women were carefully listening for, not so much the names of places their prospective husbands had been, but rather what those names could translate to. Like coupons at the bank, traded for a toaster or a new iron. Groton meant honeymooning in the Poconos. In-laws on Park Avenue meant an apartment with a wall oven. An offer at J.P. Morgan meant that there were always travel plans to discuss over Jell-O salad and children could be welcomed sooner.

She thinks about this more than she can admit to herself, having unwittingly made a trade and seemingly lost both ends. At school, as ring after ring appeared on classmates' hands, she thought, *What a dolt, what a stiff! She doesn't even like him!* And felt smug about being so in love, their long walks along the Charles, their rambling conversations late into the night. *Rodger is brilliant, and success will surely follow.*

Besides, the world of bartering, withholding, and hoarding things is her parents'. She doesn't want to build a life on acquisition. She wants to build it on the way he looked at her. No one had ever looked at her with such single-minded ferocity of adoration before.

Now she's unsure if she can steer them back there. She gets up early to iron his shirt for the day and prep dinner, trussing the chicken, making the brine, trying not to think how much like an infant the pink headless blob looks. When Rodger has to work late, she makes chicken salad. When he stumbles in after midnight and asks how her day was as he kicks off his shoes, she mumbles, "Good," even though she shares a desk with a man named Martin who's fond of liverwurst and her boss touches her more than is strictly appropriate. She does not burden Rodger with any of this.

In the morning she watches him walk, naked, to the bathroom, touched by his vulnerability, filled with longing for the man who over-slept, who has somewhere urgent to be that isn't there and a conversation to have with someone who isn't Jayne. How does she make herself essential again? Where is she needed? Where can she *do* something?

Kennedy is killed in Dallas, and the change they felt at school, an invisible key in the ignition of the twentieth century, rumbles history to life, picking up its pace. As public interest shifts, Rodger finally starts to get his name in the byline, picks up a readership, begins researching communism in Asia, starts work on a book.

One by one, Jayne's friends get pregnant and decamp for Connecticut and Westchester with half-hearted promises to meet for lunch, not so secretly relieved to shed their *bohemian* friend with the poorly paid husband.

And Jayne—Jayne makes a psalm as she tends and tidies, perform-ing her daily ablution of devotion to Rodger, to their life, to their tiny apartment with a bucket and soap. *This, this is where I am needed.* She watches Julia Child and practices cooking for sophisticated palates with sophisticated expectations. On the sly she reads *Cosmopolitan* to learn how to be a better lover to the only lover she's ever had. All the while taking her temperature and putting her feet up the wall after sex, waiting, *waiting* for her Real Job to begin.

Then, in October 1967, Rodger's first book is published.

～

What am I doing here? Jayne finds herself asking at least once during every cocktail reception, invitations her previously reclusive husband is now *delighted* to accept and slot into their diary around the dinner parties his colleagues, the not-churlish ones, throw him. Jayne is not unprepared. Once she realizes that no one discusses travel plans, or Johnny Carson, and that the cursory overview of Western thought she received at Radcliffe is not going to pass muster, in the long hours after work while Rodger is already furiously writing his next book, Jayne reads Schopenhauer and Chomsky and practices conversing, napkin-swaddled canapé in one hand, the other free to gesticulate.

Yet she is only ever directly asked one question. As soon as the person seated to her right or left has confirmed that she is not the author—of the paper, of the article, of the book—being discussed, or of any paper, article, or book anywhere: "Do you have children?"

When she smiles and says, "Not yet," the journalists and professors turn to their other side, their one gambit exhausted. The wives will begin to prattle on about their own, but eventually there is only so far they can take that conversation in the absence of any direct contribution from Jayne. And so, Jayne asks, "Have you read *The Pursuit of Justice*?" And then begins to perspire just slightly because she has deliberately tipped herself out of her depth.

"Rodger," she asks one night as she unclips her rhinestone earrings and watches him hang his tuxedo on the back of his desk chair—she's already swooping in with a hanger lest it get misshapen. "You've made money, right?"

He grimaces.

"I mean, with the book. Yes? And there must be an advance for the next one."

"Where is this going, Jayne?"

"Well, I thought it would be nice to be able to reciprocate everyone's hospitality. But this place is so small—"

"It works well enough." He sounds affronted.

"Of course it does. But when we have children, we'll need more space."

"Well, let's discuss it then. I'm tired." His trousers drop to the floor with a jangly thump. He retrieves them and deposits his wallet and keys on the desk. "Oh, I almost forgot," he says, picking up an envelope addressed to him, care of his publisher. "This came a few weeks ago in my fan mail." He hands it to her.

"What is it?"

"Look inside."

Jayne opens it along the top slit to find another envelope inside addressed to her from—

"Bunny!" she squeals.

"What?"

"My sister, Bunny. She must have seen your book, or one of the profiles on you, figured out how to contact me." She sniffs the airmail envelope, takes in the cluster of stamps—*Venezuela?*—and sits on the bed to devour Bunny's words, not having realized the full shape of her loneliness until that moment.

5

Jayne leans against the porch's support post in her yellow sundress, eyes on the end of the road, waiting for Rodger's Plymouth to come into view. She wishes she'd left some chores to today, something to keep her hands busy. But she's already rearranged the guest room, made up beds for the children, prepared lunch, and finished wrapping the toys she had to guess at. The street is quiet at this hour, everyone already down at the beach.

She hears the car before she sees it and feels herself lifting out of her clogs. "Bunny!" she cries, clip-clopping down the three steps to the short walkway as the car pulls up at the curb.

Bunny is up and out of the passenger seat before Rodger can turn off the ignition—and pregnant. Massively pregnant. It irrationally sucker punches Jayne, but she struggles not to let it show, wrapping her arms around her sister to the extent that she's able. Bunny smells different; of course she does. Jayne pushes herself to catch up to the idea of this grown woman, thirty-one years old, mother of—soon to be—three.

"Oh my gosh!" Jayne pulls back, tries to ape a happy surprise. "You're pregnant!"

"Not as far along as I look. I get bigger faster with each one." Her voice is different, too, of course, husky. Which matches her deeply tan skin and sun-bleached hair. She's wearing tiny denim cutoffs unbuttoned below her belly and a crocheted top that barely contains her breasts.

"Kids, come say hello!" she calls as Rodger opens the rear door and Sage and Huck, ages five and four, spill out. The echo of Bunny in Sage catches in Jayne's chest, and her nose prickles as she kneels to wrap her arms around the girl.

"Welcome to Broadkill, kids!" she says over Sage's shoulder. "How was the bus ride?"

"Long," Huck answers from behind his mother's leg, allowing Jayne a glimpse of dark-olive skin, black hair.

"We started in Oaxaca," Bunny explains, gently scooping Huck around her bare thigh to face his aunt.

Jayne is momentarily taken aback by the dark eyes and pronounced cheekbones of this tiny Aztec warrior. "Wow," she says stupidly. "That's so far."

"Yeah, well."

"I thought you were in San Miguel?"

"We had to keep moving," Bunny says, squeezing her son's tiny shoulders. "Anyway, we grabbed the bus to DC first," she explains, "which took a few days. Met up with some friends to attend the demonstration—"

"You took the children to the march?" Jayne asks.

"Yeah."

"Don't they sometimes turn violent?" She can't help herself.

"We can handle it." Bunny dismisses her firmly. "And then we got another bus to Wilmington from there." She looks up at the Victorian bathing cottage. "Wow. It is exactly as I remember." Her thigh muscles tense like she might spring backward and take off running.

"It's pretty different inside. I made slipcovers since Mama stopped coming, and replaced the pots and pans."

Bunny nods. She has to step forward.

"Come on in, kids." Jayne extends a hand to each. "I'll show you your room."

"Oh, that's okay. They usually just sleep with me."

"Well," Jayne says, nonplussed, "I bought new sheets and made the beds up, so maybe they could just try it?"

Bunny shrugs and follows slowly up the steps.

~

In the days that follow, Jayne hopes they'll spend real time together, like when they were little. Not catching crabs or making sandcastles, of course, but perhaps swinging together on the glider or walking the dunes at sunset. But the smell of marijuana blows up to Jayne's room at all hours from where Bunny smokes on the porch, claiming it eases the morning sickness that knows no temporal bounds. She allows Huck and Sage to run naked on the beach, inviting stares. And bristles when Jayne discovers Sage can't sing the alphabet, and again when Jayne doesn't understand how Huck could have gotten the measles. To Jayne it feels like Bunny is falling, and the house that summer is no more than a ledge she's landed on for a moment until momentum will continue to pull her down.

Rodger is in residence for a few weeks, enjoying the same seclusion that once attracted their father to the house back when Broadkill was Rehoboth's far quieter neighbor. Only Rodger isn't using it to avoid anyone cringing at a gnarled body lumbering down to the surf, but rather to write his third book away from the lure of lunch with his agent or a chat on Dick Cavett. Meaning, he spends his days tucked in the low-ceilinged room on the third floor that faces the ocean, the sound of his typewriter competing with the waves when the back door is open. At five o'clock he emerges, still very much inside his work, the ideas so much more present and real to him than the tray of Triscuits and cheese Jayne sets out, having already bathed Sage and Huck. They love how she gently lathers the sand from their hair and guides a small boat in between the bubbles, asking them to imagine where it's sailing.

Then Bunny rolls in from the porch, and she and Rodger drink and discuss the war. Bunny's known so many men back from combat—Sage's father, actually, when it comes to that. At least Jayne is fairly sure about that detail.

One night they build a fire on the beach, and Jayne helps the children make s'mores. Bunny lies back on a driftwood log, her white piqué shirt riding up to expose her tan expanse of stomach, like a swollen leather water pouch carried in one of the photos of Rhodesia in Rodger's office. Rodger is holding forth about something, some piece of research, some source who's now willing to go on the record, and Bunny reaches out and takes Jayne's hand. They listen to him like that, holding hands, for an hour maybe. And Jayne knows that on campuses and at protests across the country, there are girls who would give anything to be hearing Rodger Donoghue's thoughts as he has them. That she is privileged to be in his company. That she is privileged. But all she cares about is that hand. Bunny's hand. Reaching for her.

~

Four months after the bonfire, Bunny shows up in New York on a bitter November night, children and newborn in tow. Gone is her tan, the glow of her sexual self-confidence. Something tore in her abdominal wall during the delivery, and inches of skin hang loose over her waistband, unable to reattach. She's in visible pain. The children are hungry.

Jayne ushers them into the small apartment, feeds everyone scrambled eggs, makes up the pull-out couch for the children, creates a makeshift bassinet out of an emptied drawer, and takes Bunny into bed with her.

And just like that, Jayne finds space where there'd been none.

~

Bunny looks around the apartment the next morning.

"What?" Jayne asks.

"No, it's . . . nice," Bunny says tentatively, indicating the kitchen walls, which Jayne has newly painted avocado green. "I'm just surprised, that's all. I thought Rodger was a big bestselling author now."

"We just haven't had time to look for a new place," Jayne answers. In truth, the more successful Rodger has become, the less she wants to leave. This home, such as it is, is the thing Jayne has made, reglazing the bathtub herself, rescuing the table they're eating on from a stretch of sidewalk off Columbus, sanding and restaining it. The invitations, the friends, the social schedule, the holiday schedule—it's all Rodger's. This hand-sanded table, this is Jayne's. If they move into a place that reflects Rodger's new status from every surface . . . how would she not become their mother?

"Do you like the curtains?" Jayne asks, scrambling up a second batch of eggs in the heavy enamel skillet. "I found the fabric at Singer's." It has a pattern of brown branches and green birds. They're a tad uneven, but Jayne is proud of them.

"They're nice," Bunny says, and Jayne hears, *I made three people and got them from Mexico back to the Northeast with no help from anyone. But you made curtains, okay.*

"It helps block the view of the air shaft." She slides the yellow curds onto Bunny's plate, trying to figure out how to help, how to reach her.

"Has Mama been?" Bunny asks.

Jayne shakes her head, her newly long hair swishing across her shoulders. "She says she doesn't feel comfortable leaving Father with the nurse. I keep mailing her letters with train times, but she never acknowledges them. I'm sure they'd love to see you." Jayne sits down. "He's quite fragile all of a sudden—"

"He doesn't want to see me," Bunny interrupts, mouth half-full.

"He does!" Jayne enthuses, based on nothing. "I'm sure they both do. And I'm sure they'd love to meet the children." So many assurances. She's skating full force out to the center of the thawing lake now. "We can rent a car, drive down there—"

"Where's Rodger?" Bunny puts down the toast and wraps her hands around her mug. They look as if she's been parting brambles. "Do they give him sabbaticals?"

"Lebanon." Unable to stand the schism between Bunny's cocktail party questions and her eyes, which have gone a dull, scummy green, Jayne reaches across the table and holds her forearm. "Bunny, what's going on? What happened? You seemed so good this summer, so full of hope. Jamie—was that his name—"

"Jamal."

"You thought you might marry. You said he was so excited about the baby. What happened?"

Bunny opens her mouth and runs the tip of her tongue around the inside edge of her lips before replying. "I made a series of . . . miscalculations." Then tears leave her eyes before her face can even catch up. "I was wrong."

"About what?" Jayne asks gently.

"Everything." Bunny flings one of her scabbed hands in the air. "About sex and college and motherhood and money, and I just want to press a button and start everything over, do what you did. Just take the fucker's money and build a real life."

Jayne flinches. She's never thought of it like that.

"Jaynie, I don't know what to do." Bunny's tears build to sobs. "I'm so tired. I'm so incredibly tired. It wasn't supposed to be like this—we were building community. I was supposed to be creating a new family."

"Bunny, go *home*. Take the children. I'll drive you there myself. Enroll them in school, let Mrs. O'Malley watch the baby, sleep."

Bunny's wet eyes unfocus as she watches some imagined scene unspool.

"They'd be *completely* cared for," Jayne promises. "I know Father was strict."

"Strict," her sister echoes.

"The way he treated the boys, it was excessive, but those were the times."

"And Mother? He terrorized her."

"But he's really too weak now to cause any fuss, and he adored you. I bet he'd dote on the children."

Bunny looks at her sister. "Is that how you think of it? That I was *doted* on?"

"Well, you were his favorite."

Bunny pulls away.

~

The next morning the weight of Bunny on the mattress springs Jayne from sleep. She opens her eyes to find her sister dressed in one of her coats, the city's smudged gray light coming through the blinds behind her. Her face has the manic look of someone who's just found a solution—magic beans, a golden ticket, debt consolidation, some intervention that will allow survival.

"You're right," Bunny whispers. "They need a home, a base, and a break from me. And I need some time to regroup. Thank you, Jaynie. I'll call in a few days."

"What?" Jayne sits up.

"No, you sleep until Bodhi wakes. I'll call soon."

"What, no." Panic shoots for the surface. "Where are you going?"

"I have some friends in Arizona. I can stay there until I get back on my feet, get a job. Then I'll send for them. Please."

Jayne almost says, *But they need their mother.* And then she looks again at Bunny, gaunt, fragmented, hollow eyed. "But what will I tell them?"

Bunny considers this for a moment, and when she looks back at Jayne, her face is wetting. "Mommy has a boo-boo, and she needs some time to heal."

Jayne nods, unable to swallow, and Bunny takes her hand. "Jayne, you're the mom. You're the one who should have had the kids. You'll be perfect."

6

Minutes later, Jayne watches herself scoop the baby from his drawer before his bleating can wake the others. Thankfully, she bought bottles and formula the day before, thinking she could give Bunny a rest, never imagining they might be a literal lifeline. She follows the instructions on the canister and, as he drinks, inhales deeply from his fontanel. "Bodhi, Bodhi, Bodhi," she whispers his name. It's foreign to her, suiting neither of them.

She stares at his little face, wondering if he'll share any resemblance with his siblings. Will the three children grow to echo each other? Has Bunny made a strong enough imprint? Or are they marked more by the chaos of their conception? She tilts the baby up and turns him this way and that, like he's an eggplant she's about to put in her cart.

"Brian," she says decisively. And so, it begins.

~

At ten she carries the swaddled baby down Broadway to buy a pram, Sage's hand holding on to the home-sewn grosgrain trim of Jayne's coat pocket, Huck lagging a few paces behind, his face still tear streaked, his eyes red and wet and angry. And yet Jayne can feel it from each passerby, each woman pushing her grocery cart, curlers shrouded with a silk scarf, gnarled hands on the rubber-coated bar—approval. Jayne makes sense. Jayne's purpose and accomplishments are squirming in her arms.

At Albee Baby, Jayne is treated with deference as she walks among the options. At Zabar's a smiling gentleman helps her get her new pram in the door, an awkward maneuver that will take some getting used to.

When Huck says he "hates everything" on offer in the deli case, a mother trying to balance a jar of Polish pickles and push her toddler smiles at Jayne in commiseration.

Commiseration.

As they stand in line to pay, sawdust beneath their feet, heat flushes from Jayne's navel to her jaw, like the first time a boy smiled at her. Commiseration has been wholly absent from Jayne's life. So much so that she hadn't even realized how badly she desires it. As a child, complaining was forbidden; as an adolescent, buoyancy was prized; and now that she's the wife of the toast of New York's intelligentsia, grumbling would be unseemly—but suddenly, her need for help is so *obvious*, her struggle so bare. She's gotten three children fed and out the door, and—if the man who raised his hat only *knew*—she's done it all with no training, no instruction.

Brian starts to cry, snatching her back into the morning.

She scoops him from the pristine cocoon of the new pram and raises him to her collarbone.

"You have to change him," Sage informs her, tucking the end of her braid between her lips.

"How?" Jayne asks, trying to balance him on her shoulder and count the nickels and pennies.

"Didn't you bring his diapers?" The little girl looks up at her accusingly, and Jayne shakes her head, a cocktail of overwhelm and defeat splashing in her face. She thinks back to yesterday, the strips of soap-dabbed rags that Bunny swiped across his bottom.

"*Ai, ai, ai,*" he wails.

She hustles their noisy, smelly foursome out the door and into the slicing cold.

"We need to go home; we need to go shopping," Jayne says, her shoulders pivoting as she feels her body moving in two directions at once. "Pharmacy—diapers, powder. Then the supermarket—we have no milk. No juice." She sees her folly. She didn't understand the invisible egg timer, the crushing need for efficiency.

"Mama uses cloth diapers."

"Mama isn't here."

From behind them there's a loud slurp as Huck rakes his sleeve across his nose.

In a gesture familiar to mothers everywhere, Jayne tilts her head up to the sky, as though someone at the same sight line as the Macy's Thanksgiving Day Parade balloons might come to her aid.

When no answer is forthcoming, there's only the fortifying breath—the demanding inhale, the pliant exhale. "Okay, come on."

She lays Brian down in the pram, his caterwauling instantly intensified as if she'd cranked the knob on Rodger's new stereo speakers. That is, if she were allowed to touch the knobs.

At the pharmacy she twists the pram against the narrow doorway, over the raised doorjamb, sweat breaking across her brow. *"Ai, ai, ai."* Beside him she piles in diapers, a package of washcloths, cotton balls, baby shampoo, baby oil, Ammens Powder. She looks at the shelves intently, the fluorescents beating down on her, needing the right items to reveal themselves.

"Anything else?" she whispers to Sage, as though Bunny had been some sort of aficionado of consumer goods, as if they hadn't been living somewhere without running water.

Sage shakes her head, and Jayne pays.

~

Rodger finally returns three days later, his clothes smelling like a fire, rambling on about a deadline before his key is out of the lock. But even he can't fail to notice the two children asleep on the pull-out couch, the third in his bassinet.

"Where's Bunny?" he asks.

Jayne looks over from where she sits drinking at the dining table, running her hand over a blemish she'd been unable to sand out.

"Gone," Jayne whispers.

"Gone?" he asks.

And somehow, after the day she's accomplished, the landing she's stuck, she can't do what she knows she should, take him into the bedroom, assure him that it will just be for a few days, that it won't disturb his writing, that she'll sort it out, and could she possibly have a little more money in their account, they need things.

"Gone," she answers.

And he doesn't cross the room, take her in his arms, ask how she's been managing, ask if they're all right, ask even the barest questions that roll and roll and roll off his tongue when faced with anyone from war-torn anywhere.

"Do we need to discuss this?"

"They're here," she answers. "And they will be until I can figure out something better or she returns. Which could be five minutes from now, for all I know. Soon, I think."

"Okay." He picks up his bag and goes into their room to unpack, pretending to be asleep when she comes to bed and again when Brian wakes in the night.

~

Jayne quits her job at the museum, enrolls Sage in kindergarten at P.S. 84, and pleads with the nursery school in the basement of the church a few blocks away to accept Huck midyear. This gives her just a few hours each morning, while the baby naps in the pram, to figure out some new thing, parenting, as she is, three different dispositions at three different stages. Like a compromised spy, Jayne finds her salvation in adept mimicry of the other mothers. They bring apple slices to the park, so Jayne does, too. They make tuna fish sandwiches wrapped in foil? Jayne does, too. A rubber ball under the stroller? Got it. Oh—there it goes!

Each day for Jayne is an adrenalized whiplash of failure and achievement, the highs exalted—Brian burping, a validating crescent of white sputum flying down his front. Or Sage putting her head on Jayne's shoulder as she repairs Rodger's clothes at the kitchen table. While the lows leave her sobbing on a side street—a broken toy in her hands, a spilled bottle down her coat, a lost sock—all a final verdict on Jayne Donoghue.

By the spring, once it's become clear to everyone that Bunny is not coming back, Jayne prevails upon a neighbor for child minding, goes to Avis, and boards the artery of I-95 alone, as it's unpredictable what effect the actual children will have on her father. Better to prevail upon him with the *idea* of the children.

Jayne is stunned as she drives through Cherry Hill in daylight, in springtime, no holiday decorations suspended like gaudy earrings to pull the eye from a wattled neck. Houses are in need of shingling, gutters hang at precarious angles, and lawns are barren and neglected. How has she not noticed this before? How has she not seen what's happening here—to her father's main street? And even, she realizes as the Buick rounds the corner, to her father's house.

"Mrs. Donoghue, there you are!" Delia—Mrs. O'Malley—says enthusiastically as she ushers her inside. "Come in, come in. Lunch is on the table."

In the dining room Jayne takes her place at one end, awaiting her mother's arrival, her gaze running over the brass candlesticks, cloisonné plant stands, mantel figurines, the talisman of stature her father insisted on.

"Jayne," her mother says, entering the room, one hand wrapped around the head of a cane, allowing her to telegraph that she is focused on her gait, on attaining her seat. She cannot stop to hug, to greet. "How are you?" she asks as she sits and drapes her napkin across her lap. "We're just having consommé; I hope that's all right."

"Of course," Jayne says, already having anticipated stopping for something on the way back.

"Thank you for sending the holiday photo of the children. I couldn't put it out, of course, but it was nice to see what Bunny has . . . accomplished."

"She's not well, Mother."

"She made poor choices," Margaret answers, one arthritic hand on the carved armrest, the other holding the spoon. "And now she doesn't want to deal with the consequences."

"Be that as it may—"

"Where was she, even—one of those communal things? Where people go around in their altogether? It's disgraceful."

"I think she thought each of the men would marry her—" As Jayne says it, she has no idea if it's true, if her sister ever aspired to anything as bourgeoise as marriage.

"When I met your father, I did not *think* he would marry me. I had two small boys—a menial job. He married me. *Then* we had children."

"All right, yes. Maybe she wasn't focused on actual marriage, but at least she thought they'd help, share the responsibility. I don't think she expected to be here—in this situation."

"Disgraceful."

Jayne inhales and tries again, "Be that as it may, they're our family, and we need to do—things—for them."

"Half."

"Well, yes, half. But any child of hers or mine would only be half Linden."

"You know what I mean." Her mother huffs. "I am not blind. I see what color that baby is. And the middle one looks like a Mexican."

Jayne presses her palms together in her lap, her body rigid with the inhale she holds in her bones.

"And now you want to dump them here."

Jayne flinches. What has she been hoping? Not that, surely. Was she picturing them here and her here, and yet—it's like waking and realizing nothing you fought for in your dream makes sense.

"No, just help with school and whatnot. So, what do you think?"

"You'll need to talk to your father."

~

He's seated in his wheelchair by the window in the sparsely furnished room, a tartan blanket over his legs, his clothes hanging off his once-intimidating frame. Although, as she looks at him now, perhaps it had never been a question of height; perhaps it had all been a trick of sudden movements, scowling, and the well-timed smashing of a glass.

"Father," she says warmly, smiling, glissading across the room. She takes the cane-backed chair from his desk and slides it to face him, the leather uncomfortably worn and lumpy beneath her. "How are you?"

He looks at her with a gaze no less piercing for being milky with cataracts. "The same."

Jayne glances to the window, searching for inspiration, not sure what she expected, but certainly some small volley before she'd be pressed to carry the entire conversation. "How's your leg?"

He grimaces. "Pus in the bone. Doctor says they've done all they can."

She presses her arms against her thighs, flexing her elbows almost backward. "Well, this room is bright and cheery."

He rewards her observation with a grunt.

She gives up on preamble. "I've come to talk about the children."

There's a pause as she watches how, even at this age, this stage, he can congeal into himself when perceiving something is going to be asked of him.

"I know you'll understand this as a man who took in a woman with two small boys and raised them as his own because they were half hers, the person you loved."

He listens with the look of a cryptographer, seeing if he can match anything flying past him with what he's already established as his own set of facts.

"It seems they're going to be with me indefinitely, and, well, our place is so small, and Sage—well, Sage—"

"Sage?"

"She's the eldest. She's fiercely bright. Her teacher says she's one of the brightest girls she's ever taught. She's a Linden, no question. She should be at a top school in the fall. Huck has your strength of character—he's sharp and quick—and Brian is just a perfect baby." Is any of this true? "And we're all squashed on top of each other; we have no room for games or"—*wrong*—"studying at home." She observes his expression. Is any of this penetrating? "They shouldn't be punished for Bunny's foolishness. They should have the same opportunities as any Linden."

He nods.

She doesn't relax. Nodding does not mean assent from Joe Linden. That's a mistake everyone makes only once. A nod could just as easily be followed by a backhand.

Instead, Joe scoffs. "Opportunities?"

"Yes, the best that you made for yourself. That we had."

"Yes, I gave you the best," he growls, mouth thick with spittle, "because when *I* was pushed face down in the manure, no one helped me up. I went home and got my second beating—why? Because I'd let myself be beat. But you know what? My father was right. He made me strong and successful. I gave your mother's boys opportunities." His gray-green skin tinges pink. "Now Michael and Luke are playing cowboys out west. Bunny's made a dog's dinner of her life, and you—from what I understand—went to Harvard and married a commie."

She swallows, reminding herself she's going home to climb four flights of stairs with a gallon of milk, which she can still price to the penny. "Father, I'm sorry, that's awfully unfair. But I promise you I am trying to—right Bunny's wrongs, to create a next generation of Lindens who are strong and resilient and accomplished."

Again, he grunts, the blanket slipping off his lap, and Jayne leans forward to tuck it around his wasted legs, the sensation of his bones beneath her hands unsettling. He smells like camphor. "I need your help," she presses. "I need my money so I can move the children into a home big enough for them and put them in proper schools. You always said Bunny and I had a trust—"

"You don't have a trust." He looks at her or pretends to look at her now that her request is laid bare. "You were a hard child, and you're a hard woman. Just like your mother."

"But you always—"

He raises his chin, undignified white stubble growing like water vines from the tributaries of blue crosshatching his throat. "It's just an annuity on the income from the buildings. I've had to lower the rents or watch them stay empty. Last summer the best building I had downtown was set on fire. Those Negroes—if they want places to live, they're going about it awful funny. What little money is left, it's for your eventual children, assuming you're not barren. I don't know that Bunny's litter qualifies."

For a second Jayne feels a rush of rage, like the loud flame below a hot-air balloon, but then it vanishes, as it always did in the face of this man. Aloof, demanding, irascible, cruel, he's also the only person who can tell her that she's done well, that she's done enough. How has she ended up here, when even now that she's doing *so much*, none of it counts?

She stands and kisses the parchment paper of his forehead. "I have to get back. The children are with a neighbor, and I don't want them to overstay their welcome."

"Of course," he says, though he knows nothing about children or overstaying welcomes, other than the one he overstays with every breath.

She pauses at the threshold. "And I am going to call Mr. Tesh first thing on Monday; he's still your lawyer? I am going to lay out for him that you intend for me to access the annuity, or whatever it is, for the sake of your grandchildren, with his oversight—even a few hundred dollars a month will help. And that he is to follow up with you directly for confirmation."

He shudders, like the earth around a fault line portending worse to come.

"You will say yes when he calls. You will do that."

"And why will I do that?"

"Because, for some reason, Bunny left this house . . ." She struggles to find the word, to name the favoritism, even in her own mind. ". . . ill-equipped. That is *our* responsibility. I don't care what Mother and the Auxiliary say about merit and choices. *I* will do my part to raise these children to the best of my ability. And this is how you will help. This is what we can *do*."

PART II

7

You're fine," Jayne says to her daughter as she retrieves the upended tricycle from the grass. It isn't the typical hushed maternal whisper, the helicopter spray of mist over a wildfire. But it isn't quite a command, either. More like the nightly news broadcast, the voice authoritative, the tone unwavering whether the words are *ribbon-cutting ceremony* or *gunshot victim*. Linden's four-year-old eyes look up, searching, and her mother answers decisively, "You're fine."

Linden stares down at the blood pricking through the dirty skin on her knee in a grid pattern. Slowly, she raises her palms from where they brace her against the asphalt. They, too, have identical half-moons of red scratches dotted with tiny pebbles of grit along the heel. She offers them up for her mother's examination.

"Hmm. Let's see," she says, though she moves no closer, and Linden does not do what the other three would have—rush to her, wailing, seeking comfort in her narrow lap.

Parenting Linden feels so disquietingly different to Jayne. It wasn't just the unexpected pregnancy itself, so far past the point she'd even allowed herself to hope. It was grotesque at her age to find her body changing daily without her consent, without the piece she had once imagined—a man by her side in the privacy of their bathroom to admire her fecundity, to reassure her about the desirability of her darkening nipples and the dark line down her belly. Instead, she'd been alone and suddenly out of control. Vomiting into a trash can on Third Avenue. Belching during committee meetings. Exhausted just when she needed to be running in three directions for three children who had thoroughly sated her on wanting children.

More than all that, it's the daily revelation as those eyes stare up at her from a small version of Rodger's face that, though Sage, Huck, and Brian are not *technically* hers, being so much like Bunny, they feel cellularly familiar. Whereas when she looks for herself in this diminutive iteration of her husband, she is at a loss.

"Come on, stand up."

Jayne opens her pocketbook for the Bacitracin and Band-Aids she always has on hand, but she changed purses for this outing. "Drat," she mutters, aware that pedestrians are glancing over.

"Mommy?"

"Come on, Linden, let's get moving."

Now that they live on the East Side, anybody Jayne knows could be walking by, the asphalt semicircle behind the Metropolitan Museum being a well-trod path after church, one congregation pouring down from Heavenly Rest to the north, the other swimming up from Saint James's to the south.

As Linden tearfully pushes herself to standing on legs still dimpled and doughy, Jayne places the backs of her knuckles on her waist, making her look like the handled vases on display just a hundred yards to their right. She watches those passing—the women in shirtdresses and gold horse-bit belts; the men in dress slacks, cuff links in pockets—and holds them in her mind's eye against the article from that morning's *Times* about the ordering of a new trial of the FBI for crimes against the Black Panthers. She tried to get Rodger to discuss it with her; it was his colleague's article, after all. Instead, he muttered something Jayne couldn't make out as he buttered his toast behind the op-ed section, like one of those hopelessly muffled subway announcements that contains no discernible details but gets through the salient information: *Something is broken. This won't go how you planned.*

It seems to Jayne that, outside the triangle formed by the path from her apartment to the children's schools, to Mortimer's, the world is throbbing, just on the other side of an invisible divide that pens her in. Rodger can permeate it, of course. *How has that happened?* Jayne wonders. How have all the wives and husbands made seemingly identical choices that cram them into the same four walls and bring with them rent and school fees and grocery lists, and yet for the wives, those choices mark the end of choices, and for the husbands . . . well, it's different.

Linden has pulled a dandelion from the patchy grass abutting the walkway. Jayne can tell she's waiting to blow away the fuzz, waiting to be certain of her wish, and Jayne wants to scoop her in her arms and squeeze her tight, make all her wishes the very best ones.

"Would you like ice cream?" Jayne asks instead.

Linden gives a sad nod, as if she's just been offered tea cake at a funeral. It isn't the enthusiasm Jayne hoped for, but—"All right, let's go."

They take the path back behind the museum that will deposit them on Eighty-Fourth Street, just down from Baskin-Robbins, with its aggressive smell of bleached Formica and sherbet. It always makes Jayne long for the soda fountain of her childhood, the one with the tile floor in the honeycomb pattern, the boxes of chocolates stacked above their pin-curled heads, and the wonderful sounds—the syrup glugging from the dispenser, the soda sending its forceful fizz in after, the clink of the long spoon against the scalloped glass. Now Jayne stands in a line behind mothers in jeans waiting for a kid with acne and braces to grunt out a scoop. And the only one who would remember those egg creams is Bunny.

But Bunny is long gone. Perhaps out west, or Mexico again; perhaps downtown, or across town, or, really, anywhere outside of Jayne's loop.

Perhaps still getting pregnant. Although Jayne hopes not. Rescuing the first three—that was enough.

"Mommy?" The small, solemn voice.

"Yes, honey?"

"Does God have hair?"

A bark of laughter escapes her. "I don't know—I think—yes, I'm sure he has hair." *Right? In our image?* This is one of those questions Rodger's colleagues would absolutely pounce on—highball in one hand, Brie in the other. Whose image? Darwin? Monkeys? *You do know God is dead, don't you, Jayne?* And she'd have to smile, eyes slightly downcast. *You got me.*

Linden stares at her cone, expression serious. "What is it made of?"

"Spaghetti."

Linden nods like she has always suspected this to be true, and it is impossible for Jayne to imagine that she once didn't have these people in her home, tugging on her sleeve, asking her to watch a performance or look at lines of crayon on construction paper or spell a word, saying, "Knock, knock," or, "Watch me, watch me."

She does. She tries.

"Can I ride home?" Linden asks. Jayne sighs. If she says no and Linden walks, it will take forever, and she needs to make a batch of soup to drop off for Mr. Wildenstein in 3A—his own children never look in on him. "Yes, but carefully. No more spills. No more hurts. All right?"

"Okay."

"Okay."

~

As they return from their outing, Linden runs to bury her face in the terry cloth hip of her older sister, Sage. The nuances of sister and cousin have never been explained to her, Jayne's philosophy being that it's always better not to call attention to something. And Sage's philosophy being that it's always better to follow Jayne's philosophy.

Sage, arm raised to avoid spilling the milk that's also shrouding her upper lip, looks down to where Linden grips her terry cloth shorts.

"I have a hurt." The words are plaintive and muffled.

"Let's take a look," Sage says gently. The opening of her whale-patterned tank top reveals the tender skin of her armpit—and a crop of blonde hairs. Jayne is stunned—already? She's only eleven. But yes, there's the distinctive swell to Sage's nipples. How has she missed this? Jayne feels her face grow irrationally hot as she thinks of the year Bunny's blouses had to be let out again and again, faster than their mother could keep pace, and a year or more ahead of her classmates. Sweat prickles the back of her neck. "Is Rodger back?" she asks.

"Nope."

"Then I—I'm going to change." Jayne tries to hang on to her thoughts like a subway strap. "Sage, can you take the onion, celery, and carrots out of the fridge? We'll do the walnuts in a bit. And maybe— change your shirt."

Feeling abruptly short of breath, Jayne hastily retreats down the long corridor off the foyer. She's just crossing the threshold to her room when something makes her pause. She backs up on the carpet until she draws eye level with a picture of Rodger. She inhales and exhales forcefully through her nostrils like a matador has just flashed the cerise underside of his cape. Rodger's version of the *tercio de varas* looks like nailing up a framed copy of his *Life* magazine cover in the middle of the newly hung wallpaper without asking if she had plans for this wall, which she does, in fact, have. Six botanicals she found at the thrift shop are now at the framer. She looks up and down the hall. There will be no way to hide the hole.

All her muscles tense. Why? *Why?* He has his entire den for his awards and framed profiles, his applause and laurels and adulation, his fan letters, plaudits, and acclaim. The room is a navy-lacquered box of ego.

Why did he need to plunk this here? It's like . . . her shoulders tremble . . . like . . . the thought bubbles off the surface of her simmering brain . . . like he's put his balls on her face.

She spins and marches down to her room and slams the door against no one, gratified by the sound, even though she knows it isn't good for the paint. She peels off her slacks, drops her purse to the floor, and with a cry of exasperation, throws herself down on the bed, the blue coverlet still cool from running the AC the night before.

She stares at the ceiling, avoiding Rodger's vacation face smiling benevolently on her tantrum from snapshots lining shelves Jayne refuses to cede to more books—"Is this a home or a library?" Now nearing middle age, Rodger has become ruggedly handsome, a fact that irks Jayne to no end, implying, as it does, that he is useful in some way that, frankly, he is not. While covering the Sandinistas, he is not liberating anyone from jail, forming a junta, rebuilding roads—he smokes, that's it. He smokes Camels and spends too much time in the sun and wears fraying shirts, and somehow that has insinuated him, in everyone's minds, into his own stories. His author photo doesn't help, squinting into the sun above his faded flak jacket, torn earth in the background.

For a moment, Jayne allows herself to picture him as he'd been at school—awkward, earnest, eager. They'd been so grateful for each other then, for the discovery of a third option—not childhood, not school, but a shared life they could assemble together.

Now Jayne wonders, *Where has that gratitude gone?*

Her parents hadn't liked him, of course. But what store could she put in that? Jayne thinks back to fifth grade, to when the boys left and she started sleeping on the settee in the parlor, listening at sunrise for the heavy footfall of her father's special shoe on the stairs.

She'd sit up, listen, and wait. Wait to eat breakfast with him before he left for work. Not that she ate. That would have required asking him to help her in some way, would have risked being underfoot. Jayne knew he didn't like to talk in the mornings, not even *thank you*, that if Delia was awake, she'd stay safely in her room off the kitchen until she heard his Chevrolet start in the carport.

Jayne knew he preferred to stand in the quiet of the dark kitchen, boil the water, watch his egg hoisted aloft over and over by the bubbles like a winning quarterback, listen to the tap of the shell against the copper, the hiss of the flame. So she stood as still as possible, as silently as possible, so that he could be alone, and she could be alone, and they could be alone together.

In the dining room she sat across from him as the orange light moved in a rectangle up the tablecloth and watched him butter his toast. It was many months before he started talking to her and even then, not every day. Sometimes he read the late edition from the night before. Sometimes he attended to his correspondence, and she stared at the jagged scar that ran from his crushed nose through what should have been his upper lip and tried to blot out the feature from her mind, see his face without the foundering at its center—were the eyes kind? Were his cheekbones like Cary Grant's? No, and yes. Then sometimes, as he dipped a torn corner of toast into his yolk, he'd ask her a question. How's school? Did she like the new dog?

As she got older, she read the late edition the night before and ventured questions. Soon, she had him holding forth about stocks and dividends and why you must never accept anyone's first offer. He explained how, in the twenties, he started buying up the distressed businesses left by sons who never returned from the war. Sons who'd once mocked his face, his gait, the twisted leg that pulled his spine into a helix.

In turn she read her A-grade papers to him, told him about the kings and queens of England, the Tudors and the Huguenots, about Chaucer and Swift and Dickens. Eventually he started making a second egg for her and letting her have coffee.

The boys had been brash and brutish, careening around the house, rebuking all Margaret's attempts at refinement. Jayne, with her ability to sit and listen, had carved out a place for herself, safely aligned at her father's side in twenty-minute intervals. And yet Bunny was always the favorite.

"Give it back! It's *mine*!" Huck's cries from down the hall are only barely muffled by the apartment's thick walls.

"No!" Sage screams back.

"You *broke* it. *You broke it. Mom!*"

She lies still for one more moment, eyes closed, even as she can hear the tussle escalate. Her children. Her brood. Beautiful Sage. Brian, with those green eyes and the curls that spring back as she holds him under her chin. How he needs her, how sometimes he'll reach out, unaware he's even doing it, focused on his Lincoln Logs, and clutch her skirt, squeezing it tightly to reassure himself she's right there.

And even Huck, implacable Huck, who's so curious about how the world works he's dismantled the toaster, one adding machine, and Rodger's Dictaphone. He's the one who climbs into her bed at the first rumble of thunder. He's the one who sometimes whispers as he falls asleep, "I love you like a spaceship."

"*Ow! Mooooom!*"

"Coming."

Knowing she still has the carcass to simmer, she rises to finish this Sunday, impose order, pass judgment, repair a broken thing, get down the poster paper for Huck's ant-colony project, and show Sage how to candy walnuts.

She reaches for the doorknob, ready for the next round. So, fine, Rodger has his war and his politics and his activism, his status and stature, but she has the children. She will always be the woman in her circles who took in another woman's to raise as her own.

~

Half an hour later, Jayne looks down at the butcher-block breakfast table, momentarily confounded. "You said ant colonies."

"I said gen-e-ologies," Huck challenges. "The ants were for science. This is social studies. Every fourth grader does one."

"O-kay." Jayne holds her chin.

"And they put them in the hallway for Parents' Day with our self-portraits."

"And DAR certificates?"

"What?"

"Nothing. So?"

"So?" Huck parrots, flinging his thin arms wide.

At the bottom of the poster paper, Huck has drawn himself as a hollow, black-inked box, next to another black box and two circles for the girls. But now he doesn't know where to send up the lines, doesn't know how to connect his generation to Jayne's. There are exuberant pencil marks shooting off the circles and boxes in all directions, all furiously erased.

"Well?" Huck demands.

"Huck, we are going to do enough, okay? Just enough. We are going to do *our* family. You next to your siblings. Under me and Rodger, okay?"

"Okay," he answers, unconvinced. Then adds, "It's your funeral," because that's how he finishes most thoughts these days.

"What about Mom?" Sage is leaning in the doorway. This is new. Bunny is usually called Bunny. And Sage has not changed her shirt. A double provocation.

"*Bunny* will be next to me up here." Jayne gestures to the top of the page. "Sort of . . . watching over."

"That's it? Just watching over?" The second realization of the afternoon, that Sage's temperament is changing with her silhouette.

"Yes. But then," Jayne prevaricates, "we don't need to have . . . other lines . . . going off to . . . nowhere. Okay, Sage?" she finishes pointedly. "This is for homeroom—"

"Social studies."

"—not the IRS." Jayne is done. She has soup to deliver.

~

"Where's my girl?" Back from his Sunday poker game, Rodger bowls his baritone through the apartment.

"Hello." Not the girl he's referring to, Sage nonetheless greets him as she crosses the foyer with the badminton racket that she's taking to the kitchen for reasons known only to Sage. "Did you win?"

Rodger slips his wallet out of his back pocket and tosses it onto the oak dresser that holds everyone's mufflers and mittens. "Twenty-four dollars, and Davis has to do all my proofreading for a month. Where's Jayne?"

Linden comes running from the kitchen, hurling herself into her father's arms, pressing into the cigar-infused expanse of his broadcloth chest. Face breaking into a smile, he raises her up, her legs wrapping around him, feet meeting. "Daddy, I can almost touch my ankles!"

"Because you're getting huge. You are an enormous person." He buries his face in her neck. Peals of laughter.

"Mommy took me to the park."

"Oh, good."

"But I got bruis-ed."

"Let me see."

Linden shows him her scratched palms, and he kisses the scrumptious skin, slightly dusted with cocoa, then runs his mouth up her arm, landing with tickling kisses at her neck. "Where is your mother?"

"Making sugar," Linden answers as she squeals in delight.

Alert, Jayne stands in the doorway.

"Wouldn't that be amazing?" she asks. "If I was in the kitchen with stalks of sugarcane? Just candying walnuts to top the cake. Huck and Brian are playing a game, if you want to go check on them?" Jayne is always prodding him to take an interest, wondering if his paternalism is solely directed at Linden because she shares his deep-set eyes and square jaw? His resting skepticism? As an infant, he fed, burped, bathed, and changed her, even voluntarily stayed up when she got an ear infection on her first birthday. And all after the first three, whom he treated as though Jayne had adopted miniature dogs.

Rodger walks over and kisses Jayne on the temple. "I'm going to phone the bureau, see if there's anything I need to do tonight. Want to help me make calls?" he asks the little girl in his arms. Linden nods excitedly.

He carries her away now down the hall, tickling and giggling, past the room where Brian and Huck are playing Battleship, and past the violating picture Jayne does not mention.

8

June 1979
Manhattan, New York

An hour after returning home, Rodger hangs up the phone and looks at the floor by his desk, where Linden sleeps soundly, mouth open, thumb grazing her lip where it has fallen out. Jayne doesn't like her to nap anymore, but Rodger thinks she needs it. He knows how to help her fall asleep.

Resting his elbows on his blotter, he listens for a moment to the preparation of Sunday supper. Rodger always suggests they order in from the Chinese place on Second, but Jayne likes the family to sit down to a proper dinner, some relic from her childhood. Although, as far as Rodger can tell, there was never anything about her childhood Sunday suppers worth emulating.

He can hear Sage and Huck bickering as they finish their weekend assignments. And Brian, lying on the old rug in the middle of it all, taunting them both.

And then Rodger tunes in to the silence of Jayne. Perhaps, cake in the oven, she is threading a needle, fingertips holding steady by a bulb, eyes narrowed to a singular focus. He still finds her ravishingly beautiful. But he can't seem to get that sense of longing back.

He remembers junior year, inviting her to the Botanical Museum to see the glass-flowers exhibit, thousands of petals so detailed, down to the tiniest particle of pollen, it was impossible to believe they weren't real. Those uncanny facsimiles had been made in Dresden by a father and son over a sixty-year period straddling the Belle Époque and commissioned by the museum to further the botany scholars' studies. It was a popular place to take dates in the crummy winter months, followed by Brigham's for a float. And she had been as thrilled by them as his buddies had promised, weaving her arm in his as they walked around the galleries, her blonde hair competing with the glass for the light. And she was with him, not someone from the football team, or Hasty Pudding, or the *Lampoon*. She was holding the unimpressive bicep of the guy from the *Crimson*, with the thatch of hairline scars on his face and a cowlick that stuck up in the back no matter what he used.

Still, when Jayne took him home to meet Joe Linden, he'd understood two things instantly: that though Jayne thought they were very different men, they were in fact twinned in some terrible way. Rodger did not want to have the best house in Cherry Hill. He did not want men in the street to owe him back rent. Or for the women in his home to keep their chins slightly tucked. But he had wanted to go to Harvard—not just college, but the best college. He had proposed to the most beautiful girl there. And had gotten an entry-level position at the *New York Times*. Because it had to be that.

Perhaps, he muses, that's what Jayne can never reconcile about him—that though he wears the same blazer for years at a time, he wants things. Wants them with a single-minded ferocity. And maybe Jayne imagined he would always be content, having come from nothing and already achieved so much, not understanding that, in fact, the words pull him onward, pull him from sleep, pull him from home, from her.

So, marriage has been a series of surprises. Of course it has. No one told him how to do this. He was advised by the faculty on how to approach his master's studies and teaching-assistant work. Editors told him how to break a source, how to navigate the complex hierarchy and allegiances of the newsroom. But no one told him how to be a husband. Or that being a husband required a *how* at all. The fact that no one pulled him aside at his engagement drinks or at the wedding itself—when he was being pulled aside at every end-of-term luncheon, tea, and dinner to have some man's professional wisdom unraveled from an old handkerchief and thrust into his own pocket—created the impression that marriage would be like breathing. As they set out for New York with so many things to figure out and succeed at, marriage could be something they just allowed to be with no effort and no strain.

Surprises.

Jayne in tears over a missed dinner. Jayne floundering in a discussion of Malcolm X. Jayne unable to get pregnant. Rodger unable to fix it. The simple differing of opinion on time and how best to spend it. Jayne did not want to see *Zulu*. She wanted to see *My Fair Lady* or *Marnie*. She did not want to spend her Sunday in a church basement, discussing the Voting Rights Act. And she did not want that misinterpreted as not caring and how dare he. The miscarriages. Jayne sitting on the kitchen floor, blood seeping out from under her, face white with shock—he'd only just run out for milk.

By the time his first book came out, he found he needed things. Laughter. Applause. Being clapped on the back. It was all so easy. So easy to say yes to a tour of California colleges. So easy to accept an invitation to London. To start his next book. Take on more assignments. Throw himself at everything and everyone who seemed thrilled to see him coming.

Rodger leans back in his leather swivel chair and puts his feet up on the desk. "Rodger!" Jayne calls. They must be seated already.

"Be right there!"

He swings his feet to the floor, straightens his piles of clippings, and closes his notebook. The phone rings. "Hello?"

"Rodger!" Jayne sends her voice out again from the dining room.

"Good evening, Mr. Donoghue."

"Oh, good evening, Delores." His service.

"You have a message."

Sage sticks her head in the door, sent to fetch him before the vichyssoise congeals.

"Can I get it in the morning? My wife's about to murder me."

"The woman said it was urgent."

Rodger picks up his fountain pen. "All right, I'm listening. Go ahead."

"Her name is Barbara Galicky."

"Okay."

"And she wants you to call her back tomorrow from the office."

"Tomorrow? How urgent could it be?"

"I'm sorry, sir, she just sounded a bit—determined."

"That's it?" he asks as he writes down the number.

"That's it. Is she a source?"

"I don't think so." He looks at the name, racking his brain. "Good night, Delores."

Finally, he puts the cap back on his pen, his mind like a rescue expedition returning defeated. No, he has no idea who she is.

9

Barely perceptibly, the silhouette shifts. If not in Jayne's closet, then in magazines and on television. *Dallas* premieres. *Knots Landing* and *Dynasty* soon follow.

Inside the apartment, the Linden–Donoghue clan evolves as well.

Sage crosses into official adolescence with a buxom figure that defies her school uniform and exasperates Jayne. After too many tear-filled mornings, she resorts to stealing Rodger's old university sweatshirts—a theoretically ideal solution, if Jayne didn't then argue that the sweatshirts make her look slovenly. Down the hall, Huck is scowling as he breaks and assembles with equal fervor, rigging the VHS audio output to his Walkman to watch movies silently in the middle of the night. When he can't undo it, igniting sibling and parental rage, he retaliates by reprogramming Linden's Speak & Spell to curse. And no amount of soccer, cross-country, or lacrosse seems to be able to exhaust his mind into submission.

While far below the canopy of his tearful, kinetic siblings, on the forest floor of their apartment, Brian's Lincoln Log creations have sprawled underfoot into elaborate G.I. Joe villages, where he stages days-long battles. Until Jayne steps on a piece in the dark and, howling with fury, dismantles the lot. Patiently, he begins again.

Linden turns six and loses two teeth. Delighted, Rodger makes her sing "All I Want for Christmas Is My Two Front Teeth" in July. Jayne becomes pregnant again at the unseemly age of forty-one, fully expecting to have a Down's child. And Rodger continues his inexorable tunneling into the brains of the cognoscenti.

None of them are unreasonably unhappy.

Jayne has a comfortable lifestyle while married to a man she hardly sees, who, she strongly suspects, no longer loves her and is, most likely, inserting his member into other women. But this is also true of nearly everyone she lunches with.

When a particularly egregious transgression has occurred, when there hasn't even been an effort to shower after, or a gifted cuff link has gone missing, they hand over charge cards to be racked through carbon copiers with a satisfying *cuh-chunk*, carrying their purchases home like pelts from war. Mostly they find they smile now with moist eyes and tired lips, hurt beyond redemption to learn that everything they've given to their marriages, their unions, their families, isn't enough. Hurt to discover that what they were supposed to do was make children but never look like it, be wives but remain nubile, be stalwart but surprising. Ultimately, it is, Jayne thinks, a catch-22 from the get-go.

But Jayne is still part of a "they," and even if it isn't the "they" she'd expected, it suffices. She thinks it suffices for her friends, too. Not that any of them would ever broach the subject with each other. When a husband gets so drunk at dinner that he has to be hauled into a taxi, shoes left behind, there's no mention. When a husband berates his spouse at a cocktail party for her sheer stupidity, the wives do not put their hands on her arm over the next Waldorf salad. They sit around the table like a half dozen eggs, isolated in their shells, and discuss manageable problems: children, schools, charity functions.

How do you not see something, then see it? A widening crack in the paint, cat-shredded upholstery, one too many piles of things to be sorted, a tipping point. That abrupt and mortifying moment of recognition suddenly demanding rectification right there in our faces. A problem we have walked past, acclimated to for months, maybe years, until suddenly we say, *Oh my God, how have I lived with that? How have I let that go?* There is a mechanism whereby our brains filter out most of what our eyes pass over. We don't see what we're not expecting to see. We don't see what we don't want to see.

It makes us unreliable witnesses and sporadically effective home-owners. It means entertaining necessitates a lot of tidying up, and putting a home on the market means looking, really looking, at where and how we have been living all this time. It means that we never really know what we've seen, only what we noticed. It means absorbing that these are two different things, and living differently with that knowledge.

~

Linden is curious. With her father's eyes, she periscopes the world, his inquisitiveness burgeoning within her. She watches the girls at school make worms out of hole-punch reinforcements, studying not just their movements but their camaraderie, how their fingers deftly weave tiny white links as their words braid invisible chains. She watches Huck pry the lid off their gaming console. She watches her father smoke, chew a pencil, and eat a sandwich, unaware of any of it. From the bedspread, she watches her mother get ready to leave them. First the intricate digital acrobatics of putting on stockings, how her fingers slip in and out of the fasteners; then the extravagant explosion of scent as Jayne sprays her atomizer in the air and walks through, the stiff silk of her evening gown catching the fragrance; and, lastly, one coat of lipstick and a dash of powder.

After she departs, Linden climbs onto the sink in her mother's bathroom and stares at her own reflection, recognizing the truth—that her eyes do not have her mother's doll-like quality, but rather a slightly hunted air, so that she perpetually looks under-slept, as though she were trailing her parents through their separate corridors of New York

City nightlife, not merely left behind to watch the *Million Dollar Movie* with Sage.

And now that her mother is pregnant, she will no longer be the smallest. She hopes that the arrival of this interloper might allow her to nestle among her older siblings unnoticed, that she might be united with them, finally, by one common enemy. It's her most fervent wish.

~

Rodger recognized her voice as soon as she answered the phone. Barbara Galicky. Bunny. Now in her third incarnation as a homemaker, such as the home was, such as she could make anything of it.

A few months later they finally met at a diner near his Times Square office. The kind with Formica countertops and vinyl seats intended to hold conversations such as these. A place where boyfriends wait while their girlfriends have procedures, where girlfriends tell their boyfriends, possibly married boyfriends, they're pregnant in the first place. A place where those who have nowhere to go, who can't even sink into the despairing camaraderie of a bar, find lonely solace in overcooked eggs and undercooked bacon.

Barbara ordered coffee and a grilled-cheese sandwich that sat untouched on the green-rimmed plate, and they started to talk, about communes and Chile, about the incongruities of the antiwar movement, about seeing the Dead, and Jimmy Carter.

"I met Steve at the VA in Tucson," she said, lighting another cigarette. She shrugged. "I mean, it's not . . ." Her voice trailed away. "But I far from deserve that," she added about the unnamable thing—love? "We have a little place on the outskirts, and I teach English at the community center. Mostly to the kids who live as go-betweens for their parents. I brought in a nurse to update vaccines and help them sign up for entitlements," she said, momentarily brightening as she acknowledged trying to do *something* for *someone's* children, if she could do nothing for her own. "I never intended not to come back."

Rodger nodded, believing her.

"But once I got out there . . ." Each word was a breech birth. "I couldn't get out of bed most days." Tears dampened the corners of her eyes. "It was like my whole life had just shrunk down to . . . ow." She shrugged again at how inconsequential the syllable seemed and yet how well it did its job. "Ow, my body; ow, the kids. I just hurt everywhere, inside and out, the broken promises and the lies, all of it."

Rodger nodded again, understanding, taking her in. "How did you . . . get here?" he asked. Not *get better*, because he would never presume.

She blew out a stream of smoke as she remembered. "One day I just . . . brushed my teeth. One day I didn't cry. One day I washed my hair. One day I cooked a meal. I started volunteering at the VA. It wasn't . . . a straight line."

"But, Bunny—Barbara, why are you here?"

She looked out the window for a moment, at the streetwalkers waiting out the rain under the awning across the street. "Finally, the thought occurred to me that it might be better to have them hate me to my face."

~

After that they met more frequently to strategize how to approach Jayne, how to reintroduce Barbara into their lives. And Rodger found himself wishing he had paid more attention to the children, that, if he had known he'd be sitting across from this woman, devastating in her broken beauty, he would have planned to be able to answer her questions better. *They're doing fine in school, everyone's health is fine, they get along fine, they like their school fine.* He felt like a fraud.

And more than that, he felt that he needed to keep talking to her, to keep listening. As she'd pull back her purple sleeve to stub out her cigarette in the buttered crust of her sandwich, a rueful smile on her freckled lips, he knew he didn't want to miss anything she said ever again.

Walking the desolate paths of Central Park in January, their breath pushing ahead of them into the cold, he was able to relate what he'd seen on his travels, use words like *severed* and *festering*, words that seemed a desecration seated across from Jayne. Barbara talked about her despair, about what it felt like—really felt like—to despise yourself.

Soon he was holding her by the turtle pond, his chin resting atop her head, her face against the blazer he topped with no more than an old wool scarf each winter. But, somehow, they kept their heads from tilting, pried their bodies apart, and went about their separate business for another week.

~

Barbara began to look for a job, the act of which told her that she might not go back to Tucson. It had always been that way. She did something, and the act of doing it revealed to her that she had chosen a path. *Oh, look, I'm getting in a car. I'm taking off my clothes. I'm filling out the application. I've invited five people to a civil ceremony in the yard behind the community center. I must have said yes. I must want this.*

~

When she finally makes the call, the sisters don't know where to meet. Barbara can't imagine crossing the threshold of Jayne's vast apartment, as Rodger has described it, having accomplished so little since the last time she washed up. She knows her coat is shabby, that *she* seems shabby, which is fair—she behaved shabbily. A restaurant seems wrong—they aren't girlfriends catching up. And it's too cold to walk and talk, too cold even to pull a scarf down from one's mouth for more than a few seconds. So they settle on another diner—this one in Jayne's neighborhood. The one chosen for proximity to schools and playdates and activities, a minuscule fraction of the choices Jayne has made on their behalf.

Fur coat closed against the wind, head down, Jayne pushes open the chrome-framed door. "Table?" the man with a Greek accent asks, holding a menu. She shakes her head, gesticulating at the woman in the third booth back, the one in the lavender turtleneck.

Jayne slides in across from her wordlessly, and they absorb each other with their eyes.

"I'm sorry," Barbara whispers, tears spilling over her blonde lashes.

"I know." Jayne does believe that Bunny is sorry. For whatever that's worth.

"I failed, I really failed."

Jayne tugs a napkin from the chrome dispenser and hands it to her, peering into her face. When they were teenagers, Bunny had been an impenetrable study in contrasts to Jayne. The softness of Bunny's child self, the girl who liked to stand on her bedspread and sing along to the McGuire Sisters, had tumbled away from Jayne, separated by an abrasive knowingness and, for all Bunny's curves and Jayne's angularity, a hardness.

It's the hardness Jayne looks for now as she studies the lines around Bunny's mouth and eyes, the freckles becoming liver spots, the blonde hair darkened to a syrup color. But it's gone, decomposed down to despair, which sprouts something much more dangerous in its top-soil—fragile hope.

"Do you hate me?"

Jayne shakes her head. "I've gone through long stretches of anger," she admits, "and long stretches of worry. I've always needed you to be okay."

"I know."

"What do you want?" Jayne asks, still afraid after all these years that Bunny can do what she has every legal right to—take them back.

"Just to see them."

Jayne nods, wanting to take her at her word. "You should come over."

It's the right thing to say. It's the right thing to do. And, unlike her sister, Jayne prides herself on always doing the right thing.

~

Winter gives way to summer, like Miss America handing off her crown. One impossibility making way for the next as Jayne and the children tilt and drive into the onslaught of angry air, thinking, *It will* never *be summer, I will* never *be warm, I will never,* ever *love the feeling of air on my skin again.* And then, almost immediately, they find themselves stepping out of the whirring, mechanical chill of the lobby to feel rank and limp within seconds, thinking, *It will* never *be winter, I will* never *be cold, I will* never *need to bundle under layers ever again.* And so, they cycle.

After a few awkward standoffs, Barbara falls into a routine with the children, picking them up on Sunday after breakfast, taking them for an outing, and then staying through Sunday supper.

"Who is she?" Brian asks his big sister as they wait for their turn on the carousel.

"She's our mother."

He howls with tears. He's the one who's only ever called Jayne *Mom.* Who has only ever known Rodger as his father, even though he's patently not their biological child. But still.

Barbara drops to the ground and holds him while he sobs. "I'm so sorry, I'm so sorry," she whispers, rocking him on her lap even though he's already tall for his nine years. "But you're safe. Nothing is going to change. You just have a lot of people who love you."

Gradually, he begins to believe her. He begins to want to know where he and his skin come from. He follows along, carrying his boat, hoping they might go to the pond. They rarely do.

At newly fourteen, Sage treats Barbara warily. Who is this stranger she has intimate memories of? How could she have left? Why is she back? Sage wants to scream and claw her face and climb inside her and ignore her, all at once. Instead, she goes on the outings and answers the questions and counts the change and remembers the sandwiches and the movie times and is generally herself, as she's beginning to conceive of herself to be.

Even Linden, eager not to be left home with her new baby brother, begins joining their adventures. She loves Barbara's smell—smoke and old fur coats in the thrift shop and flowers like the ones that bloom on her mother's windowsill. And how Barbara lets her put her head in her lap when she's tired and strokes her hair. She loves going through Barbara's crochet bag, sometimes finding a solitary knitting needle; sometimes a peppermint, its wrapper half-off; and once, a circle crisscrossed like a spider web, a feather hanging from its rim. Barbara explains the Lakota tribe and dream catchers and gives it to her to keep—actually keep for her very own. Linden then steals Huck's abandoned kachina doll, which she passes along to Barbara in return.

Huck, however, is just infuriated. Infuriated that she left, infuriated that she's back, infuriated that she is the conduit to this word *Oaxaca* and all that he can neither access nor conceive of. Refusing to join, he silently ricochets against the boundaries of his world as hard as he can, trying to leave no stretch of his skin unmarred. On his skateboard or bicycle, he weaves in and out of traffic, grabbing on to graffitied buses and garbage trucks. He tears through clothes faster than Jayne can mend them, and she finally stops going to Lenox Hill's ER every time they call. It's two blocks from their house; they have her insurance card on file.

What does bring him pleasure is looking at his naked body as he dresses for school, at the patches of crosshatched skin that will never grow normally again. While his little brother looks on, alarmed by Huck's pubic hair, the muscles that seem to be rippling out from under the casing, Huck admires the thing clawing its way out of him.

∼

Then Thanksgiving comes around again, and Jayne pulls out the dog-eared *Joy of Cooking* and invites friends with grown children, and elderly neighbors from the building, and any sundry orphans in need of rescuing.

"Is Barbara coming?" Sage asks.

"Of course." Then: "I'll ask her."

Jayne has found gold acorn place card holders at a curio shop that go beautifully with the cornucopia. The five children each have a brown velvet outfit from Magic Windows, and Jayne commissions a photographer to take their portrait so she can slip a copy inside each Christmas card.

After days of cooking, Jayne slides into her seat at the head of the main table; her sister-in-law beside her on her right; the Rosensteins, Clarks, and Ortners in the middle; and Barbara seated at the other end beside Rodger so they can talk about politics without dragging the rest of the table into it. Jayne says grace, expressing gratitude for the gathered family and friends, and for the bounty they're about to receive. "God bless us, every one," she concludes.

"I think you mean, *God bless the less fortunate*," Rodger says, reaching for the haricot verts. "And for what we are about to receive, may he make us truly grateful."

Perhaps, Jayne thinks as she presses her lips together, she had too much sherry while waiting for the meat thermometer. *Perhaps* she has conflated the two holiday blessings, but honestly, *fuck him, fuck him*—

And then she sees it: Rodger glancing at her sister as he mocks Jayne—and Bunny smirks back.

～

Jayne doesn't speak again for the rest of the meal, her mind's eye staring hard at every crack, every fissure. She doesn't hug Bunny goodbye, waiting instead for Rodger in their bedroom, knowing he'll come in smelling like that god-awful patchouli stuff from a hug that lingered.

"How long?" she asks simply.

Rodger slumps inside his starched shirt. "A year." A sharp inhale. "But we've never even kissed. Nothing's happened."

"A year?" She's reeling. "How many months was she here—with you—before she called me?"

"Six? But not *with* me, there's no 'with.'"

"Do you love her?"

"Yes." As he says it, she watches him realize it's true. He drops onto the edge of the bed. The bed she picked out. The bed she made just this morning.

"Are you in love with her?"

"Yes," he acknowledges.

"Why?"

He looks up. "Does that matter?"

"To me?" Her fingers splay like she's shooting energy out her palms. "Yes, it does."

"Jayne, be reasonable. We met in college. We were children. Everyone married so quickly. We didn't know."

She thumps her sternum. "*I* knew."

"Did you? Is this what you would have chosen?"

Her eyes sting. "No. But I didn't get that choice." She takes a step back so that perhaps he can see her. "I got a prospect. We all chose *prospects*. You were like majors to us—this one seems promising. Don't you get it? You weren't just men, you were our only tickets to anywhere."

"Not for her."

"Is that why?"

He looks at the carpet, seeing the life Jayne never gained access to. "I didn't mean to split my worlds. I'm in the field, or at my desk, or on the subway—then I come home, and I don't know where I am."

"And Bunny could be one of your subjects."

"In a way, yes."

"Get out."

10

Jayne lies on the floor of her bedroom, her bed no longer feeling low or flat enough. She'd just found a trellis-patterned carpet remnant at Janovic Plaza and now enjoys the sensation of it against her shoulders, above the line of her peignoir. *Peignoirs, for God's sake!* She sleeps in peignoirs. Not football jerseys, like the moms on the sitcoms the kids watch. *Real Goddamn silk.*

Hot tears drip out of the corners of her eyes again. Now she has to get through the holidays and Linden's birthday party all by herself, and the charity circuit is building to its frothy jingle-belled crescendo. She's used to Rodger's absence on her arm, but the assumption was always that he was out safeguarding democracy—not that he'd left her for a woman who looks like—like—like if Malibu Barbie had three babies and her tits sagged and she smoked and lay in the sun and worked in a refugee camp and was just totally Goddamn sad. *And it's her own fault!* No one said, *Hey, why don't you leave your kids?* They weren't dead! Her kids didn't die! They were right here, taking ballet and piano and tennis! Getting braces and remedial-reading help!

Jayne seethes. She wants to grab her mother and shake her, because if there was one thing Margaret drilled into her girls, it was that a man wants to come home to a well-tended house, polished children, and a composed wife. This, *this* is what she's supposed to have accomplished; if not the Upper West Side and a PhD, then at least doing this beautifully. And being *seen* for it.

~

One sister lies at the center of a well-appointed room for many weeks while children ask unanswered, unanswerable questions, until, one day, a manila envelope arrives for her and in that envelope a straightforward petition for divorce and joint custody of all five children.

Meanwhile, the other sister moves out of the room she's been renting at a convent on Twenty-Ninth and arrives at an apartment on West End Avenue with only one small suitcase's worth of possessions. She places it in the bare living room beside his typewriter and file boxes and allows him to kiss her for the first time, allows herself to kiss him back. They make love on the splintering parquet and, afterward, while she cries, he says, "We really must buy a table."

"I'd rather have sex on a bed," she murmurs.

And he thinks, *This is it—the life I've been waiting for, finally about to start.*

~

"Then I'm suing right back," Jayne says in her attorney's office, lighting a Benson & Hedges. The cuff of her suit jacket slides down to reveal gaunt wrists. When some women lose weight that they don't have to spare, they look instantly older as flesh thins out and the fullness of youth is leached from them, but Jayne just looks childlike, as though she were a twelve-year-old playing grown-up.

"He's not actually suing you," her lawyer corrects, seated uncomfortably in his rolls of fat behind his solid desk, reminding Jayne of a pyramid of cannon balls. "It's a petition. You can grant it."

"I want his money."

"Child support, alimony," her lawyer responds, making a show of writing the painfully obvious words on his yellow pad when he might just as well have written *I am holding a pen*.

"No." Jayne stops him. "I want *his* money. We never comingled our finances. I paid for Sage and Huck and Brian with an annuity on my trust—or, it's not a trust, it's, it's the rents, the rents my father collected on his buildings. In Baltimore. After taxes. It isn't much." She inhales deeply. She hasn't smoked since Radcliffe; now she understands why Rodger always has one clamped between his lips. "Everything else, I've had to ask for. Ask for him to deposit money in our joint account so I can take care of everyone. Can you imagine how humiliating that is, having to continually ask for money like he's my father? Justify what I'm spending it on. Be judged. Be told, *Oh, you don't need that*. Like I'm a teenager. I'm entitled to half of what he's made on his books. Without my running the household, he would never have had the time. I want child support, alimony, and a settlement."

~

"No," Rodger spits down the line to his lawyer, head akimbo to clamp the phone. "Half is outrageous. She doesn't need it and isn't entitled to it, and I won't be blackmailed. I made that money during my marriage, in spite of Jayne, not because of her. This is pettiness, pure and simple. I'll pay child support, of course, and alimony—that's it."

"Are you sure?" the lawyer asks, not pushing back so much as nearly whining.

"What?" It's hard to hear over the din of the newsroom, hundreds of fingers bruising keys.

"Are you sure?" the lawyer repeats. He's so close to retirement, and the thought of another drawn-out battle exhausts him already. This is new, all new, this scorched-earth style of litigating the dissolution of a marriage. When he opened his practice, divorce was like a bowel movement, something that had to be done as expediently as possible, out of sight. One spouse set the terms, the other acquiesced. Now there are grievances and wounds and rage, and each has an equal monetary value, and the goal isn't the end of the marriage so much as the end of the other person.

"Yes. Tell her she'll have alimony and child support, and that's it."

~

Jayne can't believe what she's hearing, the disbelief crowding atop the weeks of incredulity and astonishment like pigeons atop a statue. Inside her red wool cape, sweat beads along her sides, the bobby pins in her French twist tugging against her scalp. "Then he can't have the children."

"Jayne, I understand this isn't the response we were hoping for—"

"He is denying that I made any material contribution? If he wants the children—who he couldn't pick out of a crowd, by the way—then he'll have to sue me for them. I'd like to see him bother."

~

"Is she fucking kidding?" Rodger shouts. No one notices as the typewriters around him fire off round after round.

"Sole custody."

"On what grounds? They're not even her children."

"Rodger, she'll have a case for abandonment vis-à-vis Barbara. Talk it through with her. Meanwhile, please reconsider the settlement. Alimony and a percentage of what you made in a lump sum."

Rodger feels it without language, face down in the yard, blood in his mouth, his new glasses in shards—there won't be another pair, not this year—and the sound of his brothers' laughter.

"No, it's ludicrous. She won't win."

~

But that night, as they sit on the floor eating Chinese food, Rodger has to tell Barbara he doesn't know when she'll be able to see the children again.

"What do you want to do?" she asks softly, unable to believe, and yet fully able to believe, that she has once again botched being a mother.

He looks over at her, sitting cross-legged in his bathrobe, head wrapped in a turban, a sliver of the soft hair between her legs visible where the robe gaps. "We'll countersue for all five." He reaches over and cups her face in his rough palm. "Fuck her."

But Barbara keeps her eyes downcast. Because, whatever Jayne and Rodger's incompatibilities, Jayne took the kids, after all, did this enormous thing beyond favor or gesture. She saved the children from both the system and their own mother. "She's the victim here, Rodger."

Rodger stops to consider this, then shakes his head. "Jayne Linden was never a victim in her life."

And something about this phrase resonates with Barbara like an echo, a thought she's never dared let herself put so succinctly, so she nods and gets out of Rodger's way. Jayne Linden was never a victim.

~

"He's suing for sole custody of all five?" Jayne asks in astonishment. "What does he want with *five* children? In his little love nest." It's a tacky thing to say; she hears the tackiness as she says it. She never attained the erudition of Rodger's circles, but she doesn't want to sound like some kitchen-sink drama, either. She rearranges her camel coat around her shoulders. On the way here she found a moth hole in the lining—another affront. "That's insane. I'm their mother. He has no case."

"There's just one thing, Jayne."

"Yes?"

He adjusts his girth forward toward his blotter, sending a shuddering adjustment down the length of the chair. "A judge will ask the older ones who they choose. Do you have confidence in who they'll pick?"

Jayne won't let the line of her shoulders erode, even as she suddenly has a vivid memory of bathing one of their mother's dogs in a tub—the soaped canine leaping out and Bunny and Jayne chasing him around the yard, laughing hysterically, suds all down their pinafores. Jayne remembers the feeling of her small hands closing around his panting middle, only to sense him slip her grasp. She reached forward, throwing her weight after him, and tumbled face-first into the grass, coming up with blood streaming from her nose.

Rodger Donoghue has left her. Left her for her older-looking, unkempt, middle-aged sister.

"He does not get to saunter out of here with as much of whatever he wants *as* he wants and just write a Goddamn check, a check that is completely meaningless to him. He has one pair of khaki pants and a moth-eaten scarf; he needs a coffeepot and a carton of cigarettes. No, he does not get to have everything, *everything* he ever wanted when I get nothing, *nothing* that I wanted. This has to *cost* him. I get sole custody of the children."

"Why?" her lawyer asks. "A judge will ask why." He stares at her.

Everything is flying past like a mudslide, and she has to reach out and grab something before it's all gone. She was wrong—so wrong. Bunny wasn't the one on the ledge that summer years ago—she was.

"They're not safe."

"What do you mean they're not safe?" He pulls his legal pad close, pen poised.

This is how this goes. Three words. And suddenly everything changes.

"I—I never wanted to put words to it, but, but—"

"But what? Has he hit them? Does he drink?"

"No, I know all about that—my father had a temper."

"Then what?"

Jayne is starting to tremble. There's a jagged breath.

"Jayne?"

She's shaking her head like a baby trying to avoid a spoon.

"Jayne?"

"Rodger is—is—"

"Is?"

A silence more pregnant than Jayne or Barbara has ever been.

He looks at her questioningly.

Her breath is trapped under her rib cage.

"Jayne?"

"In love with Linden."

"In love w—"

She holds her palm up. "I don't mean he loves her like a father. At that distance, with that reverence. I mean—" Tears abruptly break without warning. Staring at the crack, staring at the gash, staring at the gaping, gaping hole that's opened inside her own brain. "He is romantically in love with her."

"Romantically?"

"Sexually," she whispers.

His forehead furrows, pushing his prodigious eyebrows down. "Jayne, this is a very serious allegation. Why did you never bring this up before?"

She blinks at him, her eyes anguished in her hollow face. "Because I didn't know." *And then I knew.* "And then I knew."

She feels like someone is dragging her violently by one arm through the house, gripping her by the jaw, forcing her to look, *look*, at what she's walked past. This has to be it—the only explanation—afraid of Jayne, he's decided to move on to someone who'll turn the blind eye Jayne no longer can. "I thought I could protect her. I wanted to be wrong. The children had been through enough. I didn't want to subject them to more."

In a practiced move, he pulls a Kleenex from the box and extends it.

"He kisses her—all the time, all over."

"*All* over?" He hoists one of the eyebrows.

"I—I don't know. They sleep together."

"They *sleep* together?"

"He passes out on the couch in his office, and I find Linden there in the morning, spooned against him. Sometimes . . . just in her underpants." How has she overlooked this? How has she normalized this for herself? The blood drains from her face. "I might throw up."

"Do you need some water?" he asks, noting that under the blotches, she's turning the not-okay white he occasionally sees in his office—the husband handed evidence of the affair captured with a telephoto lens, the wife who learns her lifestyle has been a high-level shell game.

Jayne nods.

He presses the intercom button. "Carol, can you bring Mrs. Donoghue some water?"

"It isn't natural—how he dotes on her. It's always unnerved me." *Men don't engage this way with their daughters. Men don't cuddle. They don't console or kiss away tears. They don't voluntarily get up at five thirty to keep their early riser company. They don't pay that much attention.*

Jayne tries to slow down to sip, but her tears get the better of her, and she coughs water down her front, as though saved from drowning. "Oh, God," she says as she recovers, dabbing at her front with more Kleenex, leaving a white lint trail down her coat. "What do I do?"

"Well, the first step is to get Linden evaluated. And we file for sole custody." It's his turn to take an audible breath. "Jayne, I have to warn you, this is going to go public, and it's going to get messy."

"He made that choice. He was the one that sought fame, not me. Now he can live with the consequences."

"Okay, then. Let's get started."

~

Jayne comes home, scoops Linden off the rag rug in the den, and kneels to press her daughter tightly against her like the primal animal she's become. "Oh, baby, I love you, I love you, I love you so much." Tears flow again down Jayne's swollen face. "I'm sorry, I'm so sorry." She vows she will do nothing but pay attention to Linden for the rest of her life.

"What, Mommy? What happened?"

Jayne pulls back to look into Linden's dark eyes. "Daddy is a very bad man. But you are safe. You are safe here with us, and I will never let another bad thing happen to you, I promise."

"Why is Daddy a bad man?"

"Oh, sweetie." Jayne sobs afresh and clasps her, one gloved hand on the back of her head. She breathes in the smell of Linden's little-girl shampoo but can't pull back to look in her eyes just yet. Because now— it strikes Jayne for the first time—now she has to tell her.

~

Rodger's lawyer picks up his hat and walks out of his office like an activated toy, no word to his secretary, no explanation. He takes a taxi to the Upper West Side, even though his Midtown offices are closer to the *Times*, and assigns himself a seat in the lobby, decorated in the inexplicable faux medieval style found in that stretch of the city, with a coffered ceiling, stained glass images of knights, and straight-backed chairs framing a large decorative fireplace meant to suggest cauldrons of stag.

Then, as though seeking an audience with the king, he waits. Briefcase in lap, eyes on the beveled-glass door, he sits at attention, posture charged by adrenaline, for hours, through the arrival of dry cleaning; cases of wine and vodka; an arrangement of flowers; children returning from school, the ends of backpack straps tucked between lips; all manner of necessity parading through this lobby to be presented to the various fiefdoms upstairs. And one lawyer. Who has taken himself off the clock because some things just cannot be said over the telephone.

~

The *New York Post* runs the story first. Following a call from her lawyer, Jayne sends Sage across the street for a copy, already dissociating from her actions like a man appointing a stand-in for a duel. Snatching the copy from Sage's hands, she trembles as she reads it in the vestibule, thinking, *Never again will you be considered a good person.*

~

The following day Sage is in the middle of third period when Jennifer M. passes her a folded piece of lined paper, its edges ruffled where it's been ripped from the spiral. Sage separates the creases, trying to soundlessly peel it open; *Sage daddy's penis* accompanies an illustrated rendering of the crisis.

After school Sage boards the crosstown bus to the West Side and changes at Broadway for the 104 to Rodger's office. When she arrives, she sits on the wool-backed chair by his desk, her backpack on her lap. A kind colleague calls him at home, gets her a watery hot chocolate from the break room, and tells her to wait. Of course, Sage realizes as she looks up at the ceiling tiles, he wouldn't be here right now.

Rodger flies in twenty-five minutes later, sweaty, scarf trailing on the floor, trying to block out the eyes on him. "Sage!" he cries, skidding to a halt a few feet from the chair, momentum nearly toppling him over her. He realizes what he mustn't do is touch her and awkwardly tries to conscript his hands into doing something else, patting his pockets needlessly, as though what she's come for is in them.

But he doesn't ask anything stupid like, *What are you doing here?* or, *How are you?*

Instead, he looks into her mother's knowing, weary green eyes and sits down.

She looks at him in return, and, even as she takes in the curves and lines of his face, realizes that's what she's come to do. To look, to see if she can discern and discover what Jayne has said in his skin, his eyes, in the hairs and pores, in the twitch of muscle, in the clues we can't suppress.

He lets her look.

They stay like that for minutes, her face the face Bunny never had, not even at fourteen, wise but not hard; and his, bedraggled and stubbled and scruffy, gray and gutted. Finally, she stands and puts her backpack on her shoulders.

She will move in with them.

She has searched him, searched her memory, searched herself, and made a series of calculations. If Jayne is wrong, then they'll need help. And Sage will always go where she's needed.

~

Barbara is still in her bathrobe. Because she might take another shower. She takes showers the way some people get glasses of water—absentmindedly, and at regular intervals. Whenever her self-disgust threatens to overwhelm, she stands under the stream until she can imagine it running from brown and red to clear. Then she puts her robe back on, rewraps her turban, and takes her spot by the window to stare out at the buildings, the curtains, the plants owned by other people whose lives are untouched by her.

She knows she started all this—so how to stop it? There has to be something she can say to Jayne. To the court. But no, nothing, ultimately, that can be proven. Nothing, ultimately, that won't actually just demonstrate that everything Barbara comes in contact with is ruined.

~

Jayne arrives home from a meeting with her lawyer and drops her purse in the hallway, kicks off her wet shoes, and walks in a kind of daze down to Sage's room. She's lying on her stomach on her Laura Ashley bedspread, half doing homework, half listening to Asia. Jayne lifts the needle.

Sage looks up, prepared as best as she can be to have this conversation.

Jayne sits on the bed, removes her silk scarf, her London Fog trench still damp, her hair plastered to her skin. "You want to move in with them?"

Sage nods.

Jayne touches her ankle. "Even though you know," she says quietly, "that he is a vile, vile man who has done disgusting, loathsome things from which there is no coming back?"

Sage does not respond.

"And you know I took you in when she left? From one day to the next, I stepped in to be your mother to the best of my ability."

Sage nods.

"And still, you're choosing them?"

"Yes," she whispers.

"Why?" Jayne's eyes well. "I don't even know if you'll be safe there. I can't protect you."

Sage reaches out and puts a hand on her shoulder. "If anything happens, I'll come back."

"You promise?" Jayne sobs. "You promise?"

"I do."

And that's how Sage exits Linden's life the first time.

~

"How does she still have a case if her older daughter is *voluntarily* moving in with me?" Rodger shouts at the new lawyer he has been outsourced to, the one who specializes in things "getting ugly."

"Because," he explains patiently between bites of whitefish salad, a smell that seems to linger on him perpetually, "you're not accused of molesting that one, just Linden. As you well know, Rodger, legally one really has nothing to do with the other."

~

As far as Brian is concerned, regardless of what his siblings tell him, Jayne is his mother; hers are the arms of his childhood, and when they wrap around his middle and he looks down, their skin makes stripes. That the high-rise featured in the opening credits of *Diff'rent Strokes* is only one block west on Seventy-Ninth Street just adds to his comfort—this is what rich white people *do*, they raise lost Black boys, don't overthink it. It will be years until he deconstructs all of it.

Huck, of course, immediately carves out his own rules, which involve sleeping wherever he feels like. Which sometimes is at Jayne's and sometimes is at Rodger's, or the houses of other families, and sometimes on a bench in the park, courting the loss of his backpack and skateboard, a black eye, a broken arm.

But when each side finds him curled somewhere in their home, skateboard-wheel grease on his hands, actual fragments of leaves in his hair, they feel like they're winning—and no one wants to make eye contact and scare him off.

~

Meanwhile, Linden struggles. As Jayne paces back and forth in front of the mantel, a cigarette in one hand, ashtray cupped in the palm of the other, the sound of the receiver slamming into its cradle still vibrating in the air, she'll say to Linden, "He is a vile, vile man. And he will never hurt you again."

And Linden searches herself, knowing it's a deep shortcoming that she doesn't understand, that whatever vile thing he's done, she's missed. That missing it probably makes her equally vile.

What she knows is that she wants to touch him, misses him touching her, wants to bury her face in his stomach, feel him blow kisses on hers, loves how he rubs her stomach until she falls asleep, or falls asleep holding his hand, or his ears, she aches for him, aches, aches, aches. Aches for someone she's not allowed to ask for, can't cry for, can't name.

~

Jayne has started dropping off the children every morning and taking Linden to her dance class at Ballet Academy East and art class at Brick Church. If she could build a wall around the Upper East Side to keep Linden safe, she would.

Instead, she stretches her invisible arms in a circle, scooping as far south as the Waldorf, whose ballroom is, several nights a month, a battleground of public opinion. But Jayne is clear—if you can afford a thousand dollars for a table, you're smart enough to recognize him for what he is. *They must know, they must believe.*

She reaches around with her other arm and takes the Upper East Side and Central Park. *The children should have Central Park.* She wages her campaign at Mortimer's and private dinner parties, arriving pitied. Departing admired. All with an eye toward keeping Linden safe. With the fervor of the newly converted, she runs in her sackcloth from hut to hut. It doesn't matter that they love his column, stood in line to have their books autographed, *they must know, they must believe.*

That there are those who instantly decide her accusations reflect worse on her than him is a thing her lawyer keeps counseling her to accept, that there will be the fallen, the doubters, the heathens. *Conspirators! Collaborators!* But she lets Morningside Heights go. And everything south of the Waldorf.

And she finds herself thinking, as she pulls on her leotard in the morning, screw those smug academics and intellectuals with their *Bolshevik bullshit* and *free love* and *morality is for the bourgeoisie* and *only the small-minded Reaganites follow the rules.* She's done. Done trying to belong to the book club that reads *serious* books, trying to keep up with Rodger at dinner, fuck Schopenhauer and Neruda and Fianna Fáil and Senegal and every tiny Goddamn thing she's supposed to keep track of and have an opinion on. And who are they? Just monsters defending a monster. Not public arbiters of the righteous and the good. Thugs. Thugs who closed ranks around their own.

So she brushes Linden's hair each night before bed, determined that she know there is nothing wrong with her, that she is loved. And she whispers the questions she's been coached to ask: "When did Daddy make you feel afraid?"

Linden relishes the sensation of the bristles against her scalp, the smell of her mother's perfume behind her. She has to hold herself rigid to keep from slipping right into slumber against her warm torso, waiting until she can be tucked in under the scallop-edged sheets, her mother inserting the wool blanket's hem under the mattress, as if making the bed with Linden in it, until Linden feels safely pressed into sleep.

"I love you, little girl," Jayne whispers, silhouetted in the doorway, each night piecing together the little fragment she can cull from Linden's brain with the fragments from the nights before, trying to be gentle, trying to spare her an assault from the psychiatrist Rodger will bring to defend himself. The evaluation is approaching, and Jayne knows, in the absence of "definitive physical evidence," the thought of which makes her sick, she needs Linden to be able to speak on her own behalf.

~

On the Tuesday before Memorial Day, Linden walks hand in hand with Jayne to the psychiatrist's office on East Eighty-Ninth Street. The air is cool, but the sun is strong, the contrast like putting fresh soup in the refrigerator. The tulips in the median have passed their moment, the petals blanketing the beds, but the morning still feels full of promise.

They're met at the office by three men and one woman: The psychiatrist Jayne has selected, Elizabeth Gerstein, who impressed immediately by getting the landscape of Rodger's behavior before Jayne even had to go into explicit detail. The psychiatrist Rodger has sent, the ghoulish, in Jayne's opinion, Dr. Farber. And two officers who are there to be able to vouch for the proceedings in court. There will be a transcript, of course, but they will testify that Linden spoke willingly.

This is a process of protocols. Protocols in their infancy. Like a barn raising among people who have never seen a barn.

Jayne is asked to wait in the reception area while they take Linden into the exam room. She kneels in front of Linden and whispers, eyes wetting, "Just tell these nice people *exactly* what you told me, and no one will ever hurt you again."

Linden nods.

Dr. Gerstein takes her hand and gently leads her into the other room.

~

Here is what's known by everyone come the end of the hearing: nothing. Linden's psychiatrist is convinced of Rodger's guilt, that is, convinced something happened to Linden, but not exactly what. The psychiatrist for the defense is sure of his criminal innocence, if not his mental health; yes, he has a narcissistic organization to his personality—but is that a crime? Jayne's psychiatrist thinks Jayne suffers from latent Electra issues that create maternal conflict, and confesses to his wife late one night, when she finds him eating cold borscht at the kitchen window, that although Jayne is clearly well intentioned, it remains problematic that the accusation only came to light *after* she was left for her sister.

More perplexed than her face lets on, the judge waits for a "gut instinct" and worries as the proceedings wear on that none will arrive. And absolutely no one knows what to make of Rodger breaking down on the stand into heaving sobs—the self-flagellation of the guilty, or the anguish of the persecuted?

~

The decision, when it comes down, is Solomonic. Jayne is awarded sole physical custody of Linden and her two-year-old little brother, Clyde. The judge orders Rodger to pay alimony and child support, which Jayne instantly and publicly rejects on the grounds that she wants no interaction with him for the rest of her life. "One lump sum for the children and no further contact."

At the recess to negotiate, Jayne kneels in front of them, straightening Clyde's tiny bow tie. "I'll change our last names," she murmurs. "We'll all go back to *Linden*. We'll be the Linden family, as we should have been all along."

"Linden . . . Linden?" Linden ventures tentatively.

"Oh." Jayne's shoulders slump. Then her eyes open wide. "You can be Linden Margaret."

"Linden *Margaret?*" she repeats with passionate disdain.

"Well, I haven't thought through the details. Maybe we'll change your first name?"

Linden starts to cry. This is one loss, one change too many.

"Well, fine, we'll discuss it later. I have to go back in. Let's just see what the judge has to say."

Calculations are made—school fees plus college tuition, accounting for inflation—an amount is agreed upon for Clyde and Linden, to be held in a trust. No further contact required.

Sage and Huck are awarded solely to Barbara, with the strong suggestion from the bench that she leave Rodger. And Brian is awarded to Jayne.

Then a gavel bang and a word from the woman who has made the final determination on so many lives she won't see play out. "As you know, this is not a criminal proceeding, Mr. and Mrs. Donoghue. I am not here to decide if a crime has been committed as the law defines it. I am here to award custody. I have based my decisions on the clinical testimony, which takes into account both Linden's psychological state as well as the problematic circumstances surrounding the accusations. But better to err on the side of caution, and, in that role, and with the limited evidence and evaluations I've had to work with, I have provided as much protection for Linden as I can. Barbara is Sage's mother. It is now her job to provide as much protection for Sage as she can. I wish you all the best—and healing."

~

So, no pronouncement that comforts anyone, or vindicates anyone, or frees anyone to march out of that courtroom into a bright, certain future. The proceeding is over, the ordeal is over, but no one is released. Instead, they cast about in the blood for their limbs and pack up to go to their assigned homes, and thirty-some-odd years later, Linden will read the judge's words in a public library and wonder over having had neither—not the best, and certainly not healing.

PART III

11

Three years pass in the same school. The one that would never have admitted Linden Donoghue had they had any idea their name would be in the papers.

Slipping into the pantry during a dinner party to sneak mint Milanos, Linden overhears it earnestly suggested to Jayne that the family move. "Why?" her mother asks as Linden freezes, the ruffled paper between her fingers. "We have a rent-controlled four bedroom." This is true, and yet, rather than spread out the remaining children, Jayne has converted Rodger's study into an office for herself, the victor throwing old banners over the crenellation to the bonfire.

"For Linden's sake," Mrs. Ortner says. "A fresh start. Anonymity."

"But Linden's the victim." Linden silently slips that word in her pocket with the cookies and creeps back to her room.

Though Jayne did take the precautionary measure of instructing Linden not to speak of the court case to her classmates. As if that is how they would learn of it, as if they didn't overhear it discussed at home. As if it didn't take just one girl, awake in the back of a station wagon when she should have been asleep, the corners of her mouth still sticky from rainbow sherbet; one girl about to walk in and ask for milk when she should have been watching *Land of the Lost*; just one girl and soon the whole class knew, knew but didn't understand, because who could understand?

They just get that there is something—wrong—about Linden. Because why else would their mothers repeatedly tell them to be kind to her—but never invite her over?

The girls look for reasons. But she doesn't have a burn scar on her arm like Colleen, or slyly suck her thumb like Kate C.

She's just sad.

She has sad eyes and a sad countenance; her mouth trembles when she can't remember eight times seven, when a party favor glistens from the wrists of the other girls, when a classmate accidentally tips tempera paint on her penny loafers. And it's this sadness that sets her apart, that lingers long after they forget why she was set apart to begin with.

The why goes dormant.

Until sixth grade, until reading *Love and Sex in Plain Language*, until the awkward conversation in science lab, third period, about where penises go, and, amid absorbing this information, the inkling, as yet unnamed, of some cosmic unfairness, *They go* in *us, they go* in *us? Why? Why? Why not the other way around?* Heads turn. Heads turn toward Linden before they can even consciously remember why. But then the girls connect the words on the chalkboard, the diagram in their book, and the hand that landed too heavily on their shoulders years ago, steering them away too quickly.

Linden takes in the faces, strewn with pustules, the mouths newly cragged and scabbed on braces, the eyes blinking behind glasses, and because she never forgets, even for a day, what her father was accused of, what everyone knows she has done with him, is certain what they're thinking.

The teacher, failing, drops her eyes to her notes, and the room, with its cabinet of beakers, Bunsen burners, and resin tabletops, witnesses a different alchemic process—sadness compressing into anger.

Linden looks back hard. *Yes,* she telegraphs to each of them, *I know. I know what this thing is you will now be racing to discover.* For whatever it's worth. What is it worth?

~

The life of a child is that of a ball lobbed back and forth in twenty-four-hour cycles—a dozen blocks north in the morning, a dozen blocks south in the evening. The upside is that Linden has only two realms to master—or endure. Despite Jayne's constant prodding toward things that she never had herself—dance and tennis, riding and sailing—Linden never wants to take after-school classes or attend camp, because that would only introduce a whole new host of dynamics to navigate—*Who knows? Who doesn't know?* Do they like her because they don't know yet or because they already know and want to be closer to scandal? Or worse, their parents are fans of her father who want to befriend and liberate her.

Do they make fun of her swing, her stroke, or her foot position because they don't know how else to exorcise their feelings of discomfort or because Linden is genuinely deserving of scorn? Is anyone her friend? Truly, her friend? Whatever that means, exactly, in a class where allegiances shift like one of the wretched square dances the northeast schools inexplicably throw at regular intervals, the gyms filled with hay bales and mothers in painted freckles bobbing their knees to rouse children who'd rather be dead.

It's just too much for her to parse after a day of dodging attention at school.

~

In seventh grade, she arrives at their building's front door, drags her backpack behind her across the checkerboard marble, and sets up camp on the den's corduroy couch. If she's already missed the end of *Santa*

Barbara, then she'll make a bowl of popcorn, put on MTV, and stay there until dinner.

She loves MTV. She loves MTV the way some kids her age love books. She started watching it voraciously in third grade, when there was only a handful of videos that looped repeatedly—"Down Under," "Hold Me," "I Want Candy"—the collective impression being that the world of adults is a literal desert. Three years later and still no one else in her class has the slightest interest.

That's okay. Linden presses down the button on the brown plastic cable box, then crosses the room and settles in to wrap the future around her. She finds it all fascinating—the men in oversize canary-yellow rain-coats; the women in ripped T-shirts, their heads half-shaved. The Day-Glo colors, exaggerated silhouettes, excessive jubilance, and longing—it all exists so wholly outside of Linden's Upper East Side world. Her teach-ers, who wear espadrilles in summer and Belgian shoes in winter, her mother's friends, who have started dressing like Laura Ingalls, all seem to strive for nothing, hunger for nothing, want for nothing. It's wrong to Linden somehow.

But unlike Huck, who slams the boundaries of this want-less world until he's shivved while dozing in the park one night, forty-two stitches and a race to save his spleen, Linden wants only to sit on that couch and immerse herself in abstract yearning in four-minute increments. Whether it's U2's battle cry for social justice, a game only the lonely can play, or an understanding of why the blues are called the blues, she stares and stares like she's going to be dropped into adulthood any minute and this will be the only preparation she will ever have.

There's one song, though, that takes her on an intolerable journey over its five minutes and thirty-six seconds, that repels and compels her equally. At the beginning, as the beat finds and matches her pulse, she just wants to be that woman in the white coat and red lips, seated in the back of the taxi. That woman who has Jayne's alabaster skin and fine features, but dark hair like Linden. Who can hold a man's atten-tion and fill him with relentless desire. At the two-minute mark, his mouth connects with hers as he pins her against the wall, his strong hand almost out of frame, gripping her head, taking what he needs, wants, and the drum finds its way between Linden's thirteen-year-old legs—a cigarette in shadow, the acrid perfume that will always conjure her father. And now Linden's stomach is involved, a sour feeling at the edges—they're in bed, and she's betraying him, he takes a step in, she takes a step back, and she's hurting him, not choosing him, and Linden feels sick and aroused and lost, and the driving chorus asks Linden, *What does it mean to be a father figure*, and what does it mean for Linden that she doesn't have one?

It's on one of these afternoons when she's adrenalized to run across the room and punch off the TV that Linden decides to go to Butterfield Market, just a few doors away, and get a snack. She doesn't need a snack, isn't particularly hungry, doesn't desire anything her mother doesn't keep prodigiously stocked in their pantry. What she wants is a break from an apartment once teeming with the wants and energy of five children, and now holding only conversational dead ends. An older brother studying for the PSATs, a younger brother singing to himself in the mirror with an honest-to-God hairbrush, and a mother assiduously applying herself to becoming the Something she senses she lost along the way.

As Linden passes through the heavy double doors, there's a boy bouncing a handball from the sidewalk to the limestone and back to his glove, *thock, thock, thooock, thock, thock, thooock*. She stops to watch, curious because the doormen aren't chasing him away. *Thock, thock, thooock, thock, thock, thooock*. He has thick brown hair that sticks out from under his baseball cap, not a style so much as a fight he's losing. The bangs smother the right half of his forehead and the back touches the red trim of his T-shirt.

"You go to Saint David's?" she asks.

He nods without pausing the rhythmic flicking of his wrist.

"I go to Spence," she volunteers.

He nods again.

Sensing her presence is no longer justifiable, Linden makes a loop to the market, where she gets a chocolate soft serve and returns. People eat ice cream outside. That stretch of sidewalk is now the proper place for her. That a boy she's never seen before happens to be there as well is merely how communities form, like *227*, they're just neighbors, enjoying the warm afternoon, making a stoop where there was none.

She watches him until her cone is gone. Despite how excruciatingly slowly she's eaten it, she's been unable to eke out more than five extra minutes.

"Do you live here now?" she asks. It's her closing number.

"Yep."

"Okay, well then, see you around."

~

It's Jayne who fills in the story early one Sunday morning at the end of seventh grade.

"A new boy," she repeats. "That must be Brock Haniman's son."

"Who's Brock Haniman?" Clyde asks from where he's rearranging Jayne's perfume bottles on her vanity.

"He founded Haniman Capital," Jayne answers as she sits on the floor by her unmade bed, still in her nightgown, surrounded by yesterday's newsprint, polishing everyone's shoes. "Something with equity swaps, like Henry Kravis."

Both kids nod.

"Linden," she says abruptly, causing everything in Linden to shrink and seize. "Turn sideways."

Linden obliges in her oversize Bangles sleepshirt.

"Ha! Well, I'll be. It's finally time to take you bra shopping, young lady. I was starting to worry you were going to be flat as a board. No, wait, I may have some from the divorce that you can use—I was so thin then."

She stands and crosses to her walk-in closet while Clyde freezes like a prey animal, and Linden adds to her catalog of information about these pending breasts that they are a source of relief to her mother and that there's a correlation between thinness and bra size.

"He's just moved in. His wife—well, ex-wife, really, I think—she just died. Cancer. Poor man, he's had to leave behind the new life he was building to find a home suitable for a family and become a full-time parent all by himself. Of course I can relate."

"Which part?" Clyde whispers to Linden in alarm. "Cancer?"

"No!" she whispers back.

"Does Mom have cancer?"

"No! Taking in children! That part!"

"Oh." He puzzles over that. At seven, Clyde doesn't yet fully understand the Situation, only that his father, the Monster, caused Jayne a great deal of Distress and that Linden has been very Brave. With a thatch of thick blond hair and his mother's blue eyes, he's handsome, with natural athletic instincts and an ability to charm. Though he knows he's missing Things, not just information, but entitlements—a father, a family that matches the ones at school—he still heads out each day as though they're merely the motel he's been assigned by the Red Cross, no more a reflection on him than a foil blanket wrapped around six-hundred-dollar pajamas. *What, this? Oh, no, as soon as we get this dreadful business sorted, I'm going back where I belong.*

And it works. People treat him like a puppy sprung from a kill shelter. Always happy to see him bound their way.

"Got 'em!" Jayne comes out of the closet with a handful of black and maroon lace bras that look like sexy doll hammocks.

"I don't know," Linden says, peering at them dubiously.

"What's the problem?"

"My school shirts are white," Linden says quietly.

"Oh, it'll be fine." Jayne is instantly exasperated. Linden can't remember what her mother was like when they were little, but Jayne strikes her now as someone who has decided she is finished. At the art studio Linden will watch an older girl, who has been single-mindedly focused on detailing a piece for hours, abruptly stand, squash her clay back into a ball or abandon her canvas, dissatisfied and done. That is what Jayne reminds her of. Though what Jayne is done with when three of them are still waiting for breakfast, Linden can't put into words. "There's just no point schlepping you to the shop or spending money until we know what size you are, really. But don't you dare be huge like my sister. I can't handle that."

Defeated and hungry for pancakes that don't seem to be imminent, Linden takes the bras to her room, knowing she has been given no not-mortifying option. As she gets dressed, she confronts that come Monday, she must either reveal the budding breasts she's just been made aware of or wear a black bra under a white shirt. If Sage were here, Linden thinks, there would be hand-me-downs. White hand-me-downs. Or someone who could walk back into Jayne's room and say, "You know, Lindy might get teased."

There's a knock at the door. "Mom says French toast in five minutes," Brian shouts.

"Okay!" Linden shouts back.

They stay like that for a moment, Brian leaning his full height against her door, Linden sensing he's still there. They're the closest in age and temperament, and yet also so much like children trying to build a train track only to realize they each hold identical pieces with nothing to conjoin.

~

In the kitchen Jayne flips thick slices of challah and catches her reflection off the copper saucier hanging above the stove. A debate is starting to percolate as she stares in the mirror, making the daily evaluation of her stock before the opening bell, the depleted capital of her skin tone, the investment of a decent cream, the gain of a good night's sleep, and still—the depreciating asset that is her beauty. The men around her, hailing taxis to their banks as she walks Clyde to school, they spread and swell and striate, red veins combing their faces, and yet their value goes up with their valuation.

Then she sees the women with the scars behind their ears no clever hairstyle can ever fully camouflage. The women who look pulled, their skin shiny like putty. Nothing about it appeals. And yet she has started staring at herself, touching her fingertips to her hairline and tugging ever so gently. And suddenly there she is—the Radcliffe junior Rodger couldn't believe was talking to him.

It's tempting. Jayne is tempted.

Friends tell her that she's nuts, that she's gorgeous, that she'll be snapped up. But she hasn't been. And Jayne isn't sure. Woman plus education plus associated expectations minus right moment in history plus marriage plus social pressure plus children minus husband, what does it add up to? What is it worth? She doesn't know.

Around her, women are opening businesses. Boutiques, gourmet shops. Martha Stewart was a Connecticut homemaker; now a legion of admirers is following her into commerce. Absent an idea for a venture, Jayne still helps at the children's schools, has her weekly hours at the soup kitchen, the gentlemen who harmlessly flirt, the tears of gratitude when she slips something in their pocket, a new pair of reading glasses or denture cream.

But is it enough? And what is enough? And who decides?

"Here's the paper," Brian says, tossing it on the table while Clyde gets out silverware. As the butter and berries are passed, the Book Review slides from the sleeping bag of other sections. Rodger's latest on the cover.

Jayne is instantly flushed. "That they *side* with that monster." She hits the paper, the sound making Clyde flinch.

"He does write for them." Linden always feels inexplicably compelled to point this out. "They didn't fire him then; they're not going to *not* review his book now."

"But the court psychiatrist said you were *irrefutably damaged*. He said that."

Linden nods. She knows. It's clipped inside her like keys to her backpack.

"And the psychiatrist said something was *wrong* with him, that his attachment was *dysfunctional*, with inappropriate overtones, and the fact that he left me for my sister was practically incestuous, regardless of what happened to you, and he's allowed to go on living his life while you sit here . . ." Her words abruptly sputter out.

"While I sit here what, Mom?"

Jayne collects herself, wipes away flecks of spittle while Clyde reaches across and puts his hand on her forearm, as though he were her husband.

Linden watches them sit in solidarity, manages a few more bites, then takes her plate to the sink and slips out of the kitchen. She grabs her Tretorns from the front hall closet and presses for the elevator.

"Hey," the boy says as the door slides open. He's dressed as he was the last time, in jeans he's supposed to grow into and a school jersey.

"Hey," she answers, quickly inventorying her own self and simultaneously accepting she can do nothing about any of it now. The loose-fitting shirt, which may not be loose enough. Her hair, which has suddenly started to curl in surprising ways. And the bones of her face that seem to be drifting, the cheekbones high one day, the forehead flat the next, rendering any handle on herself impossible. The other morning, she found a jar of Jolen bleach on her sink, a gift from her mother. When she asked what it was for, Jayne answered, "I am a blonde. But you are going to need help."

What she does have are rubber bracelets, at least a dozen, and dangling heart earrings from P.S. I Love You, a high-end child-geared boutique that devours the neighborhood's allowances like a basilisk they've all agreed to keep as a pet. "What floor are you on?" she asks.

"Ten. You want to go somewhere?"

"Sure."

He doesn't ask her where she wants to go or pause to see if she's keeping step. He just struts out into the perfect June morning toward Central Park freshly hatched, cocky on arrival. Linden walks slightly slower, hoping to drag him back. The park to her is outings with Barbara, forced marches for hours with a babysitter; it's blisters and hunger and needing to pee, or it's the malevolent place that nearly killed Huck. Couldn't they get an ice cream? Or an egg cream?

But she follows. Because she's on a date. And even though school will get out on Wednesday, and there will be no time to turpentine her portrait in everyone's minds and repaint this new Linden, the one who Goes on Dates, it could still be an image potent enough to last until September if she keeps it out of the sunlight.

At each crosswalk they fall back in line, her shoulders slightly higher than his, and she spins through questions like the Rolodex on her mother's telephone table, finally settling on, "How does your school do it?" a terrible start by any standard.

"Do what?" he asks, his expression one of derision, but his torso pivots toward her because it's unexpected and maybe he feels like no one does anything unexpected.

"Your school finishes in eighth grade, right—next year?" she clarifies.

"Oh, yeah."

"So you'll be a senior?"

"Yeah." The light changes, and they cross Fifth toward the canopy of trees, the branches rustling as if beckoning.

"That's cool."

"You want a soda?" He gestures to one of the carts that line the park's entrances like sentries.

Yes! she thinks. *A soda.* Something they might have to sit and drink. In Linden's mind, this might happen on a bench swing, in the South. "Sure. Grape."

He holds up two fingers while sliding singles out of his back pocket, an obvious repetition of something he's seen his father do, and Linden feels like she's in good hands.

"We turn over in eighth grade," she says, popping the can, trying not to spill, trying not to seem like she feels—awkward and nervous. Does she have a pimple? She hadn't even looked in the mirror that morning. "It's a weird system. So I'll be a freshman."

He nods, taking that in as they start to walk into the park. It hasn't rained since April, prompting talk of drought and water rationing, and a cloud of dust hovers inches from the path. Linden only minds that her Tretorns might turn brown. "That stinks."

"I know. Only bright side, maybe, is that when I get to ninth, I'll have upper school kind of figured out, I guess."

He leads them to the left, down toward one of the short tunnels Linden always avoids if possible because they smell like pee and usually have someone lying on the ground asking for money or, worse, performing juggling tricks, and she hates the intense inadequacy she feels at those moments to fix their lives so they don't need to sleep where people urinate, or mime for money in funny striped tights.

Topic exhausted, she asks, "What are you doing this summer?"

"Everyone asks me that."

"I'm sorry."

He stops to face her as they emerge from the tunnel, deeper into the park, closer to the center ring, where, from certain angles, you could lose sight of the buildings entirely. "You know what that is?"

"No."

"It's a conversational stupid."

"What's that?"

"'How are you?' 'I'm fine.' No, you're not. It's a waste of breath. People ask bullshit all the time. Or questions they don't really want the answer to. Nobody actually gives a shit what I'm doing this summer." Just above his jawline, in a patchwork of stubble, the skin turns red on both sides, and something about that makes her breath quicken.

"I care."

"What?"

"Or, rather . . ." She draws herself up but then drops down on one hip to even out their heights again. "I want to know. I am genuinely curious. I asked to get the information. Information I want to have. That's why I asked."

He smiles, effecting a transformation over his entire face. Linden has been in the elevator with his father, Brock Haniman of Haniman Capital, and it occurs to her that, while she's a girl with a man's face, he must look like his mother—the sharp and narrow nose, the full lips with a natural pout. But the smile erases all trace of scowl and becomes her new goalpost. "I'm spending the summer with my aunt on the Cape," he says. "Tennis camp."

Her eyes trace the length of him. He doesn't seem like anyone who held Brian and her mother's rapt attention at the US Open; there's nothing catlike or expansive about him. She can't picture him covering the court in a stride.

"Do you like tennis?" she asks.

"Who the fuck likes tennis?"

She thinks for a moment. "Tennis players." And then: "It's okay if you swear. I'm not allowed, but my older brother does all the time. He'll be a senior."

The boy drains the last of his Coke, wipes his mouth with the back of his hand, and burps. "I'm going to the Cape to give my dad a 'break.'"

"From?"

"The *exhausting* work of being my father." He suddenly sounds like her mother, and she imagines he's parroting someone—his aunt, maybe.

"Are you?" she asks, wondering if she's given herself a grape mustache. And if she used the bleach right to begin with.

"What?"

"Exhausting."

He looks at her in disbelief.

She shrugs. "My brother Huck was exhausting."

"How?" he challenges, now the defender of all those perceived to cause fatigue.

"He brought whiskey to school in a thermos."

"Really?" He's impressed, she can tell.

"Everyone agreed, if he'd just picked vodka, he might have gotten away with it." Her ponytail is now sitting on her neck like a hot little animal. She lifts it up for a few moments of air, but she has no bobby pins, and her mother told her when she conceded to trying ballet that she didn't have the face for buns. She certainly isn't going to try to braid her hair right there in front of a boy.

"Was."

"Was what?" she asks.

"You said *was*. Was exhausting. Is he not now?" The sun rises higher in the sky, the trees providing no further respite.

"I don't know. The doorman wasn't permitted to allow him up after a point, and I—" She falters. "I don't know." She squints to think how to put it. "I mean, I imagine he's still exhausting, just exhausting someone else. Like, maybe my aunt, or his friends, or something."

"Your aunt? He lives with her now?" This seems to intrigue him, and she wants to intrigue because she isn't sure anything she's said yet is right and she needs more time.

"Well, she's his mother. Technically."

"So he's your brother—or he's your cousin?"

Linden takes an audible breath. "When my aunt was young, she had kind of, like, a nervous breakdown or something and left her kids with my mom, who raised them as her own, and then we moved into our building, and I was born—"

"So, she was married?"

"Yeah."

"Your mom's pretty."

Whenever someone compliments Jayne, Linden feels a prickle of pride—or jealousy, she's never sure which. "Yeah, so one day my aunt shows back up, and she looks old, my mom says she looked so old, but I don't remember, she just seemed grown-up to me, so we hung out with her for a while, you know, did museums and stuff, and she liked hard candies, but then she went again and—somehow—my dad went with her, and that was a whole big deal, but then Huck and Sage, they followed, so that's where they are. But not Brian. Brian stayed." She ends on that triumphant note. As if that's what the whole story had been about, how Brian stayed. Of course, to hear Jayne tell it, it was. If it didn't fully tilt the scales to Jayne's side, it at least balanced them.

"Brian, the skinny guy with the books?"

Linden nods. She knows what he means—her brother's habit of not putting all his books in his backpack but carrying several in his arms like he's waiting to be invited to a sock hop. It's weird.

"My dad thought he was maybe Israeli or Lebanese."

"Nah," Linden says. "The green eyes are my aunt's. But he's just half-Black. I think. We think." Jayne has never answered the question she cannot answer and that would/should begin a conversation that could/should end with *Call your mother.*

"And the little one? He doesn't look like you, either."

"That's Clyde. He's . . . well, he's Clyde."

The boy takes all this in, the torrent of words, the girl—a little too tall, a little too much elbow and knee, one hand holding her hair off her neck, the other shading her large eyes from the sun to see him—and he says, "Wait, what's your name?"

"Linden—" She catches herself. "Lindy—" And again. "Lin."

"Which is it?"

"Lin. But I'm thinking of spelling it with a *y*, and maybe an extra *n*. You?"

"Justin. I think just Lin is good. You want to run the ramble?"

He leads her expertly into the center of the park, and she wonders if this is something the boys' schools teach that the girls' schools don't or if this knowledge is scrawled in urinals or passed along on the sidelines of lacrosse games. As the canopy closes over them like dancers clasping hands, they leave behind children chasing balls and secretaries sunbathing on rocks with small transistor radios.

At a certain point Linden starts to feel tense, not because Justin is jumping from rock to rock with increasing ferocity or that she's struggling to keep up, but because she knows she's venturing closer to the West Side and her father. She doesn't want to say, "Hey, let's head back," because she never wants the day to end. But seeing the windows of Central Park West come closer makes her feel like the earth is tilting, and she needs to grab the nearest trunk. "Are you hungry?" she asks instead. "Hot dogs?" Boys like hot dogs.

Justin pauses to consider. "Okay."

A half hour later they find themselves back on Fifth Avenue, eating and drinking two more sodas as the museum traffic ambles past them, eager to see, or eager to recover from, thousands of masterworks.

"What are you doing this summer?" he asks.

"Sailing camp. It's going to be a disaster." Then she remembers her mother's maxim, that men do not like downbeat women, and catches herself. "But I'll try it."

After another minute, Justin crushes his soda can underfoot and scoops it up, arcing it cleanly into the trash can that smells precociously like August, as if the whole promise of summer has already rotted. "I better get back. Think I'm going to the movies."

She feels herself sink as she takes in that this is over, that he has plans, that she doesn't, that he won't invite her any further into his life, that this has been just this.

"Yeah," she pushes herself to agree, "I'm meeting a friend."

She follows him back across Seventy-Ninth, and once again, she trails just inches behind him. Lexington arrives too quickly.

They get in the elevator. She presses four, and he reaches across her to press ten. He smells like boy and sweat and dust. "You want a cookie?" she asks rapidly when the door opens.

He shrugs.

"Clyde was going to make them after breakfast."

"Okay."

Now he has to follow her—into the vestibule, into the apartment's foyer, into the kitchen, where, indeed, two sheets of chocolate chip cookies sit by the open window, their scent on the hot breeze.

Wordlessly, she tears off two sheets of paper towel, slides a cookie onto each, and carries them toward her bedroom. He follows in silence, the covertness of their mission suddenly electric between them.

Linden listens for the quality of the silence. Is it the silence of her mother running errands? Or the silence of her reading in the next room? Is it the silence of Brian studying at a friend's? Or studying on the other side of the wall? Clyde has no silence, so she can discount him.

They enter her room, and Linden latches her door slowly, stealthily, and turns the lock.

Justin takes her desk chair, the hard one that swivels.

In response she places herself on the carpet, leaning against the base of her bed, and looks at the room—the pegboard covered in Laura Ashley fabric that matches her headboard and dust ruffle, the pictures of Eric Stoltz and Judd Nelson, the stuffed unicorn that she keeps on her bed because the most popular girl in her class keeps a stuffed unicorn on her bed, and until that moment it had never occurred to Linden that it might be lame.

They eat their cookies.

He finally speaks. "Do you miss them? Your family?"

She nods, although the enormity of what it is that she misses is impossible to convey. He comes and sits down next to her.

She doesn't know what to do, but she knows what she does—which is put her hands on his shoulders and press him down to the carpet.

Her face above his now, she can smell the soda crystals clinging to the faint hair above his lip. He looks into her eyes, and she feels a hard pressure against her hip, uncomfortable, almost, as if someone has suddenly wedged something between them. No moment ahead and no moment behind, she reaches down and unbuttons his jeans. Then slides her hand inside the fly, taking the tent of his Fruit of the Looms in her hand—and instantly his eyes shut, shoulders shake, and a warm wetness seeps through the fabric under hand as he makes a sound—of pleasure, of defeat, Linden can't say.

She only knows, as she helps him up, takes his chocolate-smeared paper towel from his hand, releases the latch, looks left, looks right, and shoos him to the vestibule, that something has righted between them. That he can decide when they'll see each other and when they'll talk, when the silence will prevail and how it will break, which direction they'll go in, for how long, and what for. He can scowl until he smiles and say what rock they have to climb, but she—she has this.

12

Despite haunting the elevator in the days after their encounter, trying to transform sixteen square feet into a windswept moor, Linden only sees Justin again when Jayne is rushing her down to Bloomingdale's to get shorts, it having come to light, amid last-minute packing for camp, that Linden's lengthening legs have made last summer's obscene.

As her mother sprints to the Lexington curb, arm outstretched for a taxi, no time for the doormen, Justin is standing amid his duffel bags at the edge of the awning, waiting for his father to bring the car from the garage. He reminds Linden of that optical illusion question from third grade—Is Lincoln's hat taller than the brim is wide? Surrounded by the horizontal spill of sporting equipment, he looks especially short. Or her mother wasn't exaggerating, and she actually has grown since last weekend.

"Lindy!" her mother calls, one arm on the open taxi door, the other beckoning.

Linden looks over her shoulder, hoping he might glance up, smile, acknowledge her, but he keeps his gaze fixed on the ground, hands in the pockets of his dungarees. He must have heard her name, he must have.

Jayne slides into the back seat, its upholstery held shut with electrical tape, and Linden slips in beside her, the car lurching into traffic before the door can thud shut. Unable to help herself, Linden spins on her knees to watch Justin grow smaller still. And she will spend the summer wondering if, when he raised his arm to wave, he'd been saying goodbye to her—or hello to someone else.

~

She thinks about him every day, relentlessly. At camp, her mind and hormones hold her hostage from sleep. Their bayonets at her back, she stares at the underside of the bunk above, the blue-and-white ticking smattered with ancient menstrual stains, having been flipped, and flipped again, and asks aloud, "What did I think about before Justin?" She alternates between rerunning the memory of their afternoon until it loses all potency and imagining seeing him again, kissing him, what she'll say, what he'll say. She maps it out over and over like a heist she's rehearsing for.

~

It feels like she's been back at home forever, but it's actually been less than a week. Less than a week to show off the end of her tan, her new haircut, and Tretorns. It seems that her face is starting to settle into some kind of form; perhaps the worst of puberty is behind her? But, despite multiplying her odds by taking every opportunity to ride the elevator, exasperating Jayne with her helpfulness as she insists that they need more eggs, milk, and yogurt, she only encounters poodles, children, and bankers.

By Friday she's given up, her polyester uniform rumpled, her new bra stuck to her sweaty back as she hunches against the weight of her textbooks, all focus on her first weekend of real upper school assignments, guard down. That's when the elevator door opens, and he emerges into the lobby in his soccer gear, passing her with an obligatory "Hey." No smile, no warmth, no acknowledgment.

Oh.

That's all she can think, *Oh.* Her mind frozen on the syllable of defeat, of resignation, of unwanted information taken on board. Oh. The sound of a circle. The sound of a hole.

~

Thus, Linden slumps through the fall while her mother is literally humming with excitement. Debussy. The étude travels to her ankles, which tap a private rhythm as she thumbs a *New Yorker* she's finally getting around to. It's on her lips as she follows the children's conversations, shares their pizza, suggests outings for ice cream. Linden does not like changes. Even good ones. When she tries to bring up the inexplicable to Brian, he refuses to acknowledge it. His twelve-month countdown to departure has begun; he does not want to hear, nor does he care, that they're going to repaint the prison.

Needing to stay out of the apartment, she concedes to join Art Club, but only because it's impressed upon them at upper school orientation that their future college prospects will rest on their extracurriculars. Similar to having a Corey or a Patrick on the inside of their locker, they now have to Pick Something that will Define them. But art isn't her real extracurricular. Her real extracurricular is Hope. She hopes at least fifteen hours a week, more on weekends. Hopes so intensely, with such single-minded ferocity, that no member of her school's unfortunately diminutive basketball team has anything on her.

She hopes that one day Brian might be hanging out with friends in the living room, that Brian might make friends, might bring them home, and that there will be a new guy who looks like Eric Stoltz, that he will notice her, and suddenly she will have a senior boyfriend. Or that she will actually meet someone at a dance. Those horrible dances she has to go to every two months, where she looks across the mob of equally pimply faces, feeling like a giraffe accidentally penned in with horses, making unavoidable, awkward eye contact with some boy who looks like a similarly stretched version of himself. It doesn't matter that she's all knees and elbows; she doesn't want Ichabod Crane. She wants Eric Stoltz. If that isn't possible, then why do the mothers go to all the trouble of renting spaces and making invitations, paying for DJs and juice and cheese doodles?

And lastly, she hopes that, given that this is New York, she might just actually run into Eric Stoltz. And he will recognize her inner amazing and be her boyfriend.

There is no end to her hoping.

Then, suddenly, it's Christmas, and the city is Zsa Zsa Gabor in an ermine coat. On Christmas Eve, wearing her Hope like a diadem, she trails her mother and brothers into the 21 Club, as she does every year, but this time Brock Haniman of Haniman Capital and Justin are already seated at their table. Her mother makes flustered, blushing introductions, as though all four kids don't immediately understand what's being perpetrated.

Linden slaps Brian in the face with a Frisbee of a look that says, *See, I told you!* Then she looks at Justin, and Justin looks away, and Linden makes her face impassive. Her Hope drops to the floor. Fine.

That's what she thinks: *Fine.* She knows when the invitation to the sleepover isn't coming; when she won't be able to share a ride to the party, even though someone could sit up front; when the group she's standing with on the sidewalk is going to break away without her, leaving her stranded, like a discharged electron. She knows when to say *fine* and walk away fast in the other direction.

"And this is Linden," Jayne says.

She extends her hand, smiling placidly. "Nice to meet you. I must have seen you in the elevator." Justin takes her hand awkwardly, palm sweaty, looking slightly frightened.

"What school do you go to?" she inquires, a mini-Jayne.

"Uh, Saint . . . D-David's," he stammers.

She nods politely, then turns her attention to the menu because pretending things aren't happening when they most definitely are is, she is discovering, her forte.

~

Brock proposes during a snowstorm, and they're married over the Easter break at Saint James's on Madison. A small reception at the Carlyle immediately follows, Jayne being sure to start this union in vetted locales that bring with them the weight of history and assuredness, parameters for behavior, and a setting of expectation. Nothing charming, this time around, no bohemian aspirations. She won't accept a roommate's pipe cleaner as an engagement ring, drive her own moving van, chart out an apartment carved from other apartments on an unremarkable street, hoping to make a mark, the mark—did you know Rodger and Jayne Donoghue once lived on this block? From such shoddily assembled beginnings, is it any wonder things fell apart as they did? No, everything about this second marriage will be different.

In addition to house hunting for a weekend place in the Hamptons, it's decided, as the building is going co-op, that Brock will buy their apartment, throwing Jayne into a fervor of redecorating, amazed now that she never repainted Rodger's study, that the scent of his Camels still lingers in the carpet and wood. She has it all ripped up and sanded away. For the first time she doesn't have to do everything on the cheap, no hunts through the Lower East Side for fabric remnants, no compromises: she can have the new refrigerator *and* the six-burner stove. By June the apartment is upholstered in Ralph Lauren khaki and terra-cotta florals, its walls mounted with Brock's trophy heads. Brian finds them creepy, Clyde helps arrange them, and Linden becomes fixated on them, especially the elephant in the living room.

"It's just so dead," she explains, whenever Jayne comes upon her staring at their new pachyderm.

"Linden."

"Why don't we do that with people? Why can't we have Grandpa on the wall with a little plaque?"

Jayne literally throws up her hands, the light catching her Chiclet-size diamond, and keeps moving—there's just so much to organize. Everything about becoming the "new" Mrs. Haniman feels so vastly improved from her time with Rodger. Brock appreciates that she replaces his fraying pajamas, that the closet in the hallway has extra of his toothpaste and deodorant, that she doesn't expect him to start using her brand of toothpaste, that she will not lecture him, red-faced, as his ex-wife had done, about her "time" and "efficiency."

That the first Mrs. Haniman had been his ex-wife, that he was not, in fact, a widower, that he left her for some tawdry and cliché amusement—a secretary, cocktail waitress, shampoo girl—left her to cope with the death of his attention and then cancer all on her own has somehow been obscured in everyone's minds. In his circles, they still refer to his "loss," and the "blessing" of Jayne. And the fact that he's pulled that off, and is now married to a woman who essentially stood at the center of the Plaza ballroom, climbed inside a mirrored box, tapped it with her wand, released a flock of doves, revealed a fat rabbit, and unleashed a stream of sparklers, until everyone paused, chicken potpie halfway to their lips, murmuring, *That poor, brave woman*, and not, *How could she not have known? What kind of mother is she?* makes them a formidable couple indeed.

⁓

After the last day of school, Justin returns to his aunt's on the Cape while Linden is sent to sailing camp for what's negotiated to be the final time. In August, the family trip to Europe is forsaken so that Jayne and Brock can get Justin settled at boarding school and then Jayne can do the same for Brian at Howard and then onto Baltimore with Clyde to check in on Margaret.

Linden doesn't mind. She's been left money. Most days she takes herself to see *Parenthood* or *Sex, Lies, and Videotape* at the new multiplex on Eighty-Sixth Street and then to Mimi's for a slice of pizza. She likes going to the movies by herself, no popcorn to share, no opinions to match. In the afternoons, she might wander to the Society Library to look at antiquarian medical textbooks, or a museum. Sometimes she looks at the art, sometimes she just enjoys the cold, and the way air feels in large stone spaces. She leans back on a bench, dangling her sandal off the tip of her toe, pretending she's a Fragonard.

Also, museums are good places for Hoping. If Eric Stoltz is going to be anywhere, surely it will be here?

Linden has started to live in a hamster ball of her own imagination. There's the world she's standing in, one in which she is essentially alone in the city, a girl contending with ongoing breakouts and a body she's waiting to find out is enough, and what is enough, and who decides; and then there's the six-foot radius around her, crackling with an electrical storm of desire and attention. She walks the Frick like she's the mistress of the house, poised at any moment to receive her guests or servants. At the Cloisters, she frets about her children and the plague.

Linden is also determined that things will be different in ninth grade. Her class has lost almost a third of its members to boarding school. The nondenominational Bar Mitzvah bus girls, famed for giving blowjobs in the last row between the temple and the party venue, have gone off to be bitchy and judgmental in the country. Two of them will be at the same school as Justin, and Linden wonders if either of them will fool around with him. That's how they put it, "fooling around," as if teenagers with weaponized hormones trying to gain access to the genitals of other weaponized teenagers isn't deadly serious.

To distract herself, she starts bringing a sketch pad to the galleries but finds it unsatisfying. Instead, she entertains herself at the kitchen table, by the only air conditioner Jayne allows to have running while she's away, making dioramas out of shoeboxes, thread spools, corks, and scraps. She starts carving a beeline from her morning movie into the

Singer sewing shop across the street to buy supplies. Notions. That's what the women who work there call them. Notions.

Linden can't explain why she enjoys creating these little rooms so much, just knows that she wants to learn how to make them look like what she pictures—not dollhouses, exactly, but her brain doesn't have another framework, so she labors without language, without context, gluing, cutting, sewing, doing what she can't in life, create the rooms, place the people in them, make them do what she wants.

13

The following summer Jayne has the idea of a family trip to London. But Brian says he can't possibly leave his internship early—or arrive at preseason training late. He politely declines. He opts out. Justin requests to go straight from his aunt's place on the Cape to boarding school again. His aunt politely declines on his behalf. He opts out. Which leaves Clyde and Linden to trail Jayne around the National Gallery, go with Brock to Jermyn Street to be measured for shirts, and learn how to pour tea without letting the spout touch the rim.

But it's standing on King's Road beside a girl with a safety pin through her nose where Linden finds what she didn't know she was looking for. Through the plate glass sits a display of shoes like nothing she's ever seen. Black and sturdy, with yellow stitching and thick rubber soles that can make this whippet of a girl look like she's a militia of one.

~

Back in New York, while sitting by the yellow lockers one afternoon, reading about vectors, Dana, a girl she used to take tennis with, says without preamble, "We need to get you a life."

Linden looks up. This is it. The apotheosis of her Hoping.

"Okay."

"Come to my house on Saturday around eight. We'll figure out where to go from there."

It's the shoes, she knows it's the shoes. They're only just starting to become available here and still really hard to find. Only the cool kids, the ones allowed to roam very far afield with credit cards, have them. For once—she has the thing. For once, she is perfect.

~

Over the following weeks she starts "going out," meaning, meeting at Dana's house to get ready, where girls who don't talk to her at school try to figure out why she's there and then seem to accept the theorem that her being there means she deserves to be. She tries to keep up with their conversation but knows none of the players, hasn't been to any of the places, so she waits patiently until the call comes in with the location of the boys and it's time to go. Which may mean to a party—or a stoop. Or a stoop where they drink wine coolers and wait to hear about a party. She could get to take her coat off, she could not. Or she could end up in the East Village, looking for a band called the Spin Doctors. It's unpredictable.

As is the attention. There's the boy in the white turtleneck who sits beside her at a party, chats for a bit, then abruptly sticks his tongue down her throat—and never acknowledges her again. There are the boys who, for no apparent reason, bodycheck her on Fifth Avenue one night so that she's made aware of the sky from one blink to the next. She lies on the sidewalk, smiling up, so full of Coors she doesn't mind. And then there are the boys who suddenly offer to walk her home, or get her another beer, or throw enough money into the cab to pay to get her the rest of the way home—but don't call. Don't ask her out.

It's confusing, and exhilarating, and she is certain these shoes enable it all. They anchor her to the sidewalk. Standing, waiting—for the girls are always waiting—she's rooted. She can't articulate it, all she knows is that she feels deliciously heavy. She would never say, to herself or anyone else, *What I love is that no one can pick me up.*

She's fifteen—who would pick her up?

The magical thing about the shoes, though, is how they transform. Because once she starts walking, the hold releases and the rubber contracts and expands, flinging her into the air and across miles and miles of asphalt. She flies. But she would never say, to herself or anyone else, *What I love is that no one can outrun me.*

She's fifteen—who would be chasing her?

~

Linden wakes early the first morning of spring break when she hears footsteps. She slips out of bed, the dishwater light of mid-March dripping around the roller shade, and tiptoes to the kitchen, unsure what she's even spying on, except that the sound is out of the ordinary, and she always wants out of her ordinary. The fridge is open, and in the yolk-colored glow, she sees a hand on the door. Then the figure straightens and lets the door shut just enough for Linden to watch him drink the milk right out of the carton, eyes shut in pleasure, rivulets spilling down his chin, splashing on his bare chest—Linden gasps. Justin has grown probably four inches since the fall and has a body like a kouros. Lean and muscular and hairless. He is so beautiful.

He opens his eyes and lowers the carton, wiping the back of his hand across his face but ignoring the drip crossing his nipple that she wants to lick off.

"Hey."

"Hey," she says. "Did you get in last night? I didn't hear you."

"Late."

She's aware of her thin nightgown, that she hasn't grabbed her robe, that she wants him, that she's never understood wanting before, that the sight of him is doing very real and measurable things to her body that nothing, no imagining and no sopping, slimy game of Seven Minutes in Heaven, has ever done.

"I'm coming with you guys to Nevis."

"Oh." Again, *Oh*. But a different oh. A tortured oh, a jagged flip top, a tattoo of barbed wire around a bicep.

"Yeah, apparently, Brian's gonna stay at school, so I'm filling in."

"Cool. Well, I better finish packing. The car's coming at ten." She backs out of the kitchen to go die, to crawl right to the bottom of her bed under the covers and eat her nails off until they bleed. Because what kind of fuckup is attracted to her own brother?

~

It's not until eleventh grade that Linden discovers it's actually damage that's the great equalizer. Of course, no one calls it "damage," they call it "cool." He's so cool, with his MC jacket and his tickets to Jane's Addiction. She's so cool, with her cigarettes in her pocket and the twenty-six-year-old boyfriend she met at Max Fish. Linden slides among them, not quite able to fully transform herself into something effortless; being Lin Donoghue is still a work requiring tremendous focus for flawless execution. But the shared drive toward self-annihilation creates a second silent language. She's casual in the pink-lit bathroom when someone does coke off a bus pass. She's already in the party's lobby when the son of the movie star needs to run out for condoms and takes her with him. They walk for blocks in the cold, his arm around her shoulder, to buy Trojans, so he can go back and have sex on the pile of coats with the girl who's pretty in a way Linden will never be. She cannot instigate, but she can commiserate. She's no one's first call, but she's always there. It's not enough, but she has never known enough.

~

One Friday evening Linden senses something is off as soon as she opens the front door and sees her mother's wet shoes kicked off in the front hall. Then hears sobbing from the kitchen. Has word about her midterm already gotten back to Jayne—how would that even be possible? Pencils down was only a few hours ago.

"Mom?"

"In here," Brock answers.

Linden drops her umbrella and backpack and walks tentatively down the short vegetable-wallpapered hall. Jayne is seated in one of the woven-back chairs, Brock behind, his strong hands on her shoulders. "What's wrong?" Linden asks.

She steps farther in, and that's when she sees Justin standing by the oven, shoulders hunched, school tie loose, khakis hanging off his hips.

"Your brother's gotten kicked out of boarding school," Jayne says, face teary and dilated.

Linden takes in the scene. Brock, whom she would have expected to be oscillating with rage, just looks embarrassed. And Jayne, whom she would have expected to be tense but contained, is beside herself. She sobs into a dish towel.

"What for?"

"Justin," Brock prompts, "would you like to tell your sister why they kicked you out?"

He looks at his feet. His hair has changed. It no longer looks like it's crawling over itself to get off his head. It's still longer than either parent would want, but now it hangs around his face. Linden notices the dent in the back pieces—has he been wearing a ponytail?

"Drugs."

Linden swallows and nods.

"I can't even look at you," Jayne says. "We worked so hard to get you into that school." Fresh tears spring. "And now you have a *permanent* mark on your record. You can kiss a good college goodbye."

Brock squeezes her shoulders.

"No. I have done and done and *done* for these children, and it all gets thrown back in my face—"

"Jayne," he interrupts her firmly, "the car is coming in twenty, and we don't want to miss the curtain. Let's get cleaned up and allow Justin to unpack."

At a nod from his father, Justin slinks out of the room.

"Where's Clyde?" Linden asks.

"Sleepover," Jayne says with relief. "By the time he gets back tomorrow, I'll have collected myself." She stands in her riding pants and cashmere turtleneck, her fingers and wrists roped in gold. "Brock will leave money on the table for a pizza."

"Okay."

Jayne looks at her for a moment, the sheen on her eyes catching the overhead light, and Linden braces to be asked about the test. "Try not to slouch."

While her mother dresses, Linden takes the cookie jar to the kitchen table and methodically eats snickerdoodles until she hears the swish of her mother's taffeta and the front door shutting behind them.

She replaces the chipped teddy bear, passes through the foyer, pockets the twenty, retrieves her backpack, and heads to her room. Friday night. She's maybe supposed to meet up with some people later. Maybe.

From halfway down the hall comes the throbbing, menacing, enticing sound of muffled drums and bass guitar. She stops outside Justin's room and touches her hand to the door. Like leaning her forehead against the smooth, cool concrete of a nuclear reactor. She puts her hand on the knob and—

The room is red. That's the first thing she notices. The only light coming from a string of plastic chili peppers hung around one window.

And hot. They've been shut for weeks, and the air is aggressively close, dense with everything he'd left behind to ripen.

Through this searing, solid air, the sound pullulates. A harsh wall that strips her eardrums and lacerates her brain, scouring her from the inside.

Then she fully sees him. Standing in the middle of the room. Shirt off. Arms outstretched in either direction, rigid and trembling with the exertion of holding something invisible at bay. Palms facing out. Head slung.

Oh.

She drops her backpack and the money.

She crosses to him.

He doesn't move.

She slows as she gets closer. Her lips are now inches from his down-cast forehead.

He doesn't move.

She reaches out in both directions and touches the tops of his fore-arms with her fingertips, tracing them slowly in through the downy hairs, then over his elbows and biceps, his skin unexpectedly soft, softer than hers, across his shoulders, the knoll of new muscle, then down, over his pectorals, her fingertips grazing his nipples, then farther over the hard ripples of his abdomen—and suddenly his mouth is on hers, and they crush into each other, a violent victory over space.

~

Of course, it's unsustainable, untenable. An impossible situation for adults, let alone adolescents. There is heroin in the next room. Try not to think about heroin. You could sit here, attempting to write a paper on the Corn Laws, or, *or*, you can put down your textbook, tiptoe eight feet down the sisal carpet, twist open the door, and get high.

Some months they convince themselves they're entitled to this. Some months they decide together to quit. The worst months are the ones when one of them decides it's over, leaving the other roiling in intolerable shame. Justin begs Jayne to appeal to new boarding schools. Jayne thinks it better if he only has one strike against him.

And then the summer lopes back around like a kid on skates, and Justin leaves for his allotted months with his aunt. Linden leaves for art camp. They write letters. Dozens of letters. Every day there's an envelope waiting for Linden at the lodge. "Linden has a boyfriend," the other students coo.

"No," she deflects too hastily, too awkwardly, "it's just my brother."

They instantly back away, discomfited. Because they know what they've seen. They're the girls who come to art camp. What they see is their currency, the foundation of their everything. They don't know what it feels like to run for class president or homecoming queen, but they know how emotion translates into musculature, how a girl runs to get mail after breakfast, cheeks aflame, eyes steps ahead of her, when she's in love.

Thankfully the rumors don't follow her back to New York.

But neither does Justin.

His aunt takes him back to Boston with her and gets him enrolled at her kids' school. The letters stop. A clean break.

~

What does it feel like to be the thing that can be given up? Left behind? Quit? Again and again?

Linden stops eating, suspecting that there's something deeply wrong with her that must be starved to wither, atrophy, and die. Her brain does exactly what the brains of thousands of other girls her age command them to do—pick safe foods, consume as little of them as possible, repeat. What she likes is that thinking about food leaves no space in her mind for anything else, no fears about never seeing Justin again, no insecurities about friendships or boys, just a quiet, ugly sky punctuated by the occasional drifting salad. What she likes is having one thing in her life she can be the final word on. What she likes is lying on her floor after school, pulling up her shirt and running her tempera-stained fingers over her ribs, palpating her hip bone, feeling the sense of her body finally floating to the surface.

~

At Christmas, Linden sees it in his eyes before she can even ask. He's done, has made himself done, has a girlfriend at school, a normal girlfriend with normal problems. For five nights she waits, awake, legs shaved, covers up to her chin, waits for the knob to turn. On the sixth night, she knocks on his door.

"Come in," he answers. "No, wait, don't."

He's as far from sleep as she is. She enters by candlelight and sits on the edge of his bed in the black cotton jersey robe her mother gave her for Christmas. The flame makes parabolas around the room. "I miss you."

They stare, unblinking, into each other, and he's hard before he can even put his refusal into words.

~

In the morning, he still leaves. Leaves to join his girlfriend's family on their ski trip, arriving off the plane in the matching sweater she bought him. And Linden, achy and hollow, sits on the piano bench in the dark as the clock strikes midnight, cheers pealing from the apartments across Seventy-Ninth Street, from the ice-slicked sidewalk below, from the TV broadcasting Times Square, and Linden thinks, *Fuck this.*

And then she says it aloud. "Fuck. This."

She gets up, goes to the fridge, pulls out the leftover Bûche de Noël, and finishes it with a fork.

She's done.

There's life out there, and she's ready to slam into its midst.

She's ready to be chosen.

PART IV

14

At thirty-two, Lin Donoghue is aware that she's adept at doing a thing and *not* doing it at the same time, moving through space, activating her muscle fibers, objectively taking action that would indicate to casual observers *toward*—opening a door, hailing a taxi, leaning in for a kiss, a hug, a platter, buying a ticket, a drink, a condom, signs of ascension, signs of agreement, all the while thinking, *No. No. Fuck, no. Never.*

This is how Lin is feeling on the subway to her aunt Barbara's funeral, daring herself to get out at every stop. Times Square, she can get theater tickets, it's always easier at the box office. Fifty-First, she knows an esthetician who takes walk-ins, she could try her luck. Columbus Circle, shopping, the park. The train hums and rumbles, sparks and squeaks, carrying her and the man wearing a tank top and a top hat, the woman tweezing her eyebrows, the Hasid, who visibly bristles at being squashed in next to a potentially menstruating woman, the homeless, the high and the destitute, and all their collective smells and stale air, and she does not get off.

But she is not going. No. There is no way she would put herself in the same room as her father.

Absolutely none.

~

It was Clyde who called her. The family chain of information goes Clyde, then Lin, then Brian, because Clyde is Jayne's first call, her *in case of*. In case of emergency, in case of new hat, in case of decorating indecision, in case of questionable mole. Validatingly, Clyde always answers on the first ring.

Once apprised of Jayne's latest acquisition or decommission, be they basal cells or baby clothes, Clyde never calls Brian, because he has no patience with Brian's ill-named "receptionists," who are, in truth, a line of interference. Human static, sentient tall buildings, living dead zones. Whether it's the women behind the desk at his production offices or some kid on set assigned to hold his phone, his family suspects Brian uses these people to hide from anyone trying to reach him. Clyde, being someone who needs to say what he has to say, when he has to say it, finds Brian distinctly unsatisfying.

So he calls Lin, who is always only too eager for the distraction from her distractions and will start conversations with, "Have you ever watched Bette Davis on Jack Paar?"

"You are confusing me with another kind of gay," Clyde will answer before letting her know that her presence is requested at a dinner, that Mom is now thinking about *not* selling the last few buildings in Baltimore but buying *more* buildings in Baltimore because Brock says it's a good idea, that Mom wants to know if she took her oolong tea.

"Why would I take her tea?" Lin asks, genuinely befuddled.

"You like it."

"I can buy my own."

It isn't that Jayne doesn't call Lin—she calls her frequently—but she would never call to ask if Lin had taken the tea she bought in Paris last year, the loose leaves housed in a ceremonial tin made to look like a pagoda. That's Clyde's department.

Clyde is, by default, the fixer, an assignment stemming from the unfortunate fact that Jayne cannot quite bring herself to ask Clyde about Clyde, operating, as he does, in professional and personal realms of which she cannot conceive. He doesn't have a job, per se, nor a boyfriend, per se, nor a girlfriend, per se, leaving Jayne somewhat at a loss. But missing tea or outdated linens—that, they can parse.

So Jayne calls Clyde, and Clyde calls Lin, and Lin calls Brian. But unlike her little brother, Lin loves "trading calls." She likes chatting to the people who answer Brian's phone, loves getting points for calling without actually having to make conversation with her terse brother, loves that the game could go on for weeks before she's forced to ask him how his latest film is going. Brian, who, since the days of his last Ewok village, did not seem to have a creative, artistic bone among his two hundred and six, who slouches to shape them like a shepherd's crook, has somehow parlayed his MBA into financing films, deeply felt, beautiful films that Lin compliments him on after, sometimes too overcome to speak, crying into the lapels of his stupidly expensive, ill-fitting suit, and he answers, "We're recouping our investment overseas."

And yet, Lin thought as she gripped the phone, on hold again, Brian was Barbara's child. Her *actual* child. So Lin really tried. She called all the assistants—the bitchy ones, the unctuous ones, the one with the tongue piercing that clicked in her ear—and impressed upon them that he *had* to call her back this time and, when that failed, that there had been a death.

~

Lin finds herself getting off the subway just blocks from the church, her body still moving steadfastly in the direction of where she isn't going. *Church,* she thinks. How has "free love" Barbara, as her mother sometimes referred to her, always prompting Lin toward hours of reflection on the cost of love, come to cross paths with a church? And if it happens after you die, does that count as crossing paths? And then she realizes, what does she know? They went to the park a handful of times over the course of a year that ended a quarter of a century ago. Barbara might have become born-again.

In fact, Lin has to keep reminding herself that she doesn't actually *know* anyone she might see today—or the deceased, for that matter. That she has to let go of her flimsy preconceptions. That she has to let go.

She does spend hours in EMDR therapy trying to do just that by incongruously looping through her memories, it having occurred to nearly everyone that perhaps the reason all her friends have paired off and she has so many weddings and baby showers to attend but none to throw has something to do with her father. "I'm not an idiot," she'll say, lighting a cigarette on Clyde's couch or outside some bar. "Obviously I have daddy issues; obviously I choose men who can't commit."

But in the worn tweed chair, the electric pulsers in her hand for the therapy endorsed by the VA for trauma, the quest to heal from *this stupid baggage* she's been carrying around *since childhood* so she can finally *get on with her life* becomes something else. Memories swim to the surface, or images, or footage, some soundless. And sometimes sound is all there is—the syncopation of a typewriter, the flick of her father's lighter, the creak of his chair spinning, the thunk of the receiver landing in the cradle. Sometimes she hears, *Shshshshsh*, and the sense of being simultaneously comforted and silenced makes her drop the pulsers to the floor like they've overheated.

She gets up and says, "I think I've done enough for today."

And her therapist says, "This work is hard. Healing the brain is tough. But you're making great progress. We're getting closer."

Are we? she wonders as she expectorates herself back onto the street. Because when she chronicles what her brain fans out before her, the sight of her father laughing as he pushes her on the swing, the feel of him holding her tight during *Bedknobs and Broomsticks*, the smell of tobacco and Bic pens, what she never confesses is that when she accesses the memory under the memories, what she feels—primarily—is . . . good. What she feels is loved.

And that's when she needs to leap up, fling the session's check from her purse, and stumble to the door.

~

She checks her watch, a vintage Omega that belonged to her grandpa Joe, and hastens her pace. A picture, that's what Lin wishes for. A recent picture. She doesn't want to mourn a purple sleeve, or a smell she now associates with Barbara and a midnineties liberal arts education in equal measure—patchouli and ylang-ylang. She doesn't want her throat to twist over the sound of a Brach's butterscotch finding its way from the bottom of a pocket into her outstretched hand. She doesn't want to flinch whenever she finds herself on the street behind a frowsy blonde in her midthirties. Because Barbara died at sixty-six. She'd moved past Lin and Clyde and Brian into another life that lasted years longer than the first one.

But did she still have kind eyes? Lin wonders.

These questions are the surface she skims, like a water strider, in the final blocks.

~

At that same moment, across town, Jayne Haniman is surprised to discover she's sad. Desperately, almost childishly so. She hadn't realized she's been like a dog nosing a ball through the grass, eyes down, the green felt forever in front. And the ball was also a fortune teller's, and in it glowed a future where she and her sister were friends, and the past was another past. But that was always in the distance, always someday, always tomorrow.

There was no today where Jayne would have called the woman who married her husband. The husband who broke her child.

So now she sits on the floor of her closet, holding in her lap a faded-yellow box from a Maryland department store thirty years out of business. Inside are two identical dresses in different sizes—puffed sleeves, smocked front, the pattern a tight floral of tiny buds, an Easter ensemble from another lifetime, hand-sewn by Margaret and stored fancily. Jayne is sure, if she'd cared, she could have dug through the piles in her mother's attic until she found the matching ties their brothers must have worn. But she didn't.

Because when the months of work that were dismantling the house in Cherry Hill fell to Jayne, and Jayne alone, she carried a box of contractor garbage bags to the attic and filled eighty-six of them with what her mother had held on to for *someday* and *maybe*. She did it mercilessly and without sentiment. Her father's winter suits, her brothers' school clothes, dresses in various shades of emerald and various sizes, depending on her mother's success with "reducing" that year. All of it went in the bags. Every single item Margaret had assembled to barricade against poverty when it knocked once again on her door. Tea sets, foo dogs, embroidery, candlesticks, letter openers, doilies, antimacassars— all hauled onto a truck and directly to the local thrift shop where her mother had bought much of it in the first place. All except this box. This faded cardboard, cracked down one side, that Jayne inexplicably could not part from, except that it was outings to town, the promise of penny candy, the promise of adulthood, the scent of the perfume counter, the sight of gloves modeled on graceful ceramic hands. And the little dress. The one she can see Bunny in if she squeezes her eyes shut. Bunny, age four, all marzipan arms and ringlet hair, and a smile that popped with ease on all alike—caterpillars, dogs, fresh biscuits, and siblings.

Where did that smile go? Jayne wonders as she rocks on the floor, little dress in her arms. *When did I lose her?*

～

Meanwhile, Lin is completing the final component of her maneuver, like the requisite finger flourish after a triple back handspring. She is now late for the funeral, forcing her to run where she doesn't want to go.

"Hey, little lady, slow down," says an unhelpful man as she rushes past, the kind of unhelpful man found in cities the world over, who park themselves like buzzards on telephone wires, waiting to comment on the comings and goings of women just trying to come and go. "Lucky man you're rushing to. Mm-hmm."

Somewhere in time Lin stopped being tall for her age and just became tall. But five feet nine, when at last men are at least five feet ten, isn't terrible, as Jayne reminds her often. Her strong face is lovely "at the right angles"—Jayne, again—and even Lin can appreciate on a good day that having her father's probing eyes, strong jaw, full mouth, and pronounced cheekbones means she could be a latter-day Anjelica Huston or Anh Duong, that perhaps the adjectives the art critics use to describe her, like *captivating* and *compelling*, may just be accurate. But to carry it off, she must walk, shoulders back, chin up; she must own it. For when she falters, when she is tired or sad or unsure, her features fly apart, and she is certain she is ugly.

Lin sometimes tries to look at herself from the vantage of a passerby. Do they see just another woman going about her day, preoccupied, perhaps, with needing a haircut, or remembering to send an email, or a date to ready herself for, or a date that's failing to materialize, or, oh God, maybe her small dog, or worse—cat? Or maybe it's okay, they might hope, sighing on her behalf, maybe she's divorced and on her way to school pickup. Maybe she has a life after all, someone to get her out of bed and out of her brain. Or maybe she has such a high-powered job that this Tuesday is the first day off she's had in months. She needs an emergency root canal—what else could tear her away from her desk?—and has given herself the rest of the hours to wander around the neighborhood, catch up with herself after so much wheeling and dealing.

In truth, she's just a woman, trying to leap from each sunup to sundown with as much grace as she can muster. In truth, she is just someone stretched to the end of her tiniest particle, throwing her body over a grenade that is always about to go off.

~

As she clambers up the church steps, her raincoat audibly flapping, a sheen of sweat on her forehead, she hears the organ playing Pachelbel's Canon and wonders loudly in her own skull, *Oh my God, who is throwing this thing?* And before she knows it, she is holding a program she took from someone she doesn't know and is seated in the back where she can bolt.

The organ ceases and the priest—*priest!*—takes his place at the lectern—*altar?*—and Lin dares to look around the church. Where are Sage and Huck? Would she recognize them? Which bald head is her father's? She tries to count the assembled. A hundred, maybe more. Colleagues, Lin thinks. Professors, journalists, commentators, and their wives, their circle, the wagons they circled after the trial.

"Friends and family of Barbara Donoghue, we are gathered here today to mourn the passing of a beloved wife and mother."

We are?

Right, of course we are.

"And now," he concludes the homily, "her daughter, Sage, will say a few words."

The program is instantly mulched in Lin's hands.

A woman, a full-grown woman in her late thirties, with big green eyes and sandy-blonde hair in a waist-length braid, approaches the lectern. She is unmistakably Barbara's daughter—the same perfectly symmetrical face—but whereas Jayne has always striven to look like a Hitchcock heroine and Barbara looked like the blousy version on a *Where Are They Now?*, Sage looks like an *Oprah* special—the star behind the scenes at her horse ranch, tan skin, muscular arms and legs, a vegan lifestyle, a return to nature. She is even wearing her namesake color, a knee-length wrap dress with additional plackets of fabric across the bust. She has her mother's bust, too. *She looks comforting,* Lin thinks. And she wants to run up the aisle to her and say, "It's me! It's me! Your cousin! Your sister!" And she wants to drop to the floor and crawl out.

"Thank you all for coming today." Sage's voice is, of course, deeper than the one Lin remembers, and rough from tears. "It would have meant a lot to my mother. Those of you who knew her knew she didn't like a fuss on her behalf, but when one was made, it meant a great deal to her.

"Huck and I were talking this morning about my wedding, how my sister-in-law had to throw Mom in a taxi to take her dress shopping at the last minute because she thought getting a new dress was self-indulgent, and Huck finally looked her in the eye and said, 'Looking like shit in your daughter's wedding photos won't win you any piety awards.' Harsh, right?" Sage smiles warmly at the first row, where her brother must be seated. Where one of her brothers must be seated. "The punch line is that she found that so uproarious she told the story to everyone who would listen. And more than that, she changed a little after that day. And I think that's what I loved best about my mother; she was still trying to grow and change, to be a better person, as she put it.

"And she brought that out in those around her. Always asking of some impossible situation, well, what *can* you do? What part *can* you control, focus on that. Hate your job? Take lunch by the water. Hate your apartment? Put wrapping paper on the walls."

Lin can sense the crowd smiling knowingly to each other; they've all clearly been recipients of this advice at one time or another. Lin thinks about Jayne's advice. Hate your job? Well, why? Why did you pick something you hate? That was silly.

Who would I have been, Lin wonders, *if someone had suggested I eat lunch by the water?*

Her focus returns to Sage's words as she struggles to finish. "And that's my mother. That she'd been in the house less than an hour but already figured out that Blue Bear was her granddaughter's favorite, already knew to keep track of it." Sage swallows, breathes, tries to compose herself to say the last few words from the page she is clutching. "She was that kind of in tune with her, with us, with everyone. I hope we all continue to sense her presence. I love you, Mom."

As she returns to her row, a man—*her husband? Huck?*—half rises to take her in his arms and folds her down to the bench in his embrace.

Lin wonders what that would be like, as she always does when she sees a man instinctively rush in like that, to be solid to a woman's dissolving. A few months before, Lin saw a couple in SoHo, the woman heaving with sobs that began at the soles of her feet. And this man, also wet eyed but stoic, held her. Held her as the grief racked her and wrecked her, and Lin openly watched from twenty feet away. Had they lost a child? A friend?

Lin couldn't stop staring because, despite the life-rending information clearly being forced on this woman, she still looked to Lin . . . safe.

~

At least weekly, Lin gets on the computer and types in *heart*. She doesn't want a double-humped triangle; she wants to see the skin severed, flapped and pinned, ribs cracked and splayed, exposing the muscle itself. She looks closely, closer still. Where is it? What is the origin of that feeling, like the fibers are being scoured with steel wool? What is it that oscillates at 3:00 a.m.? Nerve impulses? A horrible Morse code gone awry, tapping *death death death*?

Lin made the decision to medicate her anxiety, as nearly everyone does, in the middle of the night. More than the constant awful flutter under her breastbone or the relentless hard push of adrenaline that could be triggered by running for a train, the subject line of an email, or her mother clearing her throat—what she was completely and totally over was the middle of the night. As experiences went, studying the walls of her East Village walk-up between 2:00 and 4:00 a.m. was one she was eagerly willing to forgo.

Therapists, acupuncturists, energy healers always asked, "When did you stop sleeping?"

She'd push her mind to think back over her childhood, promising it a strong drink after if it would just cooperate for a few minutes. *No*—she'd shake her head—*I don't think I ever started.*

It was the summer after Lin turned twenty-seven. The year 2001. The last simple summer of simple times was also the same summer her friends were getting engaged. And at the end of each meal, as the check was waved down by a bangled arm, one of these women would say casually, as if it were an afterthought and not something they had wanted to broach with her for years, *Have you considered medication?*

What had she been saying? *No, no, no*—she'd quickly produce a laugh—*I was joking about*—*everything, don't take me seriously.*

She didn't need medication. She was fine.

Knowing, as she said it, that if you ever catch yourself using such a disgustingly banal word as *fine*, you are most decidedly not.

So she would walk home to her one-room apartment, considering. She strove. So hard. To succeed in her work. To succeed in her friend-ships. To make it simultaneously to one's opening and another's birth-day, make each feel seen, to help anyone moving or raffling or pickling. Her hands, the ones copiously burned by the hot-glue gun, were the ones they could count on. She was fine. By daylight, she was fine.

More importantly she'd never wanted to be one of those tortured-artist types who drive everyone crazy while they nurture their art like it's an exotic plant that they keep alive under their coat. Her mother hates those people. When they were children, Jayne would come home from some museum gala, fuming as she tossed her beaded silk wrap on the couch. "He ate the salad with his hands!" she'd vent at Lin, who was still awake, reading on the living room rug. "Like he was raised in—what's worse than a barn? I don't care how brilliant you think you are, there are rules!"

Her mother has a very low opinion of rule breakers and unconven-tional thinkers, alas, cursed to have not one but three unconventionally employed children. Brian and Lin eventually tired of pointing out that Aeschylus, Matisse, and Mozart were the rule breakers of their time, and Lin often thinks if she'd just been dead a hundred years, her mother would probably love her work. As it is, Jayne finds the dioramas "deeply upsetting." Frankly, so does Lin, and yet she's compelled to make them. *ARTnews* described them as miniature sets for horror films, which she supposes is accurate enough, although she certainly aspires for more subtlety than that.

The walls are made of lacquer, layer upon layer, using the traditional Japanese urushi method. The people, she casts in resin; the clothes, she sews by hand, some garments no larger than the wasabi peas she snacks on while listening to NPR. The furniture, she makes from dangerous objects—noose rope shredded and rewoven into tiny carpets. Knife blades bent and welded into an Art Deco dining table the size of a playing card. Her favorite description was from a brief *New York Magazine* profile of her first show out of art school, which said, "If Wednesday Addams had a dollhouse, she would want Lin Donoghue to design it."

Despite Clyde's constant cajoling—"Come on, Mom, Lindy's work is so fuckin' cool"—that article did not make Jayne Haniman's scrapbook.

As insurance against her own mental tendencies, Lin tries to approach her work with some semblance of structure and sunshine, like nurses who wear scrubs with kittens on them that end the day spattered in all forms of fluid. Every morning she goes to yoga, puts on proper clothes, and tries to get to her studio by eleven, a coffee and salad in hand. Yet some days are, admittedly, more productive than others. Some months, too.

Even at group shows, with artists who make work from their urine, she feels slightly apart. They stand there in their found clothes, even if Prada was where they found them, looking cool, like they've lived. She worries she looks like she works at the gallery. She tries. She even hired a stylist at one point, who, after asking Lin what her work was about, made her wear a cuff bracelet.

At that particular show, Clyde arrived with his date in tow, some girl dressed right out of a magazine for better or worse, and Lin found herself thinking, like an anthropologist carrying a found object back to its tribe, *Oh, that's how you wear that.* And Jayne stood in front of her, looking her up and down while the art advisers looked her work up and down, and flipped Lin's collar, flipped it back, adjusted her necklace, adjusted her part, asked to trade shoes, and then just gave up.

At the end of the night, she pressed the cuff into a friend's hand. And went home with the gallery owner, who should have gone home with his wife.

~

Suddenly the hymns and scripture are concluded, and people are standing, awkwardly milling around, handing each other Kleenex, handkerchiefs, and Lin has another decision to make.

She edges up the aisle, sweat soaking the armpits of her blouse. *What would I say,* she asks herself—not *do,* not *What do I say,* but *What would I say*—*were I ever to find myself in the extraordinary situation of having voluntarily and knowingly placed myself in the same room as my father, which I would never do because that would be insane.* So, on *that* day, she thinks as she inches farther, passing people with a vague smile of commiseration, *What would I say? I hate you? You ruined my life?*

Lin pauses to consider as she shifts herself to pass a portly man in a tartan jacket that was new and fit well sometime around her birth. Is her life ruined? she wonders. *I mean,* she thinks, *I have issues. But so does everyone.*

No, she decides, with the pragmatism only accessible in daylight, she is not ruined. And then she catches herself. That wasn't the question. Was her *life* ruined?

~

The psychopharmacologist's office was on the Upper East Side. He was quiet and thin-lipped and bearded, and asked probing questions without making eye contact. She politely took him through how pedestrian things seemingly everyone else could manage set off the scrub, scrub, scrub of her muscle fibers, and, of course, she had to touch on her History. She imagined her words in toe shoes. Touch, touch. This was Upper Fifth Avenue. The lobby was marble. In the limestone building above her, there were powder rooms with toile hostess napkins that matched the wallpaper. It wasn't the place for her History.

Of course he already knew. Everyone did. She was famous. Footnote famous. But still. If you knew who Rodger Donoghue was, then you knew what he was accused of.

"I just think," she said, "that if I can recover the memories—" She cut herself off. "I have the memories *around* the memories. But I think if I can just connect the dots, everything will fall into place, and I'll feel—"

"Feel what?" he asked.

"It's like I've walled something off, but the wall is flimsy. Like five roommates in a one bedroom, and I've just thrown up a cardboard divider, but whatever is next door is—huge. Or I'm standing in the water, holding up a shield—*yay*, a shield. But a *tsunami* is coming. A fucking tsunami. Filled with sharks. Did I mention I'm terrified of tsunamis?"

"Not sharks?"

"Of course sharks."

He made a note on his yellow pad and gave her a prescription for Celexa and his number. "Leave a message, and I will always call you back within the hour."

On the sidewalk, she pressed the rectangular white paper to her chest. Who in her life had ever said that to her?

Even though she filled the prescription immediately, she waited until Saturday. She poured a few of the peach-colored tablets into her palm and held them there, excited, hopeful, and slightly afraid. Was she throwing out her angels with her demons? Would she sit at her drafting table and see only an inky nothing? Would she get fat? Would she be unable to have an orgasm? Was this a horrible mistake?

She caught herself. The whir of questions, the sensation of her skin starting to dance on the surface of her—all symptoms. She took the morning dose as instructed and went to the gym, went to see a movie, bought a dress, all the while waiting, waiting, waiting to feel—bigger? Smaller? Different? Eight hours later she was ready early for dinner, so she sat down on her scavenged couch. Her room faced a small community garden with a wall of windows open on more of the treetops with every passing year—

The next thing she was aware of was her phone buzzing underneath her head. She had fallen asleep. Without trying, willing it, rubbing her temples, massaging her feet, using essential oils, crystals, magnesium, or that stuff Clyde brought her back from Thailand—she had simply drifted off. She staggered to standing, checking her BlackBerry—her dinner had gotten moved back; her friends were still drinking at the bar—and stumbled to the door, disoriented, but euphoric.

"Oh my God," she said aloud. "Oh my God."

She swept her gold clutch from the console by the door and checked her makeup. She had her phone, money, ID, keys, condoms, Altoids, and lip gloss.

"Oh my God," she said again, being bathed over and over with the sensation, and the Truth.

This is what other people feel like.

~

In the nave, Sage is greeting and hugging Barbara's friends, taking in their grief, their stories, their fear, the urgency in their eyes so intense, asking, *You miss her, right? My children will miss me, too?* Lin can see now that the man is not Huck. Where is Huck?

Lin stands awkwardly, now actively craning to find people she never wanted to see. Where is Huck?

There is an old man seated in the front row, liver spots on his crown, thin strands of silver, a cane in his right hand, the gnarled claw squeezing the carved ornamentation as though it were bearing his weight, a blanket draped over his lap. A young woman is crouching in front of him, wholly bright faced, speaking slowly, someone's daughter or granddaughter, telling him she's just written a paper on him, most likely. But Rodger would only be Jayne's age.

There is no one, she realizes. No one she recognizes. No one she fears. No one she's missed. She thinks, *I will feel something later. I will take this moment home with me, along with the crushed, illegible program and my wet blouse, and I will inventory it all later.* She can sense her ribs squeezing themselves together, closing the space between them, the space where something could slice in.

Later, she thinks.

I will feel this later.

"Linden?" the voice to her right cries out.

Heads whip around, faster than she could have believed possible, sharp, hostile eyes on her, Linden, the daughter of the woman who had tried to desecrate their lives.

Because theirs had been a religion of Zabar's, of French wine, then, later, Italian, of season opera tickets, chamber music, and QXR; they wore shirtdresses and trade beads and combs in their hair to rage, rage against the dying of the light. The light being not life but culture, history, a world and time and place when the price of dinner was fluency. And that woman, Linden's mother, had suggested they were worshipping false gods, that, perhaps, among them, were not so much the rightfully neurotic, the angrily awake, the stridently conscious, but the malformed. She rebuked them and their comfort with blurry social norms, their embrace of the louche, the "edgy." She said that what their decades of intellectual rebellion had culminated in might not have been a new Vienna, but a crime.

They stare sharply at Lin, vulture eyes in mottled faces.

In her mind, the mind that will render this later in miniature, the man with the cane turns his spotted, stripped head and looks into the depth of her, him inside her, and she him—and at the same time, her sweaty, trembling body is being wrapped tightly in strong, soft arms.

"Oh, Linden," Sage whispers in her ear, "I'm so glad you're here."

15

May 2007
Manhattan, New York

S he's waiting for her gallerist's name to be called by the hostess in a scrum of people, umbrellas dripping on squelching shoes, wet wool evoking childhood games of hide-and-seek, women pointlessly fussing at hair they correctly suspect has betrayed them, a tight pool of light corralling them all together, tired New Yorkers who are all somehow vying to pay to eat.

"Haniman!" the hostess calls, her eyes unfocused. "Party of two?"

"Here!" a man answers.

Lin has only to slightly twist her head, and she is inches from his face. His face, his adult face, so confusing, so inevitable.

"Hi."

"Hi."

Everything stops, the jostling, the music, the menus waving him on, her date, his date. They are both simply clinging to the driftwood of now in waves of then.

"You want a hot dog?" she asks.

His man face breaks open, and a fourteen-year-old smiles back.

∼

Hours later they are in a room upstairs, sheets wrapped around them, eating room service ice cream.

"You broke your toe," Justin observes, staring at her bare foot.

"I broke a lot of things. Pass me the chocolate."

"Have you become sporty?"

"You mean, *did* I become sporty?" She rises up on her knees, the sheet hanging off the tips of her breasts, the ones Jayne unsuccessfully lobbied for her to reduce before college. "Do you really want to hear this?"

"Yes, why not?"

"We have fifteen missing years, you want to slow down on my toe?"

He reaches behind her, grabbing her ankle, swinging her onto her back, and puts her foot in his mouth. "Tell me about the toe," he says, lips open, teeth pinning the scar tissue. "We have to start somewhere."

"Okay." She looks up at the silver-foil ceiling that reflects just enough of them, a wash of skin, the ribbon of her hair, to suggest that might be all there is. "I was in Miami for Art Basel. I was so nervous."

"Why?"

The question makes her insides warm and runny. No one ever asks her why. And certainly no man, also half-wrapped in a sheet, eating ice cream, looking down at her like he really wants to know while he sucks her toes. "I'd never been invited before. It seemed like—oh my God, where to start? When last we left, I was—what? Cutting shapes out of construction paper?"

"You have a career."

"I have a career. But I'm only just really breaking through now. To do that, you need the museums to buy you. But I—I had switched galleries. Anyway, I was nervous, and I'm running around, setting up my work, which I was hanging on walls for the first time, instead of each one on its own pillar. So I'm using staple guns and nail guns, and at every second I am a Tarantino movie waiting to happen, like, I'll spend the rest of my life wearing an eye patch or have a scar in the dead center of my forehead."

"Instead, you broke your toe."

"Instead, I got the show up and the response was great, and it sold out, and I went out for sushi and got drunk, and some guy invited me out to the beach, and we were sitting on chaises, watching the surf, and when it was time to stand up, I just hit the frame of his at the wrong angle and—crack—it snapped to the side."

"And?"

"I reached down and snapped it back," she says simply.

Justin removes her toe and inhales through clenched teeth. "Yowza. And the guy?"

"Went for help, never came back." She shrugs. "I limped to the emergency room."

"By *yourself*?"

She just looks at him. Lets the question sit between them. Does what she could never do then: reach up, pull him down toward her, brush his hair off his forehead, stare into him.

"I thought you were in Hong Kong," she whispers.

"I was. I came back."

Their eyes lock as though they have to for the world to move, like Jayne's ancient Cuisinart.

"I thought—honestly, Lin—I thought, New York is huge. I'll never see her."

"Silly bear." She gently bites his lip.

"I've always thought I misremembered. That you couldn't possibly have been—my therapist says I use the memory of you to avoid intimacy. Really . . ." He smiles his sexy half smile, the one that shows off the tooth he killed playing hockey, the one he never got fixed. "We're arrested."

Lin flings the sheet away, slides her warm, naked body against his, wondering how long they can stay suspended here.

"Are you still the same?" he whispers.

"How the same?"

"Do you still look at the faucet and see a hunched man, or the shampoo and conditioner are the Chinese dancers from *The Nutcracker*, bowing to each other."

"I'd forgotten that."

"Everyone else just sees what's there, what's right in front of them. Do you know that?"

Lin considers this. "I learned how to do it manageably."

"What does that mean?"

"It means I go to work and turn it on, like, like night-vison goggles, I guess. But I turn it back off." She finds a smile. These are the words she's waited fifteen years to say. "And I come home from the studio and watch TV, or meet up with friends and go out and have fun." Matching sweaters, matching sweaters. "So, yes—and no," she answers in his ear with the fullness of confidence 2:00 a.m. will allow. More banter, more ice cream, more sex. Because she knows 4:00 a.m. will come to start tidying up, and 5:00 a.m. will betray her. The city will leach black to gray, and she will have to ask questions, she will have to care about the answers. Because if this goes away again, it will kill her.

"We can't do this," she'll say, half-dressed, half-undressed, half *of* this room, half-ready to be of the rooms and rooms and rooms that are not this one.

"Why not?" he'll ask this time. "We're adults. We're not, technically, related."

"Really? You're ready to go to work and say, 'I'm dating my sister. But, I mean, *technically*, she's not. Our parents have just been married forever.'"

He'll rub his wavy hair hard and fast, his suit half-on, half-off. "Fuck it. Let's move to Seattle. I don't give a shit. Europe. I just want to be with you."

What she's been waiting to hear her whole life: *We will surmount this, whatever this is. You are not alone.*

"Okay," she'll say.

"Okay."

~

Four months later, Clyde and Lin meet at a diner, which is, in and of itself, weird. Usually, they meet a few mornings a week, halfway between Clyde's place and hers at somewhere new and notable, taking over a table with two laptops, multiple newspapers, orders of food, coffee, and, if the weather is nice, ashtrays, camping as if they're regulars. Which they will be until some other place comes along with younger, hotter, more beguiling, more tolerant servers or better lighting or crisper bacon.

But that day Lin suggests a diner, not knowing that, decades prior, a man and a woman set the course for her life at a diner, as if life were paper folded and folded again, the cuts strung out to reveal the same scene. But Lin needs something. Something that will require Clyde's undivided attention, which can only be attained if he's eating unremarkable eggs brought to him by a hairy old man, under fluorescents.

Clyde bounds in at 11:00 a.m., sunglasses firmly in place despite the clouds. "Hey, Lindy Hop."

"Clydesdale."

Greetings exchanged, they peruse the menu that starts with the dishes people order reliably—bagels and pancakes, bad coffee—and then takes off like a jazz solo into pages and pages of things like veal piccata and lobster thermidor, as if someone had just been pressed to list all the food they'd ever heard of.

Lin is trembling slightly. Like her aunt before her, she knows she needs an ally against Jayne. Like her aunt before her, she chooses questionably.

"So, whassup?" he asks, his leg bouncing under the table.

"Oh my God, are you still high?"

"*Peut-être.*" He pouts.

"Jesus." He's twenty-eight. Accredited. And aimless. At family gatherings Jayne tries to keep them tucked behind her skirt, the tall girl who makes disturbing art and the beautiful boy who makes nothing.

"Jealous?" he asks.

"No." She shudders. "That sounds like having an erection that won't end."

"Much better." He flashes her the grin that has always absolved him of all sins, the one that got her to let him crash at her studio senior year, buy him a fake ID, and let him tag along to Machu Picchu.

"Have you heard from Brian?" she asks absentmindedly while another part of her brain debates a bagel.

"Have I heard from *Brian*?" he repeats, mock aghast. "Why on earth would he reach out to me?"

She shrugs. "Mom's birthday is coming up; sometimes he wants suggestions."

"His assistant calls to get those, I'll have you know."

"Oh, come on, you two had such a nice time when he was here for Tribeca."

"I think I make him uncomfortable."

"Everything makes him uncomfortable—he always looks like his chair has sharp lumps and he's starting to suspect his clothes are poisoned. But that's just Brian."

"Mom called this morning." Clyde is done with the subject of their significantly more successful brother. "Ashely Gordon is engaged."

"Fuck." Lin scowls, knowing what this will mean for the next few months. "Can't she just start telling her friends that I'm married? That I eloped?"

Clyde sighs and shuts his menu. "She doesn't want to *tell* people you're married, Linoleum, she wants to throw you an engagement party and watch the table in the entryway fill with blue boxes. She wants to spend months planning your wedding and call all her friends to complain about it every day. She wants the caterers to be so *difficile* that she has to fire them, lose her deposit, and go to all the trouble of hiring a new one. She wants the bridesmaids' shoes to come back dyed the wrong color, the wedding band to break up, and the calligrapher to get carpal tunnel. She wants problems to solve. Frankly, whether or not you're married is beside the point. And you have a gray hair."

"Where?" Her hands fly to her scalp as though she'd be able to find it by touch alone.

"At your hairline."

"Do you have tweezers?"

"Do I have *tweezers*?"

"It is within the realm of possibility that you carry them in your wallet."

"True. But no. I'm starving. Let's order." He waves the burly man over. While Clyde orders for both of them, Lin steels herself.

Leaning in, she feels her forearm touch a sticky patch on the Formica, and says, "I need you to talk to Mom about something for me."

"Okay, great, yes, because I need to talk to you about something—"

"I'm seeing someone," she says, twisting her elbow up to her face for inspection.

"Reaaaaaalllllyyyy?" He drops his torso over the table.

It's syrup—she hopes. She dips the corner of a napkin in her water.

"Do tell."

What can she tell? They've enjoyed four idyllic months, walking the city, going to museums, slurping ramen on the Lower East Side, and eating pastry in the West Village that dusts their coats in powdered sugar and splurts *crème pâtissière* on their chins. And they touch. Long journeys taken by mouths down spines.

It's the happiest she's ever been. So happy she can't sleep. So happy she can't eat or work. It's all-consuming, this happiness, requiring new outfits, buying heels she can take such long walks in, getting her hair blown out at the salon around the corner. Waxing. Keeping her house ready, the fridge stocked, his favorite vodka in the freezer, his brand of toothpaste in the medicine cabinet. There's so much to remember.

So she pretends to drift off beside him, then waits until he's out to sit up, not knowing what to do, scared to wake him by moving but more scared to fall asleep, have one of her nightmares, and rouse him with her screams. She's had that complaint before. But not now. No, it can't happen now. Because it's enough. Enough that she's the woman who wants this—him, her stepbrother. She doesn't *also* need to be the woman who was the girl her father wanted. That person, that crooked person, can get left out of this.

"He's wonderful," she says. "He completely gets me. But it's—complicated."

"Is he married?"

"No."

"Russian?"

"What does that have to do with anything? No."

"Amish?"

"No."

"This is a fun game." Clyde claps his flexed palms so that only the base of each finger and the heel of his hand touches, making a hollow flapping sound. "One leg?"

Lin throws her hands down, exasperated.

"Poor!" Clyde shouts. "He's poor! That's it, right?"

Lin squeezes her mouth shut.

Clyde looks befuddled. "Short?" he asks softly.

"Look, he just isn't someone Mom will approve of. But I love him, and he loves me, and we're planning to move away together."

"Oh, God, you are all really leaving me with her, aren't you?"

Lin arches an eyebrow. "You can handle it. Besides, you treat her like an ATM; think of it like your annual fee."

"Meow."

"If the withdrawal slip fits . . ."

Clyde sits up, suddenly all business. "Look, I have a diversion."

"A diversion?"

Clyde starts emphasizing each phrase by tapping the sides of his palms against the table. "I need to ask you something, and I think it might help. It'll keep Mom occupied, and that'll get her off your case."

"O-kay."

"I'm trying to get traction for my blog."

"Your blog?" Lin's head tilts like a canine's.

"Clyding with the Truth."

"You're still doing that?"

"Yes, I'm still doing that. I have two hundred loyal readers, I'll have you know."

"Uh-huh."

"So, I want to write a piece on Rodger."

"What kind of piece?"

Clyde takes a pre-spiel breath. "Just, with everything in the news this year about Polanski, and with Dad's new book coming out, and all the coverage he's getting about his career fighting for the underdog, his smug fucking picture everywhere, I thought it's also worth bringing up that the case against Dad was essentially undecided. He lost physical custody of us, but there was no criminal investigation. And everyone acted like nothing happened."

Lin nods slowly, not saying *yes, you can,* so much as, *yes, you are right.*

"So, I think that the time is ripe—historically—to say something back. A rebuttal, if you will."

She narrows her eyes. "To your two hundred readers?"

"Yes."

Lin leans back, extending her arms, wrists crossed. "Clyde, I don't know. I don't think it's a good idea to rehash—"

"Don't you hate him?" he cuts her off, waving his unused fork.

"Of course I hate him. With every fiber of my being, or whatever. He got off scot-free, essentially, and I—I—"

"So let me do it. Let me speak truth to power. It will give Mom huge gratification and take the heat off your indigent dwarf."

Lin looks across the table. He's impossible. She's negotiating with a supernova, a sinkhole, the IRS; resistance is futile.

"Fine," she caves. "One essay saying that the horrible man is hor-rible, and then you back me the fuck up when I introduce my Amish drummer and shit goes down."

"I love you, pumpkin."

"I love you, honey bunny."

RODGER'S LETTER

September 15, 2007

To the Readership of This Esteemed Paper,
My estranged son has been endeavoring as of late to dredge up an ugly and unfortunate period in our family's history. Ostensibly he is doing this on behalf of his sister. Though whether or not that is the case, I cannot say.

His allegations require that I respond this one time, on the record, and then I will never speak of it again.

First, I begin by acknowledging that I am not a perfect person. I drank heavily in my youth, have struggled with fidelity, and have been accused of having an overweening ego. All that is true. But I have never inappropriately touched my daughter, ever. The suggestion that I did was the product of an adult woman's mind, a woman so devastated by jealousy that she was determined to take away my happiness, my family, and my reputation.

Second, let me say that I fully submitted myself to psychological testing and neither side's psychiatrists could find any evidence of pedophilic tendencies. Third, the story my six-year-old daughter submitted as testimony was only provided after her mother removed her from the room. Prior to that she was unable to affirm that the incident my wife accused me of had taken place.

The incident that, empirically, makes no sense. Pedophiles have psychological profiles. They groom their victims; they are slow and strategic. Methodical. My study didn't have a lock on the door. What's more, Linden testified I had her lie down between my desk and a rocking horse. I can assure everyone I have never owned a rocking horse. Certainly not as a grown man typing copy for this very newspaper.

Why would I do something so risky? The answer is, I wouldn't. I didn't.

What I did do was leave my wife for another woman.

Cruel, yes. But a common-enough occurrence that it should not have warranted this kind of retaliation.

That my estranged son continues to harangue me about it in the media is a mystery. One would think he would want his sister to be able to have some kind of normal life. Perhaps he doesn't know what that is. Perhaps I don't, either.

But I am old now, and I would like to finish my books in peace.

This is the last I will speak of this, but it was important to me, as a public person, to put on public record that, as far as I see it, I am innocent.

Of this at least.

Yours,

Rodger Donoghue

16

Lin shakes, the newspaper audible in her hands. Her mouth hangs open, the corners wetting, sounds punching out from her solar plexus, unable to form syllables—*how—I—he*—the words try to surface from her macerated brain, but they can't.

Gingerly, Clyde grips the paper's top edge in his fist and lets it drop, the section splaying across Lin's floor. "No more," he says.

"But, but—" *That's not fair. You've had hours with this. I'm seconds in.*

"You have a drink? A Negroni?" he asks, flopping down on the tattered leather couch.

Lin opens the freezer to get ice. She starts to mix him a drink until she realizes she can't actually make sense of the bottles in front of her, then crosses to Clyde and sets them heavily on the coffee table, which is as close as she can come to saying *Make your own fucking drink.*

"This ran today?" she asks. It's a conversational stupid; it's the Sunday Review on her floor. She wants to talk to Justin. "Has she seen it?"

Clyde pulls his weeks-old iPhone from his shorts pocket and sets this new contraption next to the liquor bottles, lighting it up so Lin can read that he has numerous voicemails and missed calls from Jayne.

Clyde, playing Come Here, Go Away with his own mother.

Lin takes a deep breath and crosses to her purse, where her BlackBerry is buzzing. Her voicemail is full. Nothing from Justin. She tries to figure out what time it is in London.

"Hi, this is Beth McKee from the Today *show. We'd like to have you on tomorrow to discuss the allegations against your father and his response piece."*

"Oh my God," she says, rolling her neck.

"What?" Clyde asks, one leg up on the couch, checking his own voicemail. "Yes! They want me on *Today!*"

"This is insane. How do these people have my number?" She looks across the room at him as if he might offer some suggestion as to how to navigate this or, at the very least, offer to delete her off the web. No, at the very, *very* least, make her a drink—

Pound, pound, pound.

"Linden, let me in!" It's Jayne. Lin can hear her summer-weight turtleneck.

"You have a key!" Lin shouts, unable to cross the six feet to the door. Whatever is going to happen next is going to happen—she doesn't need to invite it in.

"Oh, for goodness' sake." They can both hear scrambling through wallpaper samples, wallet, datebook, makeup bag, receipts. The lock turns. The door swings open. "A *rocking horse*? That's what he's hanging this on? He is vile, and he has always been vile." The bangles she's thrown on clank loudly as she gesticulates, reminding Lin of those elaborate wearable musical contraptions she saw on buskers in England, the drums wired to a harmonica, knees tied to cymbals. She'll have to ask Justin what that's called. "We are going to sue him and reopen the case and bring charges and ruin his life."

In the face of Jayne's rage, Lin goes limp, all anger chemically neutralized in her mother's presence. She slumps onto the couch next to her brother.

"Yes!" he says into his phone, as if it's asking for his opinion, which it probably is. "Traffic on my site is finally exploding. *Vanity Fair* wants to reprint my original article—this is *huge*. Would you like a Negroni?" Clyde crosses to the kitchen to get tumblers. Thick-cut crystal from Tiffany's because Lin thought men would like her to fix them a drink in a solid glass, a Hemingway kind of glass, only men had never come over sober enough to need a drink.

"Yes, please." Jayne drops her purse to the floor. "Linden," she asks, "who is cleaning your apartment?"

"I am."

"Hmm," Jayne murmurs, perching on the edge of the armchair as if avoiding something invisible to the naked eye. She pulls out her flip phone and her glasses case. "I'm calling Brock's lawyer. Arthur will know what our options are."

"We have to respond," Clyde says as he hands over their cocktails. "We can't let him have the last word."

Lin takes an eager gulp of her drink, hoping it might quell her nausea. Nothing Rodger said matters. She has the memories around the memory. She can see his office floor, smell his cologne, the scent of typewriter ribbon on his fingers, feel him on top of her—"How can he do this? Can he just do this?" she demands.

"So, what do you want to do?" Clyde asks Jayne. "*Nightline*? Or *20/20*? Maybe morning shows?"

"What do you think will have the biggest impact?" Jayne asks in return.

"I won't be on camera," Lin says quietly.

"Oh, honey, don't worry," Jayne reassures her, "we'll get someone nice—Diane, she'll do it as a favor to me."

"No. Print, okay?" Lin finds herself pitching something she's equally averse to.

Jayne looks to Clyde.

"It might be classier," he concedes.

"Okay, good, yes," Lin says quietly. "Let's find the classiest way to reply to my father denying molesting me in the *Times*. Let's be really elegant about this."

Ignoring her, Clyde extracts his laptop from his leather satchel, and she feels a sensation creeping up around her torso, the urge to pick at her skin, peel it away in strips. The drink isn't strong enough.

"Excuse me," she whispers, getting up and going to her medicine cabinet, thinking, *No, no, no. Tonight we're supposed to have dinner, and Clyde's going to help me tell Mom about Justin.* She finds Cetaphil and Peter Thomas Roth and one very old Valium. She rummages in her purse, her travel bag, her bedside table, yielding only a Klonopin and one tissue-lint-covered Xanax.

She washes all three down with the rest of her Negroni as a kind voice says to her, *You don't need to be here for this.*

PART V

17

Lin holds a miniature brown shopping bag, the kind of ridiculous thing that has rebranded itself as chic in its utilitarian simplicity, like twine and Ball jars. The Brooklyn boutique, whose bestselling item is a cologne called Gun Residue, can't even be bothered to stamp its logo on one side. Or, perhaps, it's the girl with the tattooed eyelids who can't be bothered. As she lackadaisically rings up Lin's purchase, Lin stands in her baggy sundress and stares at the black curlicues, feeling lost, a sensation she's familiar with. Typically, it's brought on by an announcement in the paper that one of her former contemporaries has a solo show, has sold a piece to the Whitney, has made it into the Biennale. But to have it brought on by eyelids is a new low.

Lin marvels that this girl had so much conviction when she plunked down hard-earned money for an arguably excruciating experience. At that moment, she knew herself, what she needed, and had some vision, however faulty, of what she would need in the future.

Lin tries to imagine having that much certainty about anything anymore. Without her gallery, her collectors, she feels like a fraud in her asymmetrical clothes, her hand-forged jewelry. But take those away and she's just one more Upper East Side private-school refugee who never found her footing.

Whenever she is summoned uptown to dinner, her mother will invariably look over the top of her menu and ask, "Why do you always wear that glittery black stuff around your eyes when we meet?"

"Because I don't want anyone to think I live here," she answers, ordering the first of the three Palomas it will take her to get through dinner in a neighborhood she no longer belongs to, before returning home to a place pullulating with a creativity and talent she can't measure up to.

The small shopping bag in Lin's hand contains sage, dried and tied with string. *Too on the nose?* she wonders as she double-checks the address on her phone and rounds the leafy, shaded Park Slope corner. She remembers learning years ago, when the Brooklyn Museum commissioned a diorama for a group show, that stoops were initially built because the sidewalks were so deep in animal waste that it felt more hygienic for the living quarters to be raised above the street. What perplexes Lin is that they deliberately left the kitchens below the level of sewage.

Then she thinks of her mother, who seemed to never want to know what was happening in the less savory parts of her house, so long as everyone arrived in the dining room on a gold-rimmed plate with combed hair, and a good report card.

Before pressing the bell, Lin smooths the front of her black skirt, runs her tongue over her teeth, hunting for strawberry seeds. The September afternoon is humid, and it occurs to her that she may have raccoon eyes. She runs spit-tipped fingers under her lids, then, resigning herself that most likely *something* is wrong—gum on her sandal, a splash of her earlier iced coffee somewhere on her person—she rings anyway.

She can hear thunderous footsteps. And small—young—voices shouting, "Aunt Linden is here!"

Aunt Linden?

Sage opens the outer door barefoot, in cutoffs and a striped T-shirt, and, once again, Lin is disarmed by her appeal. Unmade eyes bright like the backs of baby frogs, her waist-length hair half-up. She is so profoundly appealing, exuding, as she does, a quality Lin has never viscerally understood until this moment. Grounded. Sage is just so *of earth*, like no one else Lin has ever met. How has that happened? That a child so *up*rooted could become a woman so firmly planted? It's unfair. Unfair in a way that makes Lin feel like she can't swallow properly.

"Come in!" Sage wraps Lin in her arms again, then pulls back to take her in. "I am so happy you're here!"

"That's what you said last time," Lin blurts, voice small. "Um, at the funeral." As if there might be some other time that they've seen each other.

Sage cocks her head.

"You probably don't remember. You—had a lot going on." Lin feels blood in her cheeks.

But Sage smiles, and Lin realizes she hasn't cocked her head unkindly. She genuinely wants to know if that's Lin's recollection and, if so, its significance. "Well," Sage says, her hand still on Lin's back as she steers her through the vestibule and into their apartment, "it's true both times. Come in—don't mind the boxes. I'm still figuring out where to put things."

Lin follows Sage into the brownstone's parlor floor. Brownstones, in Lin's experience, are curious things. Externally uniform, internally a profusion of depths and widths, air and light, and the absence thereof, much like the families within. They could be in need of just a little refreshing or demanding full cornice repair, joist replacement, new boilers, roofs, ventilation, brickwork, and electric. Hundreds of thousands of dollars before even one fun decision is made. As Lin's friends have married and moved to Brooklyn with the repetitive chorus of *We bought a brownstone!* she has learned to reserve her envy—of their homes, at least.

The apartment Sage's family is renting is composed of the parlor and garden floor of a house gutted and opened up to feel as much a transplant here as they are. Past the open kitchen, the back wall has been replaced with glass facing their garden and the gardens beyond.

And the decor is like a beach house—white canvas couches, jute rugs, and driftwood end tables, all strewn with toys, and parts of toys, and adult objects repurposed as toys. Boxes line one wall with labels like "back to school" and "games," while on the living room floor, discarded newsprint lies all over, surrounded by crusting paintbrushes and pots of bright colors. Blank rectangles reveal where the "work" must recently have been created.

"It's gorgeous," Lin says.

"Oh, thank you, we lucked out. I mean, we're renting it furnished so we can sublet our place in Seattle furnished in case this is all crazy and we have to go home next week, blah, blah, blah. Come on, I'll open some wine."

Lin knows there are questions she should be asking, would be asking of any friend. *Why have you moved here? How is your stepfather? You've come to look after him? But you didn't want to be any closer? Or even stay with him? Why?*

Instead, Lin follows her past the living area to the open kitchen. "It's not ideal—for the kids, it's not ideal. A rental and the upheaval, and moving, knowing we might have to do it all again soon," Sage explains as she opens the fridge, the satisfying suck of the seal being broken, sliding out a bottle of rosé from a display of more yogurt cups than Lin has ever seen outside a grocery case.

On the counter sits a platter of prosciutto, olives, and soft cheese. "But it had to be done. It had to. I came out a couple of times—" Sage blushes. "They were fast trips."

Lin waves her hand. "I understand." What does Sage owe her?

"Looking in on Dad. Checking in with the nurses, his PT people, and house hunting." *Dad?*

Sage drops her eyes to the corkscrew, and Lin can't believe they're here so fast. But are they here? Or are they just alighting on the water's surface before jaws can snap?

"Anyway, the second I walked in—I thought, okay, this feels as close to home as we can get, and the two/three is just a couple of blocks away; I can be on the Upper West Side in forty-five minutes. Which isn't five, but it's better than trying to triage everything from Seattle—kids, come say hello! Anyway, I think the owners are an acting couple. They were in a rush to move back to LA, and I don't think even really bothered to research what places are going for out here." Lin admires the birch-patterned wallpaper, the lithograph-printed dish towels, the professional-grade stove, and Sage looks around her new kitchen for a moment, seeing it as Lin might. "It's weird to be using another woman's home goods. Hopefully Adrian's job will okay his transfer soon, and we'll have *our* things, which aren't so fancy, but at least they're familiar."

"He's not here?"

"In six months—hopefully. He's in the middle of this big rollout, so . . ."

"You did the move by yourself?"

Sage goes to the cabinet for plates, putting her back to Lin. "It ended up being a really bad week for him to be away, and they've cut *so* many people, he didn't want to give them any excuse. So we flew out and waited for the boxes with the kids' stuff to get here. We explored the grocery stores and found a local pharmacy and made friends with the dachshund next door."

"Will he visit?" Lin cannot wrap her brain around this, the idea that people could choose to be apart when animosity isn't a factor.

"He'll go back and forth."

Lin keeps her eyes trained on the counter, the plates, the cheese, as if at any moment they might *do* something. "You must be exhausted."

Sage startles as she turns back around. "No. No, I'm good. I'm a machine." She smiles again. If Lin were a sommelier of Sage's smiles, she would say this one was light bodied. "Anyway, I hated to leave Seattle, but it was the right thing—"

"Oh, I brought you this." Lin cuts Sage off to hand over the gift, not ready to hear about anyone doing the right thing.

She opens the bag. "Sage!"

"To smudge your house. It doesn't look like it needs smudging, but you never know; you might just want to—be on the safe side." Lin feels uncomfortably, inexplicably young—adolescent, almost. Her right shoulder is sloping toward the counter, her left foot has lifted up behind her right calf.

"Thank you. I love it. It will get used. Kids!" she shouts down the stairs. "For the love of criminy Christmas, come say hello!" Her hand still resting on the doorframe, she whispers, "They were working on something for you." She returns to the marble island. "Here, take this."

Trusted with the platter, Lin follows Sage onto the patio and down a steep metal staircase to the garden, settling herself on an aluminum wicker couch. Eschewing the armchairs, Sage sits next to her, tucking her muscular, bare legs under her on the canvas cushions. Lin regards the house, its back transparent, and realizes Sage has moved into one of her pieces, that they've merged somehow in this, a desire to see in—to see out.

Then Lin watches Sage watching her, uncomfortable in the silence, uncomfortable in her gaze, reminding her as it does of sitting on a bench with Barbara so long ago while the kids waited for the carousel, of Barbara asking, *How's school, Lindy?* like she genuinely wanted to know, genuinely cared about the answer—and then blew her life to smithereens.

"How *are* you?" Sage asks.

Lin looks away into her wineglass, funnily prepared to answer every question but this one.

Sage tries again. "Are you happy?"

Lin looks up. "Are there a lot of happy people in Seattle?"

"A few. More than we have a right to, given the rain." She touches Lin's ankle. "I want to know, truly."

Lin can't find the words.

Truthfully, Lin can't even find the question. How are you? *No one* asks her that. Her mother asks, "How are things going?" which is not the same and really means, *Has your work started selling again?*

Do you need money? Even her therapist asks, "How was your week?" which is also not the same and really means, *Let's get going.* Clyde asks, "Whassup?" which could mean, *Oh, look, Dean and Deluca marked down that chocolate you like,* or, *I'm giving up porn for Lent.* Her friends ask, "What's going on?" which means, *Give us the latest on your mom,* or, *Sleeping with anyone?*

But just . . . *how are you?*

"How am I?" Lin finally repeats. "Well . . . the last few years have sucked."

"It's been hard on Dad, too," Sage says intently, warmly, as if they were all flood victims in different districts. As if *he* wasn't the hurricane. As if *she* hadn't been quietly living in her dry house.

"Has it?"

Sage presses her lips, looks away.

After Rodger's rebuttal, it seemed like every New York City publication weighed in. They ran long articles on her father, on his oeuvre, on her, on her oeuvre. They crassly dissected her work. And they all included the same photo of her from the gallery brochure the previous year, her somber, black-shirted self, seemingly lifted from an Edward Gorey cartoon, all large, lost eyes and jaded despair.

Lin started getting looks, incurring double takes, on the street, at yoga, in the supermarket, at restaurants. Not every day. Just exactly at the moments when she'd have relaxed and talked herself out of it. And while she was spurring double takes, the intelligentsia was honing *their* take: Naomi Wolf, Katie Roiphe, Camille Paglia, and countless others felt a call to arms. It was time to hold men like Rodger accountable. No, actually, men like Rodger weren't the problem. Linden and her outdated revelations were the problem; it was an attack on thinking in the age of stupidity.

Linden's desire for Rodger's accountability was somehow simultaneously symptomatic of a sexual inversion, a cultural Electra complex, and an Ophelia-like hysteria that could only ultimately consume itself. One writer in *Vanity Fair* even managed to tie Linden Donoghue into her feelings on Girls Gone Wild and American womanhood in the post-divorce boom. Many journalists just seemed to be angry that they'd been pulled from opining on the financial crisis to consider that one of their own might be an asshole. And still others lumped their defense of Rodger into their abiding love of Wagner, despite his anti-Semitism, and *Star Wars*, despite Alec Guinness's anti-Semitism, and isn't this the same thing?

Admission to anywhere by the who's who suddenly seemed to require an *opinion*. Did he—or didn't he? If he did, then his entire subsequent career was a paean to the patriarchy, and he was no better than Allen—

Manhattan makes me physically sick. How anyone thought that was okay—

Or Polanski—

Polanski! I love Polanski!

Yes, but he had sex with a thirteen-year-old.

But it was supposedly consensual.

You look at a thirteen-year-old, and you tell me if you think they're capable of consenting to sex.

So now we have no agency? When do we get agency? You tell me at what age we are capable of developing agency over our sexuality!

It got ugly. Tears were shed over kohlrabi carpaccio.

The market collapsed for Linden's work. "Well, now it's a bummer," her gallerist explained. "It was one thing when people could look at the pieces and guess, but now that they *know*, well, it's taken all the fun out of it." Lin murmured an apology for killing the fun and left, an unsold piece under each arm.

She went to a tarot-card reader recommended by a neighbor because apparently even the way she did her laundry invited an intervention.

"You had great success before your Saturn Return."

"What does that *mean*?" Lin asked, looking around the apartment done in high Lucite Louis XIV while the reader consulted her astrology books.

"It means," she said, pulling her glasses off and twirling them by the tip, "that you are about to go through a very hard period."

"No. No, I'm here because I am *in* a very hard period, and I want to know when it will be over."

"Five . . . six years, tops."

"Six *years*?"

"But then you will be reborn. You will be free."

Lin went home, fell on her bed face-first, and slept for twenty-four hours.

~

Now she blinks, touches a canvas cushion, finds a hole in the piping, unsure what else to say, but Sage is a mom—she perseveres. "Are you in a relationship? Anyone special?"

"No." Lin smiles. "Many, many unspecial people. Some antibiotics and one AIDS scare, but no—no relationship." She presses her palms together between her thighs and flexes her arms, hyperextending her elbows and making the tattoo of a vine that wends its way down her forearm jump. She is unexpectedly having a reckoning with herself here over cheese and olives under a colorless, limp September sky. A sky that is adjacent to, merges somewhere with, a sky of hope and expanse. But not here. Not above Lin.

"How's Clyde?" Sage comes to her rescue.

Lin exhales. "Oh, Clyde—wait, how well did you know Clyde? How old was he?" *When you left.*

"Little," Sage says, reaching for the olives.

"Well, he's exactly the same."

Sage spits a pit into her palm. "I tried subscribing to his—whatever it is . . ." Sage waves her hand away from her face.

"Clyding with the Truth."

"Yes. But I just couldn't . . ."

"No, we are *not* the target audience. I'm not sure who the target audience is, just that they're under twenty-five and love him in a low-key restraining-order kind of way."

Several times a day Clyde uploads a video of his response to the news as it happens—no time to second-guess, type, spell-check. As he recently explained to Lin: "Sometimes I'm louche, sometimes I'm in tears, I'm always honest and always on—fucking—point."

News shows follow him to see what they should cover that night. Election handicappers follow him to see what to think. And when he walks near his apartment, people just—follow him. "We live pretty near each other, but going out with him downtown is impossible. Mom won't do it. She makes us meet near her apartment, where people either don't recognize him or are too polite to stare. He hates it."

"She's still in the apartment?"

"Oh, yes. It's too big for her now that Brock's dead—her second husband. But she will leave that place feetfirst. Can you imagine her anywhere else?" Lin takes a sip of her wine. "She only makes sense on the Upper East Side."

"And Brian?"

"He hasn't called you?"

Sage shakes her head, eyes clouding, smile shifting. "I often think how different my moving out would be now. I'd go across town but still be able to text with Brian a hundred times a day. But then we had to call landlines. Anyone could answer—any angry adult. Jayne hung up on me once."

"No."

Sage nods. "Yep. And I assume Brian didn't want to risk talking to Rodger. Or he tried, and Rodger went off on some diatribe—*you tell that woman* and—" She stops herself again, threads her right fingers between her toes. "I guess I might as well have moved to France. I just didn't think it would be so—permanent. Didn't think he would see it as such a betrayal." *He did. We did.*

"What's he like?" Sage asks, returning those eyes to Lin. "Is he married? Does he have kids? I've seen all his movies, they're beautiful."

"He is married to his job and is nothing like his movies."

"Really?" Sage turns away, losing the flimsy thing she thought she had.

"You know flowers," Lin jumps in, "like, an amazing arrangement of flowers in a hotel lobby?"

Sage nods.

"And they're in a giant vase. And the vase is on a table? And under the table, there's a sandbag to keep it all from tipping over? Brian is the sandbag. Integral to the operation, yes, but utterly devoid of poetry."

Sage bursts out laughing. "I don't believe it! He could be making action things with robots and cars and car-robots. He must have soul."

Lin looks skeptical.

"Somewhere? Deep down?"

"Deep. And Huck?" Lin asks in turn.

Sage shrugs, the tips of her shoulders transforming her chest into an ark, carrying all these sadnesses two by two. "Well, you remember."

"Yes." Lin takes a sip, thinking of that half-naked feral boy found curled up on the floor of his old room, his skateboard still in the front hall. Until Jayne barred his entry. "I tried looking him up on Facebook. I've always hoped that he found God and went on a whole spiritual quest and now teaches yoga or something."

Sage shakes her head definitively, lips pressed tightly.

"I mean, he'd probably be one of those angry yoga teachers, but still—"

Sage whoops. "What is up with angry yoga teachers?"

"Right? What is up with angry yoga teachers?" They are suddenly smiling stupidly at each other, and worlds unfurl: playing lava as kids, leaping from couch to coffee table to ottoman, suddenly finding themselves both balanced on a needlepoint stool, hugging each other to keep from falling. And the others are never-beens, might-have-beens—Lin coming home from a dance and Sage is there, Lin coming home from college and Sage is there. They laugh together at Jayne's new winter hat. They smoke pot together in the country-club bathroom to get through dinner—confidantes, friends, sisters. "What a fucking mess," Lin says softly. As though she weren't the apotheosis of said mess.

"What a fucking family," Sage murmurs back before they seem to shake themselves out of it. "And, what's his name—your other brother—Josh?"

"Justin," Lin confirms, feeling a hard stab through her sternum that she waits to fade into a dull ache and disappear, like the peal of a bell. She remembers with such all-consuming fondness those first months of high school when he moved in—how she was able to decide to turn off her feelings for him. *Dissociate,* her therapist says. *You dissociated.*

Well, why can't I now? she demands.

Because you're integrating; that's this process.

I don't want to integrate. I want to not feel.

"We don't see each other." Because each time Justin called in the aftermath of Clyde's Molotov cocktail, offering to get on a plane, she put him off. She picked fights. She jumped down his throat, lodged herself there, palms and feet pinned against the walls so he couldn't speak even if, by that point, he'd wanted to.

He arrived anyway, surprising her when her legs were unshaven, hair unwashed, take-out containers on the counter, a stack of op-eds about her on the little farm table where she ate breakfast. She couldn't bear it. "Lin, I love you," he said over and over, but she knew that couldn't be true. She stood in the bathroom in the dark, shoulders hunched, vision tunneling, breath coming in insufficient spurts. She'd read about the earthquakes in Sichuan, buildings reduced to powder because they were built around nothing—no foundation, no rebar— and thought, *Yes. That's me.* She was failing. Failing as her mother had always predicted she would. Failing to be normal. Failing to be lovable. Or even likable.

She sent him back to London confused, anguished, desperate to help yet without much scaffolding himself. He made his unreturned calls every day, then every other, then weekly, then not at all, finally conceding that maybe this wasn't the time for Lin to try to publicly date her brother.

"And what's the significance of the vine?" Sage gestures toward Lin's arm.

Lin shrugs. "Part *Sleeping Beauty*, forest of thorns, and part laurel wreath, anointing myself when the world turned its back on me." She smiles shyly. What she doesn't say is that when she took Justin in her mouth, her hands on the base of his rib cage, she'd feel a pulse where the tender skin under her right forearm met his hip bone. There is a leaf there now.

"I see."

There are legions of incidents and miscommunications, slights and misperceptions surrounding them. They don't need to stop at Justin. "So how did you end up in Seattle?" Lin asks.

"College. A theater program." Sage snorts. "I mean, it was good for me—" She abruptly lashes her hand in the air, catches a mosquito, and fans her palm, revealing the crush of blood and mangled wing. Lin passes her a cocktail napkin. "Thank you. I made my own bug spray from essential oils and bought calendula plants, but none of it's doing jack shit. DEET, that's what works." She lets out a resigned sigh. "Anyway, theater, yes, I think I just really needed to crawl around on the floor and growl for a few years, you know?"

For a second their pupils align. Yes, she knows.

"But the actual business of it?" Sage shakes her head and pulls a face. "I worked with a theater troupe out there for a few years, doing experimental work. It was well received, which was cool, but I was having a thing with the artistic director, so that was—complicated."

Lin understands.

"Mostly, I made cappuccinos and learned how to handle baked goods with tongs. And once I became completely sick of being looked at, I got a job at a gardening store, and that kind of took off. And then Adrian's firm hired me to landscape their campus, and here I am, mother of three."

Lin isn't sure if she's supposed to ask questions—what kind of art, what kind of complicated, what kind of baked goods? Instead, she says, "I can't wait to see them. Forgive me, what are their names again?"

"Sarah is my six-year-old. She has never met an opinion she doesn't like. She just arrived with so much conviction." Sage nestles deeper into the pillows, her knees up in front now, her tan shins forming a beautiful barrier between them, the muscle flaying out behind the bone like a king cobra. "Cal is five and has only two modes: lightning and stone. He's either running like he's trying to trail flames on our wood floors"— she slaps her palms past each other—"or he has taken a magnifying glass to a speck, and there is no budging him for love or money or chocolate."

Lin loves these descriptions. They make her wonder how Jayne described them at that age. What was her summation? Perhaps it was more a generation of, "Sage is the pretty one, Brian is the brain. Huck is my handful."

"And Henry is just trying to keep up."

"Those are such sweet names."

"I think all Sages pick names like Sarah and Henry, and then they'll name their children Sassafras and Temerity. And they'll name their children Harriet and Richard. We always want what we didn't have."

"True." Lin has never thought about baby names. At thirty-six, she thinks about freezing her eggs. She thinks about trying to create routine and structure for another human being when she can't create it for herself. She thinks about how broken she is and that she's fairly sure if she had a baby, she'd drop or molest it, because that's what the statistics say, so better not. But if she was to want what she didn't have . . . or, rather, to give what she never had, where would she even start?

"How did you know how to do this?" Lin asks, meaning life.

"Well . . ." Sage thinks for a moment, mulling the question. "I'm a little bit Jayne."

"No!"

"I am. The routine, the consistency. We never wondered if there'd be milk in the fridge."

Lin is about to say, "Big deal," but then remembers what her mother used to say, about how gaunt the children had been when they'd arrived. That somewhere Sage remembers hunger and uncertainty. So instead, she retorts, "I think she just made a list."

"Well, it was there. Everything was organized. At one point there were *five* of us, Linden, and yet we opened the closet and there were shoes that fit; we opened the medicine cabinet, there were Band-Aids."

Lin realizes how little she understands of motherhood because— isn't that the bare minimum?

"She was wonderful to me."

"She was?"

"Yes! Until I went through puberty," Sage concedes. "And then it was like she couldn't look at me."

"Why do you think that was?" Lin asks, remembering her mother's discomfort with her own changes.

"Probably I reminded her too much of Mom. Which I didn't understand at the time."

"Free-love Barbara!"

Sage laughs. "So, I just hid out at the barn. See! She got me horse-back-riding lessons!"

"Honestly, Sage, did you *want* to learn how to ride a horse?"

"No," she admits. "But when I got good . . . it was powerful—the freedom. Nothing felt like that again until I got my own car."

"Did you keep it up?"

"No." She snorts again. "Oh my God, Barbara and Rodger could not have figured out riding lessons! I'm amazed my tuition was paid. Actually, that's funny, I haven't thought about this in years, but it popped into my head today. Of course, Jayne immediately transferred my tuition bill to Barbara. I remember, I came home from school, and she was standing in the vestibule, holding one of those slivers of paper the tuition bills came on, in those little envelopes—did you ever see them? As if printing it all on child-size stationery made the numbers smaller. Anyway, she was shaking. Visibly shaking. *Fourteen thousand dollars,* she kept saying. She was appalled and, I think, embarrassed. I don't suppose she'd ever really thought through what she'd expected Jayne to be doing all those years. Of course, Dad was like, chill, I'll pay it, no big deal. But she was really undone." In a point between Sage's eyes, Barbara is shaking, and Rodger is comforting her, and Sage is watching it all, fourteen and forty-three all at once. "Something about the fuck-you of it and knowing she deserved it."

"Not that Jayne would ever say *fuck*."

Sage smiles. "No, of course not. Neither of them. Still, I don't know why, of everything, I thought it would break her."

Of everything.

"Anyway, parenting, yes, it was really the women in my theater company who had children before me, wearing them to rehearsal, nursing them as they walked and swayed and ran lines—it was something else entirely. It inspired me."

"I'm glad you chose Park Slope."

Sage laughs. "Yes, that recommendation was made to me very emphatically."

"And not the Upper West Side?"

"I'm close enough." They both look around at the neglected, frizzled flower beds Sage is spraying with biodegradable, organic bug repellent, all of it a world away from Jayne Haniman's East Hampton garden, with its meticulously tended beds, the annuals she staggers to let the order of color unfold week after week, month after month, until it produces her winning entry into the garden show.

"I think about Barbara all the time," Lin admits. "I'm so sorry."

Sage gently shakes her head, a small smile cupping its hands over the flame of her words. "I think of death like the H2O floating in a kettle with its fellow molecules, and then suddenly some of them turn into steam. Those left behind can grieve. But the released molecules are just fine—they're still right there, hovering around us, simply harder to see."

"And that's comforting?"

"Well, it only sucks when you really need a glass of water." She lets out a small laugh. "When you can't read their handwriting at the bottom of a recipe, or you can't remember what year something was. But most of the time steam will do." Sage leans forward to reach for a cracker. "Let me go see what they're up to." She takes the cracker with her and swiftly crosses the garden.

Lin sits and thinks of the wool scarf she knit years ago in a loose tartan pattern that created deliberate finger-size holes. When she loops it around herself, layering the design, she can either hide or double the holes. That's what it feels like to be sitting here with Sage. Depending on how they arrange themselves, they can mask each other's limitations, or expose them.

"Here they are!" Sage calls brightly, leading a production of *Peter Pan* down the stairs. Having seemingly forgotten their initial excitement, they now file solemnly behind, resenting having been wrenched from whatever they were creating in their room.

"Stop it!" Sarah cries, violently tugging her arm away from Cal.

"I wasn't doing anything! Mom, I wasn't doing anything!"

"You farted," the baby says, and Lin bursts out laughing.

"Welcome," Sage says. "It's like living in a John Belushi sketch that never ends."

"I'm Sarah." The girl holds her hand out. She has white-blonde hair, blue eyes, and a stocky build that must be Adrian's contribution.

"I'm Lin. It's lovely to finally meet you."

The boy regards her. He has the same coloring but is lithe like his mother. "And I'm Calvin, two syllables. Cal-vin."

"Got it."

Henry just climbs up into Lin's lap, the first child ever to do so, the first child she has ever held, if providing a human cushion can be called "holding." But within seconds Lin has wrapped her arms around his middle, rested her chin on the top of his head, and finds herself immediately thinking, *Delicious*. And then wondering why people use adjectives of consumption to describe children.

"I should get dinner going."

"Let me get out of your hair," Lin offers.

"No, don't be silly. I'll just whip up some pasta. Stay."

"Stay, stay!" Sarah and Cal jump up and down as Henry twists around to look at her.

"Okay. Can I help?" she asks, as though she can cook.

"No, no, it'll be quick. Come upstairs, and we can talk while I chop. Kids, clean up your room. Has everyone done their homework? Are your backpacks hung up? Are you ready for school tomorrow?"

"I am homework," Henry answers emphatically, and the women laugh.

"Yes, yes, you are." Sage gently touches her fingertips to his downy hair.

In the kitchen, Sage extracts ingredients for dinner the way a clammer might slip mollusks from a bed, swiftly recognizing the ripe and ready. Within a minute, water is on to boil, a tomato is being sectioned, and olives drain.

Lin takes a big breath. "So, him. Rodger. What happened?" She is ready to take it in, a piece of information not available on his Wikipedia page.

Sage looks up, pushing her hair behind her ear with the back of her tomato-juiced hand. "Stroke."

"Stroke?" Lin repeats.

"With his chain-smoking and hypertension and just regular old tension, it's a miracle it didn't happen sooner. And in some far-flung place. Thank God I didn't have to get on a plane to Myanmar in the middle of the night."

"When?"

"The first one? The day before the service. But people were already flying in and—Huck only stayed for part of it. The service, not the stroke. He left and went back to the hospital. I wasn't sure, who was it all for?"

"Your mom?" Lin offers.

Sage lays down her knife. "She would have barely been able to stand it. But they had friends—really *his* friends and their wives—and it just seemed the thing to do. I was on a plane and organizing a funeral before I ever even wondered if we needed to have a funeral."

"What did she die of?"

"Breast cancer. It was so advanced. Which is not what she told us, of course. We flew home after Presidents' weekend thinking she'd start treatment, and she died a few weeks later. I honestly don't know that she ever got checkups." Sage stares off again, and momentarily Lin is left there with her body, but the woman is elsewhere.

"After the funeral he recovered, had a couple of good years, and then—this last one really took him down. So now I have a dead mother, an incapacitated stepfather who wants to be a dynamic young man, and a brother who cycles through two modes: using, when he's homeless and useless; and sober, when he is encouraged to not so much as lift a toothpick if it might compromise his sobriety, and equally useless. And I have Adrian, the kids, *so* much." The overwhelm Lin has suspected is finally writ on Sage's face.

"The trappings of success," Lin suggests, and Sage cocks her head again. "Just funny that we call them *trappings*. Because I cling to, I enumerate mine. In the middle of the night. The ones that are left. Desk. Home. Accountant. Gym membership. And I think, this is what makes me *not them*, the ones who don't make it. The ones you see on *Oprah*—Huck. But it also does feel . . . confining. Right? Because I have to keep them all to maintain the distance between me and what I've struggled not to be."

"And what's that?" Sage asks.

"Crazy."

18

November 2011
Manhattan, New York

Jayne worries about her children. She worries with the fervor and commitment her daughter once Hoped. In the morning, as she walks to and from her Pilates studio, she worries about Brian. That he is in his early forties and unmarried, that nothing in his lifestyle seems conducive to making that happen, that his last film was a critical success but a financial debacle, that his neighborhood in LA hasn't gentrified as quickly as he assured her it would, that he doesn't have a headboard.

She reads an article in the *Times* about potentially removing Asperger's from the DSM-5 and sends it to Clyde with the subject line "Brian????" which he promptly forwards to Lin and Brian, prompting a rare moment of instant sibling bonding. Within minutes they're on a conference call, wondering what she'll diagnose each of them with next.

She just never imagined that Brian would be so far away. He was so good with numbers, was supposed to be her stalwart, working in finance, living in the neighborhood. He'd had every advantage; there'd been no reason he couldn't have had everything any of her friends' sons had, a second home, children in a nearby school she could babysit. Instead, she gets one-line emails from him, no capitalization, no punctuation, as if film sets were the western front and Yahoo were a telegraph.

And when she does get him on the phone, he says something accusatory. Most recently it was, "Mom, I understand you thought you were doing the right thing pretending that you couldn't see the color of my skin, but it was a complete abnegation of my history, my identity."

"What history? *I'm* your history. I held you in my arms from practically the moment you were born. I gave you everything. Don't let anyone make you feel like you're not the same."

"But I'm *not* the same. And by pretending I was, it made me feel my Blackness was something we couldn't talk about."

"Don't be ridiculous. Look at you. You're fine."

She remembers how he clung to her the day she dropped him off at Howard. Clung to her. Snot on the shoulder of her blouse. Or how he fell asleep against her that very first day he became hers, one small victory in a string of defeats she isn't sure how she survived.

Three children. No warning, no training, no real explanation.

Whatever else, she thinks, she did that. She "nailed it," as Clyde says.

For whatever that's worth, she thinks as she comes in the door to the silent apartment, the rooms long emptied, the walls scarred by Scotch tape from posters long gone. *What is it worth?*

Five children. By that math, she should have been the doyenne of an enormous clan, grandchildren and in-laws and holidays to coordinate and a reason to reclaim the Broadkill house. Instead . . . well, she wasn't supposed to be here.

As she puts her breakfast dishes away, Jayne turns her worries to Clyde, even though by that hour he will already have sent her three of those images that repeat in a loop, a cat holding a microphone or Joan Crawford lighting a cigarette.

She worries he won't leverage this silly internet thing he does into a real job with a real network before something shifts—tastes, the internet itself. Or, worse, one of those words that spurt from his mouth like a chemical spill might be the wrong one, and he could find himself on the receiving end of his own spear, hoisted on his own petard. Or he will simply piss off the wrong drunk in the wrong hour of the wrong night and find himself beaten to the edge of life in some alley.

She worries. She makes her way to her dressing table, six feet from Brock's old dresser, and she worries.

Before lunch Jayne will have correspondence to attend to. Emails to return. Or actual letters to write. Customer service departments to navigate. There was no pre-authorization for her MRI. Could she pay out of pocket? *We're so sorry the iron has stopped getting hot after only two months, but you have to speak to the manufacturer.* And Jayne thinks back to Linden's debutante season, the names that presented with her— Corning, Decker, Dow, Proctor, Johnson—and thinks, *Perhaps I can speak to the manufacturer?*

She assembles the errands, the swatches she'll need if she's matching a color, or the jacket that needs to be rewoven. She misses doing things for Brock. Getting his shoes resoled, his watch cleaned, buying the caramels he liked from that tiny shop in Midtown. She enjoyed making his life run.

She knew full well when she entered into the marriage that it would have one of two endings. Either, ever ambitious, he would leave her for a younger version of herself at some wholly distasteful age. Or he would collapse on the tennis court on an August afternoon when the dull heat had lulled even the mosquitoes down for naps; that she would be resting on her matelassé bedspread with September *Vogue*, the phone book–size magazine giving shape to an otherwise amorphous month. That he would leave her to figure out how to be in the world again. That her entire existence would abruptly feel like one long August.

Worse, there is the stress she has inherited. He wasn't running a Ponzi scheme, thank God. At least, that's what the forensic accountants have at last determined. But as Arthur tried to explain, "Jayne, there were people who saw ahead, who shorted the market. Brock—he got shorted."

She tries to understand how so much can become so worthless so quickly.

As she fastens her earrings for her lunch date, she moves on to worrying about Lin. She used to be so proud of her that she would tell anyone who would listen. Making a living as an artist. Of course, it always made Jayne anxious—art money *is* fad money. It's like tulips. Jayne begged her to get a master's so she could at least teach, have something to depend on. Because, let's face it, love seems to be eluding her. And certainly, the kind of men her friends' daughters are marrying are not going to look twice at Linden. They want bright, ambitious girls, the kind Jayne smiles at on the street, not her tattooed daughter with the jet-black hair, who seems to be hiding that now-trendy figure in her layers of ebony as though she were the stamen of a wilted flower.

And she's closer to forty than thirty. No children. Not that Jayne thinks Linden would be a particularly good mother. So perhaps it's for the best. Apparently, Sage is a good mother, according to Linden. How she can stomach it, helping Sage, "babysitting" so she can be uptown looking after *that man*. How she can even *stand* Sage, for that matter—

Jayne clamps her hands over her ears, a makeup brush between her fingers, her eyes squeezed shut.

Then, with an exhale, she collects herself. Keeps moving. Making up the stranger in the mirror. The old woman. Carefully massaging in the creams. Applying mascara with her glasses halfway down her nose. Staring at the face she never did, in the end, alter.

~

On the way home in the afternoon, eager to put her feet up, Jayne's mind turns to Justin.

She doesn't hear from him very often. She knows he's in the city, living the life she once envisioned for Brian, but his invitations to dinner always ring as the obligation they are.

She wonders where she went wrong with him. She took him in, made him a room, steered him through adolescence and onto a reasonably good college. The damage, the fault, the injuries and injustices, all predated her. Surely, after all this time, he could recognize that she was the best of what those years could have looked like for him?

She was the best of what any of this could have looked like for any of them; how has everyone seemed to forget that?

~

Home, she opens the closet, where school uniforms still hang in dry cleaning bags as though another semester looms. Where did it all go? There was always a project, a line on a list, a piece of equipment to order, an instructor to check in with, pocket money to remember, checkups to track. What she racks her brain for are memories, the children getting in bed with her, a school play, a food fight, even simple . . . laughter. But it's like reaching through mist, like those fogged-in mornings at Broadkill when she couldn't see the gate and misjudged it by feet, lunging against nothing, falling to the gravel.

And so, she worries now, to the benefit of nothing and no one, if they had fun.

19

February 2012
Brooklyn, New York

In February, the walk from the F train to Sage's apartment holds no charms. Typically, Lin goes first to the schoolyard to collect Sarah and Calvin, while Henry prefers to accompany Sage to see PopPop. That Rodger could be a *PopPop* is something Lin still can't assimilate, like any number of things Jayne has delivered to her apartment—a fabric steamer, a waffle iron, or pillows that are too big for her couch.

She slogs against the lateral sleet, the wind feeling malicious and personal, and waits with the other parents for the chain-link gates to open, funneling in like factory workers needing to punch their cards, no smiles, let's go, go, go.

But once inside the apartment, they drop their heavy boots and coats to the floor, molting, unwrapping scarves and shaking snow off backpacks. Lin makes hot chocolate and gives them slices of apple and homemade oat bars. *Like feeding horses,* she thinks. They do their homework, they get distracted, they make messes. Lin brings a huge bag of art supplies that she eventually stops lugging and just leaves there, believing in tomorrows and next times. She shows them how to make their world out of shoeboxes and dowels and corks and twist ties. She shows them pictures on her iPad of less gruesome pieces she once exhibited. They ask to create miniature people out of resin. "When you're older."

She prepares dinner and gives baths, invites them onto her lap for story time. She thinks, maybe. *Maybe I would have been good at this.*

Sage comes home, caked in snow, a sleeping child in her arms. She puts them all to bed while Lin cooks, her new skill; then the women sit by the fire and watch the eddies and drifts in the yard.

It's a strange time, born of crisis and need and not knowing, and yet, for both women, it seems to feel that, somehow, they were destined to do this together for these three children, as much as their mothers were destined to do it in tandem for them. And again, Lin wonders, *Is this what it felt like for my mother?* Long lonely months while Rodger was in Southeast Asia, and suddenly this surfeit of love arrives in an unruly package? Did she feel proud of herself?

She calls on her way to the train. "Mom."

"Darling, I was thinking of you. *Vogue* says highlights are in for spring."

"Yes?"

"So that black hair does you no favors."

"Mom."

"Honey, you're so pale. Listen, I'll pay for it. I think it would be good for you."

"I don't know—"

"And have you given any more thought to taking a poetry class?"

"Why would I take a poetry class?"

"You could meet someone."

"What straight man my age is taking a poetry class?"

"What about salsa? My neighbor met a man—"

"Mom!"

"You're so negative. Just try it. You don't know until you try."

"I do! I do know!"

She never gets to ask Jayne if she's proud. Jayne never gets to say, "You get soaked getting them out of the bath? Me, too! I finally kept a butcher's apron hung in there that I wore just to survive the bubble fights." Like an artifact crushed to dust, it is another connection lost between mother and daughter.

~

One night, Sage comes home especially shot. "The aide quit," she says as she serves herself the truffle mac and cheese Lin made with not just cheddar but also Gruyère she grated herself. "Her back is giving her issues and . . ."

"Sage," Lin ventures, dishing salad for them both, "you know you don't have to shoulder this alone. Have you considered just—"

"Don't *you* start." She cuts her eyes at her.

"Don't me start what?"

"I'm sorry." Sage exhales, her posture an overcooked noodle. "Adrian wants me to come home."

This catches Lin off guard. *No*, that isn't what she wants. More. More meals, more nights, more time, time when Sage doesn't look drawn and drained, when she can finish sentences, when she has something left over to ask Lin how she's doing.

"I thought he was coming here?"

Outside, the strong wind has blown the snow on the terrace to cover most of the glass, making the little dining area feel like an igloo. "That isn't proving so easy. It's hard on the kids. And the flights are hard on him. And the cost of all of this is hard on everyone. I didn't envision supporting two households."

"Dad will leave you money." *Dad? Is he "Dad" now?*

"He could live for years, Lin. He's incapacitated, but his heart is strong. I use my power of attorney for home health aides and groceries; I'm not drawing down on his account to live on."

"He would want you to," Lin finds herself saying, as if she knows this person at all.

"His retirement fund lost half its value in the crash, and that was *after* his poor investments—there isn't enough to cover this kind of care indefinitely, and I don't want him to know that it's hard for me to be here."

Lin raises her eyes, her expression like Henry's. "Why?"

"Jesus, how do I answer any of this?" Sage flings her hands in exasperation. "Night after night we talk about how tired I am and how hard this is, but we don't actually talk about what I'm doing. How surprisingly heavy he is if you're trying to turn him so he doesn't get bedsores. The hours I spend massaging his limbs to maintain circulation."

It hurts, all of it. "Why?"

"Why do I do it? Or why don't we talk about why I do it?" Sage picks up her fork. "Are you ready, Linden? Are we going to do this?"

Lin looks at her and knows that the only unsaid thing is the one she cannot hear, that Sage decided at fourteen that Rodger was innocent. That, to her, he is the only father she remembers, a man who took her mother in and spent the rest of Barbara's life trying to love her to the best of his ability.

Because once Sage has said it out loud, Lin won't be able to come back. Won't be able to finger paint or help spell tricky words or read about taco-loving dinosaurs. So she shakes her head no.

"I told him about you."

"What about me?" Lin asks, scissored by conflict.

"That you're watching Sarah and Henry. He smiled. Half smiled. Half his face smiled."

Lin leans in. "Sage, what if you weren't here? He'd have to figure it out. *Somebody* would have to figure it out."

"Not Huck. I haven't heard from him in a few weeks."

They sit in the sound of the candle's flicker.

"Disappearing," Lin whispers.

"What?"

"Disappearing. Disappearing! It's what we do. You know, other families aren't like this. They keep track of each other."

Sage touches Lin's arm. "We aren't like other families."

~

Spring returns, a batty aunt running late, shaking out her wet coat, flowers on the brim of her hat. Lin wakes early. The kids have soccer at eight on Saturdays, and getting them up and out the door is such a palaver that each week, Sage threatens to quit the league, and each week, the kids protest, begging in one shoe, hair uncombed, toothbrushes sticking out of their mouths.

Lin lets herself in at seven with bagels and coffee beans. She puts on the kettle, gets out the French press, puts out the salmon, then tiptoes downstairs to wake everyone—

In her research, Lin learned that the stomach has its own intelligence. That there is a vast web of neurons connecting the brain and enteric nervous system, so afterward it makes sense she remembers this as if her stomach saw it first. Saw a half-naked man asleep in Sarah's bed. And Sarah, not in the pajamas she was put to bed in the night before, but also naked and splayed atop him.

Lin's skin is instantly irrigated. She opens her mouth, summoning air—

"Aren't they cute?" Sage whispers, tying her kimono shut beside her in the doorway.

Lin jumps.

The man stirs, rolling over, taking Sarah with him so she nestles in the crook of his arm.

Sage takes in Lin's face wild with alarm.

"That's *Adrian*."

"Right, right, of course," Lin says, as if calming down. As if that assuages anything for Lin.

"The kids fell asleep with me. Sarah must've heard him come in." Sage claps her hands. "This is such a great surprise."

"Where are her pajamas?" Lin asks.

"Oh, God knows, she's my little hotbox. She never wakes up in them. Are you making coffee? Bless you."

Lin extracts herself, feeling as if she's duplicating with every step, leaving one Lin firmly planted in the doorway to watch over Sarah and another to listen just outside the door, another to back up that one, and so on, until she is toasting bagels so dissipated that she burns her finger.

"Ow, shit."

"Hey," a man's voice says behind her.

She jumps again.

"Sorry, I'm Adrian." His hair is askew. His gray undershirt is riding up above his boxers, revealing a belly. Sarah is walking in front of him, naked, or not walking, forcing him to shuffle against her, his hands crisscrossed in front of her for balance. "You're Lin."

"Get your hand off my nip-ple," Sarah says, pronouncing it with a bouncy inflection, as if in a Noël Coward play.

"My hand was not on your nipple," Adrian contradicts.

"You hand was on my nipple!" She cracks herself up.

"Sarah, babe, if you insist on walking in front of me and holding my hands, your entire torso is the size of my palm."

Calvin bounces into the room from the stairs, soccer uniform already on. "Dad! Dad! Dad! Dad!"

"Thank you for helping Sage out so much while I'm not here," he says, scooping Calvin in for a hug as Sarah keeps throwing her weight back against him and Henry has started hitting him in the thigh with a cleat.

"Dad was touching my nip-ple!"

"I'll touch your nipple." Calvin reaches around and squeezes Sarah's nipple.

"Ow! Mom!"

What is happening?

"Nobody," Sage says as she emerges from the stairs, "is touching anyone else—anywhere. Eat your breakfast." The kids fall on the bagels as Sage adds quietly, "When she was five, she went through this phase of basically needing to hump Adrian's leg like a puppy. I thought he would die. Do you want to come with us to soccer?"

"Actually, I should go," Lin manages. "You have enough hands for today, and I have work to catch up on."

"You sure?"

"Totally."

Lin looks around, trying to remember what she came with, what she has to take with her. Is this okay? Should she be staying? Did Sage unconsciously move across the country to get Sarah away from her father? Is this the consequence of living with Rodger?

Lin's hands are shaking. She drops her keys as she tries to get her bag together. "Okay. Well, you guys have a great day. Adrian, nice to meet you. Enjoy your visit."

Adrian rubs his face. "Yeah, actually, I have a surprise. Guys, I'm here! I'm staying."

"What?" Sage asks, her smile instantly finding an expression of itself lost in the months of snow and care.

"I just said, fuck it. Nothing is worth this. If I'm in New York, they'll have to find me a spot in the operation or lose me—and hiring is starting to pick up. The broker is handling the house. Whatever, I'm here!"

The kids explode as only kids can—they wrestle him onto the couch, a pile of limbs and tickles and squealing, the frame squeaking beneath them.

"I should go," Lin says again to her hands. She picks up her purse and walks out, knowing she may have left her keys—and so much else—behind.

~

Over the following days and weeks, she finds she can't call Sage back—and she can't pin her thoughts down, either. She tries to anchor herself with her work, the pieces that once sold for thousands of dollars now displayed on a folding table in SoHo, in the hopes that European or Japanese tourists might think they're cool. She stands behind the table hour after hour in the sun, and it's like she's trying to look at life through a spinning telescope. At one end she is huge, and it's life that recedes. Adrian is hurting Sarah, and Sage must be made to see, and everything falls in line behind that fact, behind the orientation of how Lin was raised to see the world. But it feels—it feels, with the instinct that makes you retabulate the bill—it's not the answer.

At other hours, it is life that is magnificent, Sage's family that is whole, and Lin who is small and broken and worthless. She is approaching forty, and even her most fucked-up friends are finding people to have children with, getting their own Christmas trees, finding a way forward. And she fears she will spend the rest of her life lying on the floor in unbearable pain.

Suddenly she hears, "Lindy Hop?" A look of surprise on his face, Clyde rounds the corner, a latte in hand, the *Financial Times* under his arm. He assesses her. "You were wearing that when I saw you Sunday."

"Yes."

"Have you showered?"

"I don't know. I can't take my clothes off."

Clyde gently pinches her elbow and leads her away.

"But my art," she protests limply.

"This is some hoarder's lucky day. Come on."

~

He takes her home and walks her right in under the water, then sits on the tile floor with her, letting her cry through his designer sweatshirt.

"There, there," he whispers.

She heaves and sobs, her face a doily of broken capillaries.

"When did you eat?"

She tries to find enough breath to speak. "I can't."

"What about a movie? We could walk to the Angelika?"

"No."

"What is it? What's happening?"

"I don't know, but something is wrong, it's so wrong, and it's either them—or it's me."

"No, no, Lindy," he says firmly. "You're fine."

"What?" she murmurs.

"You're fine, Lindy. You're fine."

Her eyes fly open, a thousand cumulative wounds pulsing on her body, scars from bumps and bruises and scrapes and violations, each one always met with the same pronouncement from a woman standing above it all.

"No," she says. No, she isn't. "I'm not."

PART VI

20

April 2012
Brooklyn, New York

As Sage huffs up the block, arms straining with unwieldy grocery bags, the last thing she's expecting to find is Lin on her stoop.

Sage swings the bags to the steps, wiping her brow. It's one of those spring days when the temperature starts in the low forties and climbs rapidly. Untying her jacket from her waist, she sits beside Lin, tenting her waffle-weave shirt away from her skin. They stay like that, in silence, for a few moments, listening to the house sparrows and the trucks rumbling on Flatbush. They sit long enough to commune over Lin's absence, her presence, and her appearance, still disastrous. Under-slept, salt crusted, she looks like moms in pediatric ICUs, wrung out, functioning on the fumes of a determination to find the end of a nightmare.

"I have ice cream," Sage says at last, meaning she needs to go in.

"Sage, I'm sorry."

Sage pivots to her. "I don't get it—are you jealous? This was always the plan—that he would come."

"Yes, no, I know. No, that's not it." Lin struggles, the words that coursed through her mind in bed this morning, that made sense on the subway, now eluding her. All she knows is that Sage and Sarah and Henry and Calvin made her feel—better. "I don't understand things, and I want to. I want to, and I don't know how."

"What do you want to understand?"

"What's normal."

Sage's shoulders release their barricade of her neck. "Come in." Lin picks up one of the bags and follows her up the stoop.

Sage doesn't offer her tea or coffee, just starts emptying the groceries into the refrigerator and cupboards.

"I've been thinking, when I started Celexa . . . ," Lin begins. She is standing on the other side of the kitchen island, between the couch and dining table, her weight on the outside of her right foot, like she did the first time she came over. "It was probably something I needed years earlier—I really had an unmedicated anxiety disorder I masked as being productive."

Sage nods, putting the sprouted bread into the freezer.

"I didn't know what being normal felt like. I didn't know how to sleep in, or not break into a sweat if the train was running late or a package didn't get delivered. I thought everyone hated me all the time. It was exhausting."

"Uh-huh." Sage crams a cereal box in where there isn't space for one.

"So, I didn't get it. Without medication, I didn't even know what to shoot for." Sage drops out of eyeline, burrowing through crackers and broccoli, looking for cheese and sour cream. "In therapy, or yoga, or whatever, I didn't know what I was supposed to feel like. And I don't know now."

"Don't know what?" The voice echoes inside the brown paper.

"If I can trust myself. And, if I can't—what that means." Lin takes one last fueling breath. "I—I saw Adrian lying naked with Sarah."

Sage instantly whips her torso up like a bird of prey. "What?"

"Y-you were there, you saw it, too. And yet you were so—relaxed. So I don't understand what I saw." She wilts under the intensity of Sage's stare. "I mean, I thought I did—I was sure I did."

At that moment Henry toddles in from his nap dragging a stuffed bear, his hair fluffed and askew like a pint-size pop star. He walks over to Sage and wordlessly raises his arms. She nestles him up.

"Oh, Adrian's here," Lin says.

"He's working from home. He's had to so I could get up to Dad's. I will find a sitter, it's just been—one thing too many. Dad has an infection. It's not uncommon. But it's been a lot of emergency room visits."

"Oh. Do you want to talk somewhere else?"

"About what?" Sage asks.

Adrian walks in, his reading glasses up in his lank brown hair, a smudge of ink on his nose. "You're up! Hey, little buddy." Henry jumps like a tree frog from Sage to Adrian, his naptime diaper falling off in the process. Adrian swings him up like a platter. "Oh, that tushy!" he exclaims, biting it. Henry bursts into peals of laughter and snorting, his nose congested.

"No, no! You can't eat me!"

"I can! I am going to eat you!" He runs kisses up and down the boy's backside. Sage is smiling.

Adrian swings him back to the floor. "Go use the potty and get some clothes on; we'll pick up your brother and sister. Hey," he acknowledges Lin.

She smiles back because she was raised to.

"Did you get peanut butter?"

Sage passes him the jar from the cupboard. He pulls a spoon from the drawer and helps himself to a large mouthful, returns the jar to the fridge, the spoon to the dishwasher. "It's nice today, I'll take them to the schoolyard for a while."

"Thank you," she says.

"Okay, cool. Lin, good to see you." He disappears back down the stairs.

Lin is abruptly sobbing. She drops onto the edge of the sturdy coffee table, uselessly raking her nonabsorbent fingers across her face. "Is that normal?"

"Yes," Sage says simply. "In this generation we kiss and cuddle and bite tushies, and Sarah can't stop talking about her nipples or asking to touch Calvin's penis, and that doesn't even cover that kids masturbate—constantly. In toddlerhood, boys walk around tugging on their penises like candy is going to come flying out, and girls lie on their stomachs at day care and rub themselves to fall asleep. And we are the first generation not to slap hands away and say, *That's dirty, you're dirty.*"

"What *do* you say?" Lin asks meekly.

"'It's your body and you can do whatever you want to, but in your room, sweetie.' And I am so excited. I want to see who Sarah is at twenty, having never been shamed about making herself feel good. Though, God willing, she will have grown out of talking about her nipples. And none of that makes Adrian a child molester."

"I understand." Lin tries to catch the foaming horse of her breath. "It's two different paradigms. You live in a paradigm where he's innocent. Where he just loved me—is that what you think?"

"Sometimes."

"But do you ever consider that maybe you're *wrong*?"

"Of course!"

Stunned, Lin looks up, eyes wide. "You do?"

"Yes!" Sage slaps her hands down on the island marble, arms forming a triangle. "I sop up his drool and I question why I went. I question how young I was. I question why I was allowed to make the decision. I question who was in charge."

"B-but," Lin says, "you could have let them go—*nothing* would have changed. We barely saw Rodger as it was. Why did you leave?"

Sage continues to look calmly at Lin. "I wanted my mom."

"Oh." Lin lets that sink in. "Did you go to protect her?"

"From *him*?" Sage's jaw drops in her closed mouth as she slowly shakes her head. "He was incredibly gentle with her." She thinks for another moment, another time and place playing in her mind. "I think she was what he needed." She pauses. "He could come out of his office, at capacity with the misery and cruelty of the world, and find her sitting there, a broken soul to reflect it all back to him. She'd be waiting on her slipper chair, in this purple bathrobe—I don't know what she had with purple—and he'd raise her gently by the elbows and then enfold her in his arms, and they'd stay like that for minutes. Every night—before cocktails were made or Chinese food was ordered, this embrace, this communion."

"Why was she so sad?" Lin asks.

Sage shrugs. "Because I wasn't enough."

~

There is nowhere left for Lin to walk.

There is no route that soothes her, no bed at the other end that offers a few hours' respite. She has tried that, smiled at stories through music too loud to hear them, bought herself some time outside her skin, but these men never feel like Justin, taste like Justin, or anyone, or anything. They are paper towels, Handi Wipes, plastic spoons. And the worst part is, as she redresses, she knows she is, too.

There is nowhere left to hide.

There is no inch of her apartment that will allow her body to trick her mind into thinking she's somewhere else, someone else. Years ago, she could switch to the couch at 2:00 a.m. and leave her nightmares behind the bookcase concealing her bed. Then, when that stopped working, she could hitch a few floor pillows together with a sheet, pretend she was on a plane. Apartment full of moonlight, she dragged that setup to her kitchen, the front hall, and even under her drafting table. But no more.

There is no drug left to take.

She has been on Celexa—off Prozac—on Zoloft—off Valium—and it all feels like wrapping a drum set in a gauze scarf. Her brain won't let her sleep because somewhere there is an emergency. What she doesn't know is—is it in 1979? Or the next room? Is it the day she told Justin she'd understand if he was done? Or is *she* the emergency?

For the first time she is willing to take *any* information on board, do what she has never been able. Instead of shrinking life so small that she can't fit in it, then shrinking herself in the hopes she might, she will reinflate all of it, every memory, hers *and* theirs, climb in, flashlight and black light in hand, until she has finally reconciled it all.

She stands under the shower until it scalds her, pulls on Justin's track pants from high school, a men's wool sweater she once found in her grandma's attic, and thick socks. She orders Chinese takeout—and a pack of Rodger's cigarettes. She turns on the computer.

She starts with the background. She splits the chopsticks and dives into reading her father's thoughts. Rodger Donoghue's unflinching recollections, razor insights, and minute observations about the world he moved through, from the early sixties until his stroke. Then she orders his books, all fourteen of them, from his analysis of the Vietcong to Bosnia, Belarus, Rwanda, then Myanmar. If it's a total travesty of human rights, Rodger has three hundred pages to say about it, embracing all the nuance of every issue, examining the regimes of oppression with equal detail.

She reads the work he did for the *Crimson*. She reads the articles published years later by his students. She reads a history of the *Times* and learns he'd order a hot soup from the deli every day, forget to drink it, and then usually spill it on his papers like a little baptism of his revelations.

More than that, she comes away with the disconnect that drove Jayne crazy: people on the other side of the world, their plight, their suffering, were always more real than Sage's dyslexia, Huck's latest fracture, or even just the need to get an answer to the question, "Will you be home for dinner?"

That he could care so deeply for them—and do so much damage to us— isn't this enough? Doesn't it justify Clyde's crusade? She poses herself the question, but no answer comes back, other than to crack another book.

The false promise of spring gives way to the raw heat of summer, the heat that always beckoned her from her studio to rooftop bars. Instead, she hires a private investigator. She tries to track Bunny's whereabouts between 1957 and 1972, records made by crossing borders, delivering babies.

"Oh my gosh," she whispers, a copy of Sage's birth certificate in her hands, counting backward, doing the math that has always been right in front of her. She calls Sage. "You were born in 1967."

"Yes."

"When your mom was twenty-six."

"Yes." Lin can hear her loading the dishwasher, can feel her desire to hang up.

"But if she was sixteen when she ran away, that would mean she left in 1957."

"So?"

Lin clutches the phone with her shoulder, the illicit Xerox in her hands. "Mom always said Bunny was a hippie—made it sound like she just ran off to join the counterculture. Like this was normal sixties teenage rebellion, but this was *years* ahead of that."

"I don't know." There's a pause and the water shuts off.

"Which part?"

"Any of it, all of it. Honestly, Lin, she *never* talked about it."

"Never?"

"No. She didn't talk about our fathers or how she got us from place to place. She'd tell us stories from when we were babies, but in a vacuum. Like the time I made a whole puppet theater from rice sacks. But did that happen in San Miguel, or San Antonio, or San Francisco? I don't know."

"Why did she run away from home?"

"I don't know, Lin! I don't know. Sarah has a stomach bug, and Calvin lost his soccer jersey, and Mom is gone, and Dad is incapacitated, and *no one* can tell us why any of this shit happened."

There is a pause, a silence between them bouncing from phone to satellite to phone, Sage thinking they are blessedly, finally done just as Lin recognizes the opposite.

"No, Sage, that's not true."

~

Girding herself, Lin surrenders to one of her mother's invitations out east, and it proceeds like all the weekends she succumbs to coming here. The ride out to the Hamptons is forever, and Clyde somehow takes up two seats, and Lin has to fold herself down into the size of a magazine-subscription-renewal form and slip herself in the air vents.

Lin invariably discovers clippings piled on her bed, articles her mother wants her to read. And clothes, items she wants her to wear. Some new, some passed along. The articles rarely pertain to anything Lin cares about. The clothes are nothing that would suit her. She stands by the bed, duffel still on her shoulder, sensing this other woman beside her, the one with the right measurements to look good in Jayne's cast-offs, someone who wants to read a twelve-page article in an old *New Yorker* about art consultancies.

Saturday morning, Jayne is invariably put out that they want to go to the beach. The beach is sandy. She thought they would play cards by the pool.

Lin and Clyde get back from the sandy beach in time for dinner, sun rouged and tipsy, but Jayne is going out. She has plans that can't be amended just because her children are here.

On Sunday it's raining, and they want to make eggs and strew the paper across the living room, nap on the window seat, drool. But Jayne has read the articles. She has eaten already. She wants to discuss if Lin is going to freeze her eggs. She wants to know where Clyde stands on Israel.

Clyde escapes for a sodden run. Lin wishes she'd taken up running. Instead, she washes a bowl of grapes and makes an effort, sinks into the salmon-colored couch. She looks at Jayne's profile, her glasses pushed up into her gray-streaked bob. Even now, she is beautiful, the skin softened to the consistency of dough almost too pliable to hold a cookie's shape. The eyes large and blue, the force of intelligence behind them that animates and recedes without warning, never having found a perch, an outlet.

The rain patters against the French doors. It's so hard to stay awake.

"How are you, honey?"

"I'm good."

"I saw Jenny Mahoney's wedding announcement in the *Times*."

"Oh." Lin pulls a pillow onto her lap, missing the old ones with fringe she could worry.

"She seems happy."

"I haven't spoken to her since we graduated high school, but I'm glad her wedding announcement makes her sound happy. Because if it didn't, someone should be fired."

"I'm just saying—she's your age—and she just got married."

"So there's hope."

"Linden!"

"What? Yes, okay, I'm lonely." She gives in. "I'm desperately, horribly lonely. It's like a giant Afghan hound living in my apartment, my loneliness."

Jayne tuts. "You know, none of you ever ask me how I am since Brock died. It so happens, *I* am lonely."

Lin just wants to eat grapes. "You are? Of course you are."

"I don't make a big thing of it, I keep busy, but I thought we still had years and years."

"Of course. I'm sorry. That's hard. Do you want to date?" Lin releases her death grip of the pillow's corner.

"Do you like the shape of your nails?"

"Sorry?"

"Your nails." Jayne peers at them, and Lin curls her fingers in for examination.

"What about them?"

"Well, they're very square."

～

At seven the skies clear, and they sit down for dinner as if this is their weekly two-hour tithe—and not the culmination of forty-eight hours

Lin silently vows never to repeat. Candles are lit inside hurricane lanterns. The place mats have a sand dollar pattern.

Lin girds herself. "Mom, why did Bunny leave home?"

Jayne looks at her daughter open mouthed. "How should I know?"

"She never said?"

"She was young. She wanted to live on a commune. It was a fad." Jayne gives the pasta salad a last toss and flings the serving spoons at Clyde. "These are all from my garden. Help yourselves."

"Why did she leave the kids with you?"

"What's with the third degree?" Jayne sits and takes a sip of her Perrier.

"I'm just curious."

"Well, I was her sister—she had nowhere else to go."

"I know, you've always said—but *why* didn't she have anywhere else?"

"She moved around a lot, and it's not like she could wash back up in Cherry Hill and say, 'Hey, I decided to tune in, turn on, and drop out, and now my womb is hanging out of my body—'"

"Wait—what? You never told us that."

"It wasn't her womb—something to do with her abdominal wall during Brian's delivery, I think. It's not uncommon—only in Bunny's case, it was pretty extreme—and it's not like we knew what we know now. Women didn't talk about"—Jayne gestures toward the linen napkin in her lap—"back then. Now the conversations I overhear in Pilates . . ." Jayne dishes herself a portion that somehow manages to avoid all the pasta in the pasta salad.

"It just doesn't make sense, Mom."

"What doesn't make sense? It happened, therefore it makes sense."

"But it seems like something is missing."

Clyde kicks Lin under the table.

"No, I just think it's important," she presses. "I want to know why Bunny left home—why she wouldn't go back."

"Oh my God, why do you care?" Clyde asks, thoroughly exasperated.

"Because if there hadn't been so many of us, maybe what happened to me wouldn't have happened."

"That's absurd," Jayne protests. "Are you accusing me of neglect?"

"No!" Lin retreats. "No, that's not it. I just want to understand—for me, for Sage—why a woman leaves her children. Why another woman takes them in."

Jayne's lips are suddenly trembling. "I loved them—all of them. You. I loved you. And I owed her . . ." She trails off.

"What? *What* did you owe her?"

"She wronged you," Clyde cuts in.

Jayne pushes back in her chair, avoiding eye contact with her children and the sunset itself. "We wronged each other."

"How?" Lin asks, sensing with urgency this last question is at the crux of everything.

Jayne just shrugs again and looks down at her paltry serving. "She was my sister. It was my job to look after her."

~

When Clyde gets off the jitney at the Third Avenue stop farthest downtown, Lin stays on. All the way to Seventy-Ninth Street.

The apartment has only been closed up for a month, but the air is stultifying. It isn't just the trapped heat—it's everything that can't escape. The Herbs de Provence from the last meal cooked, the citrus tinge of floor wax and furniture polish, the tang of bleach and scouring powder. The sour smell of fresh paint coming from the den. And under all those are the spines of books, dust jackets quietly going brittle, and the fuzzy smell of electricity where Jayne left her printer on. It's the lining of the emptied garbage can and the mildew by the washer. It's a spot on the carpet and the dust that can never be beaten out of the pillows.

And beneath all this, another layer fills Lin's nose and mouth. Jayne. Jayne's skin, her scent, her choices. And below Jayne is—all of them. Below this year—last year. And all the years before that. Sage crackles through the hallways, as do Huck and Brian, and Clyde and even Justin. Brock is there. His elephant head. His safari cologne in the headboard.

It's all there, their history, collected in a series of rooms.

Lin drops her bag heavily on the front-hall carpet. She doesn't open the windows, but she gets herself a big glass of water and walks back to the master bedroom that no longer has a master. She turns on the light.

The entire space is lying in wait for Jayne's return. Not like a dog, not with that much enthusiasm, but like a cat. It curls around Lin's ankles. "Welcome," it seduces. "Admire me."

"Okay," Lin concedes, as if admiration is the coin to be ferried across to the closet. She takes in the new drapes, the verdant trim picked to echo the Art Nouveau perfume bottles and vintage frames that hold childhood images of Linden and Clyde on bright-green lawns under cloudless skies, the colors matching the bed's throw pillows. It is all so well thought through. For the first time, it occurs to Lin that this room is her mother's diorama. It is the little box where she has control.

"What's your story, lady?" Lin whispers as she turns on the lights in the carpeted walk-in. She looks up, past the rows of tweed jackets with gold buttons, the rows of ballet flats, to the boxes on the high shelves.

She drags in a chair with a needlepoint seat, kicks off her sandals, and climbs atop. There are three of them—an old Tiffany box, large enough for a bowl; a Gimbels box that could have held a set of wineglasses; and a flat one from a Baltimore department store Lin has never heard of, a dress box, yellow and white with a sepia photograph of a horse-drawn carriage on its front, an image meant to evoke an agrarian history in a postwar mechanization revolution—and now both are almost beyond anyone's first-person accounting.

She takes the Tiffany box down first and sits on the tan wall-to-wall. Lifting the dusty lid carefully, she reveals black-and-white photos. Lin doesn't understand—in the den is a shelf of albums her grandmother made. There are portraits of her uncles as boys in short pants and knee socks, the girls in wool coats that reveal dimpled knees, the house in its heyday—formal, curated.

These are snapshots. A couple having a picnic. Who is the couple? Who took the picture? What year is this? Lin squints. Is this her grandparents? No. It's her grandmother, yes, but the man is different—no scar. Didn't she have a first husband? Is this him? The one who died? Laughing at the camera, they hold hands over a lattice-topped pie.

Lin can't ever remember her grandmother laughing.

Lin combs the box, finding vellum baby books for Michael and Luke with little snippets of hair fastened to each. On the first page is a woman's handwriting, tight cursive: "This is Mrs. Eleanor Ellison writing for Maggie Leopold."

What did that mean? Why did Margaret have baby books if she couldn't write in them herself?

Mrs. Ellison, whoever she was, dutifully recorded each boy's birth weight, his one-year growth, his sleeping and eating on the translucent pages edged with illustrations of flowers and rabbits. At the back of Michael's book, she added, "You never did see a happier mother than Maggie."

Lin tries to reconcile this with the unsmiling woman with the formidable bosom who wouldn't allow Lin or her siblings in the parlor. "What happened?"

On the last page of Luke's book, Mrs. Ellison wrote, "I am teaching Maggie her letters and trust that by the time baby number three is with us, should the Lord see fit, that she will be able to do all the writing herself."

Below the books is a stash of letters to Margaret Linden, return address Wyoming—unopened.

Was Margaret left husbandless *and* illiterate? She would have to ask her mother. Would her mother know?

She lifts the lid on the horse-drawn carriage. It's a small dress, for maybe a four-year-old. Spring flowers, a smocked front. Was it Jayne's?

Why has she kept it? And then she sees on the box, someone has shakily written in pencil *Bunny Easter*. Which doesn't mean that it was Bunny's Easter dress. But it might have been.

So many things might have been. What *was*?

She picks up her sandals and walks out of the house, duffel over her shoulder, stash of letters and picture of Maggie in hand, leaving everything else strewn behind her.

21

Ladies and gentlemen," the pilot says over the loudspeaker, "we'll be making our approach into Jackson Hole in a few minutes. Passengers on the right side of the plane should have a beautiful view of the Tetons."

Lin closes her magazine and looks out the window. They have perforated the clouds, and he is correct—the mountains are impossibly perfect. Honestly, she hadn't been sure what to expect. In fact, she deliberately *didn't* bring any expectations, as if they exceeded the weight limit for her suitcase. It's enough that she's nearly here, in a town she's never visited, in a state she's only flown past, to see a man who doesn't know her—and may not want to.

She didn't even need her investigator this time. She simply googled *Luke Michael Linden Wyoming*, and up popped the listing of the facility the brothers co-own and operate. She didn't call, afraid that—what? They'd get a heads-up and flee? She simply booked the first direct flight to Jackson Hole, committing herself to—something, even if it's just visiting the airport.

But unlike her typical tour de force of doing the undoable, she is not simultaneously doing and *not* doing this, deplaning and not deplaning, waiting and not waiting for her bag, standing and not standing with four or five couples for a car. She is simply surprised at each turn to observe herself committing further, like inching ambivalently into cold water.

The taxi drives along the miles of raw-wood fence. Two parallel beams, a spoke every six feet, so quintessentially Western it almost feels fake. Then they take a right under the wooden arch with the sign swinging from two metal chains—CHEYENNE RANCH AND WELLNESS CENTER—and up the mile-long drive to the center itself, visible for acres in the uninterrupted scrub. A rehab facility masking as a spa—or vice versa, she can't tell yet. Regardless, it definitely isn't what *My brothers moved out west to be carpenters* conjures, reminding Lin this is exactly why she's come. Because Jayne's world is cut into neat categories—good, bad, with me, against me—and Lin is starting to suspect that sanity might be the ability to hold a dichotomy, embrace paradox. Perhaps your brothers are wildly successful carpenters. Perhaps you love your sister *and* hate your sister—but if you only hold one of these truths, where does that leave you?

The cab lets her off in the circular drive that seems to suggest people change their mind up until the last second, simply slingshot around without slowing, try another day. But Lin has tried enough tomorrows to have a fairly good sense of what this one will feel like if she retreats. Whereas she has no idea what it might feel like if she doesn't, and so she climbs the three porch steps with her wheelie suitcase, the bag itself a source of so much internal debate she almost didn't come. Arrive with a tote, she told herself, you mean brisk business. Arrive with a suitcase and you could be asking for anything. The embarrassing truth of the suitcase prevailed.

The entry is double-height and shaped like a beehive. From a central umbilical cord, an antler chandelier dangles over a table of brochures on local hikes and recreation.

"Checking in?" the man behind the counter asks gently.

Lin looks across at his silhouette, her eyes adjusting from the shadeless sun. Then looks again. Stunned. And not stunned.

"Hi," she says simply.

"Hi." He smiles. His age is hard to pinpoint just by looking at him. He is older than Lin, to be sure, but at a glance—how much older? His gray hair is thick and standing up at all angles as if mimicking the horns above them. Under his denim work shirt, he's wiry and hollowed out, like somewhere along the line he's had to trade parts of himself, shaving them off, until only the incontrovertible remains. His face is pockmarked, and his nose looks like it was broken more than once. But his olive skin is robust, the color of vegetables and sleep consumed in the right ratios.

"I don't have a reservation," she says automatically, all reservations gone.

"That's not unheard of. Sometimes you just know what ya gotta do at the spur of the moment." His voice has developed a soft twang that matches the logs and antlers and mountain peaks.

Unable to figure out what to say further, Lin crosses to the bust-height desk, slips out her wallet, and hands him her ID.

"Oh," he says and looks up. Oh. That one syllable. The circle of recognition. The birth canal, a newborn reaching blindly for the perfect ring of its mother's areola. A homecoming.

"Hi," she says again.

"Hi," he replies, this time in shock. "Is everything okay?"

Lin lets out a quick bark of a laugh. "Well, I'm here, so . . . no."

"How did you find me?" he asks.

She looks into Huck's eyes, overcome suddenly with so much . . . love, more than she imagined she could contain. "We're family."

~

An hour later Lin is sitting with Huck on the veranda outside her ground-floor room, sipping cactus juice and staring at the mountains that invite staring like pageant winners.

"I can't get over it," she says. "It's so beautiful. I don't know what I was imagining—but it wasn't this."

"It's the words *Jackson Hole*," Huck acknowledges. "Just makes you think of a horrible president or an outhouse, and it used to make me think of that diner on Ninety-First and Madison—"

"Oh my gosh, yes!" Another marble from her past shaken loose. "The one that got away with the bowls of pickle slices on every table! The welcome-mat health-code violation."

"I still ate them, though," he says slyly, touching the tip of his boot as if it was his old pair of Chuck Taylors.

"Of course. We all did. Braced for someone's gum to come floating to the surface."

They smile at each other; a smile that should never have happened in a place it was unlikely they'd be.

She turns back to what her brain keeps telling her is a movie-set scrim. "But this makes me feel small in a good way."

"That's the idea when you've come to surrender," he says softly.

"How long have you been here?"

"This time?" He squints. "Eighteen months."

"Does Sage know you're here?"

He touches a length of leather cord wrapping his wrist. "She knows I'm getting help. She knows I'm staying sober."

"I don't understand."

He sets his boot back on the decking and rests his elbows on his knees. "Mom sent me here in college—or what should have been college if I wasn't too high to work." He speaks slowly, deliberately, with the practice of someone with a daily habit of accountability. "But I didn't get it then." He hunches his shoulders. "I was a kid. Kids get high." He blows out a breath. "I didn't see the problem—I thought they just wanted me to be like them."

"Unappealing."

He smiles again. Sitting beside him now, she sees that he's lost a few of his back teeth and has a bridge. "But somewhere in my twenties I tried heroin, and then . . ." His hand floats out from his body. "Everything slid away." His head drops for a split second like a dog heeling. "I won't bore you, but it was disgusting." He looks directly at Lin. "That's my word. I was doing things to get and stay high that should have disgusted me, and they didn't. But they do now, and I hold fast to that." He clenches his fist around the moment.

"So, this is a rehab facility?"

"Partly." He looks down. His hands are webbed in micro-scars, as though he put them through a window over and over and over, and dotted with what look like cigarette burns. "In the other buildings we detox, and we take people through their twenty-eight days, but we also welcome those who need to reset. Ultimately what we're finding is that the old model of addiction treatment doesn't serve enough people."

"I understand," she says, thinking of all her compulsions, the times she chooses to get drunk or laid rather than sit with her discomfort, her fear. "That sounds valuable. And you work with patients?"

"Nah. I just lead a couple of low-stakes workshops, crafts and what-not. I'm taking engineering classes at the college and looking to get my old credits from Columbia transferred—I want to finish my degree, but I don't want to go back to New York."

"I get that." She takes in the length of him, wants him to know she sees the effort he's making. "You seem really good. Peaceful."

He allows himself a quick smile. "Yeah, I know I was so angry—you remember."

"I do. Was it my mom?"

"Nah. I mean, yes. But it started before. The moving around. There was a guy—Brian's dad, I think. And he was suddenly supposed to be our dad. But I had a dad, and no one ever explained why we had to leave him. And the more Sage played along—with Mom, with Jayne—the angrier I got."

"She misses you, you know."

"One thing at a time." Huck abruptly stands. "Michael is leading a woodworking class, but he'll be here soon."

"So, he *is* a carpenter?"

Huck gestures. "Made that bench you're sitting on."

She half twists to look just as there's a knock.

"I'll leave you two to it." Huck places one hand on the balustrade and effortlessly hops the fence into the dust. "I'm gonna go check on the horses. See you at dinner." With a wave, he ambles off, and Lin rushes inside and past the king bed with its red Pendleton blanket.

She flips the lock to find a man filling the doorway. Even in his late seventies, even slightly stooped, he is over six feet, with broad shoulders. But Lin immediately perceives with her artist's eye a conflict between his yeti presence and his energy field. Despite literally looking down at her, his chin is tucked, his eyes are questioning, as if he were looking up, waiting for an invitation, for permission.

"Hello," she says.

"My, my." He takes her in. "My niece. In the flesh." His voice is friendly, with a rasp like sawdust. She suddenly wonders what her in-the-flesh amounts to. Making no concession to the journey, she's wearing a black tiered skirt, tank top, and cardigan to match her hair, eyes, and nails. And for the first time she catches herself wondering if she really needs to try so hard. If her mother is right, if it wouldn't kill her sometimes to just throw on a pair of shorts.

"Would you like to come in?" she asks.

"Let's take a walk, if you don't mind. We have a policy of never going in guests' rooms—you understand—and I'd feel uncomfortable."

"Of course, let me get my shoes."

Flip-flops on, she follows him through the dining room, off the back porch, out onto the lawn.

She stops. "Are there snakes?"

"In life?"

"On the property."

He replaces his hat on his head and resumes his leisurely stride. "Probably, but they shouldn't bother us."

"Great." Lin isn't sure if he means the snakes'll stay away or they won't, but she shouldn't be bothered if one slithers by. Pretending not to have authentic reactions is something she's trying to become less adept at.

"Luke is sorry to miss you. He's at a conference in Santa Fe."

"I'm just so grateful that one of you is here, that this wasn't a wild-goose chase—and Huck! Oh my gosh, I can't believe he's here. I can't wait to tell Sage I saw him. He seems like he's doing really well."

Michael allows a pause to follow her torrent of words before asking, "How is my sister?" as he guides her away from the treatment outbuildings toward the paddock.

Lin watches her feet and pulls her sweater closer around her, though the setting sun is warm. "I would say the same, but I have no idea what she was like when you knew her."

Michael smiles, his deep wrinkles making the aerial map of a subdivision. "Well, she was just barely a teen when we left. She was beautiful—I gather she stayed beautiful."

"Yes, she did."

"She was always striving, Jaynie, trying to find her place. One year it was winning the spelling bee; one year it was organizing a book drive. One year she was determined to win the juniors baking contest. I don't remember who won, but I do remember thinking you can't *force* something to taste good."

"Yes." Lin smiles. "She is exactly the same. What do you think she's looking for?"

"Someone to tell her she did a good job."

Lin considers this as she scampers, having to take a step and a half for each of his to keep up, the one possibility that never occurred to her. Then she thinks of Sarah's and Henry's and Calvin's little faces and Sage always ready with a thumbs-up and a *"Yay! You did it!"* Is it really so simple? That we need food, water, shelter . . . and just someone to say, *"Go, you."*

"How did you come here?" Lin asks as they approach the paddock.

He rests his forearms on the fence and watches for a minute as two women canter in a circle under the watchful eye of a trainer. "We had a child's idea of what 'out west' was. If we could've boarded a rocket, we would've done that, I suppose. That house was just so damn *small*."

"The house was small?" she asks with gentle incredulity.

"It was while he was alive."

"Grandpa Joe?"

He nods.

"I'm sure you're wondering why I'm here."

"Not really. You all seem to wash up here sooner or later."

"I want to understand why you guys left, why Bunny ran away—and Mom stayed. Growing up, she only let us have the barest interaction with them. Yet when we ask her, Joe was a pillar of the community, and her mother was the soul of industriousness and charity. I don't know what this all has to do with me exactly, but—"

"What has my sister told you?"

"Nothing, really. Just that Bunny sort of took off to join the counterculture movement, but I think there's more. Is there? Is there more?"

His eyes hold the horizon while Lin waits for him to answer her question. After a minute he says, "I just want you to understand things don't have to stay bad—they don't have to stay broken."

"Okay," she agrees, having no idea what he means.

"People check in here all the time, and their lives seem beyond repair—but they heal. They put things to rights. Not always. Not for good. But some do. Remember that."

"Okay."

"My mother—well, when our father died, she was left with nothing."

"Oh—I brought the letters you sent her. They were unopened. Did you know she couldn't read?"

He smiles faintly, mirthlessly. "That makes sense. She never checked our homework, can't remember ever seeing her with a book. Gosh." He shakes his head. "I'm sorry she never got to know we were doing okay. Too much pride to let anyone read them to her, I guess."

"What was she like? When you were little?" she asks.

"Well, that was an awful long time ago, and I don't remember when my pa was alive so much. I really just remember her as tired. Too tired to pay us much mind."

"So, when a man comes along and wants to marry you—*any* man . . ."

Michael nods. "Especially one who was quietly buying up the town, determined to put out every tenant who'd ever bullied him."

"What was he like?" she asks. "Mom describes him as a little cold, a little hard to get to know, but inspiring. She says he set high standards."

Michael snorts and the nearest colt snorts in return.

Lin's face breaks open in delight. "She thinks you're talking to her!"

"Always." He reaches in his pocket, pulls out a sugar cube, and the colt trots over. "Look, I don't know you, Linden, and ordinarily I'd say this wasn't my place, but it's not like you're a kid anymore. He wasn't 'inspiring,' he was a mean sonofabitch who punched us until we got too big to punch."

"Oh." The circle of a bruise.

"In sixth grade Joe came for him, and Luke put his fist up and knocked the wind clear out of him." The other colt trots over. "I should have brought apples." He places a sugar cube in Lin's hand and encourages her to extend it over the fence.

"After we left Cherry Hill, I saw Bunny two times—once, she passed through after Sage was born. My goodness, she was a precious baby." He smiles at the memory. "I think Bunny thought she'd settle here, but at that age she was so beautiful. And wild—it was as good as asking one of those tumbleweeds to slow."

"Was she just rebellious? Is that all it was? Is that why my mother judged her so harshly?"

"Then maybe twenty years later," he continues as though he hasn't heard the questions, "when she brought Huck here the first time. We really talked. I apologized for leaving them." He stares away, hard to the memory of it. "And you know what she said?"

Lin shakes her head.

"'You have nothing to apologize for. Who should have said sorry was Jayne.'"

"Jayne?"

"'She left me with him,' she said. 'She left me all alone.'"

"He beat her?" Lin asks.

"No," he says, angling the brim of his hat down so Lin can't see his eyes. "Worse."

22

Lin spends the flight home accounting, absorbing, reconciling. Was the abuse why she and Barbara shared so many sympathetic silences that year of park visits and carousel rides? Did they both vibrate at the same unsettled frequency? Was this why Jayne was attracted to Rodger? Because he was horribly familiar? Because she was doomed to repeat the cycle?

"I don't know," is all Sage can answer in her garden the next day, holding herself as though she might hug the part of her that is Bunny. "I feel guilty."

"Why?"

"I was so hard on her. I assumed she just never forgave herself for leaving us—because she took too much acid or picked the wrong men and everything went from bad to worse—but it never occurred to me that she really was running from something, something unbearable."

Lin sits down beside her in silence for several minutes of shared mourning, like firefighter widows lined up at the service. She considers that description, "something unbearable," and how it applies to her.

"Your mom suffered because no one wanted to know what was happening," Lin begins.

"And by the time the world caught up," Sage continues, "she felt the suffering she had caused outweighed the suffering she'd endured and there was no one left to comfort her—except maybe Rodger."

For a second Lin feels a flicker of gratitude for him—in the next her gums water and she feels sick. "And I'm the same but somehow the inverse because everyone knows, yet there's no comfort." Worse, some part of herself is still trying to get her attention. Every night from two till five.

"Where are you going?" Sage asks when Lin stands.

"To the library. I have one last piece of research to do before I talk to Jayne."

~

Even though everything is online, Lin needs to do this properly—meaning, not on her fritzing laptop with the Andy Warhol banana sticker. Not sitting on her bed. Not on the couch where she once ate breakfast with Justin.

She claims territory at one of the Formica tables of her local library branch on Crosby, surrounded by people from the methadone clinic up the block, killing time in an air-conditioned room requiring no proof of purchase. While they picture lengths of rubber tubing, charred spoons, and fresh needles, she lays out her own accessories to enable the thing she is compelled to do—a stack of yellow pads and a fresh pack of pens, a bottle of water and Post-its.

The man next to her gnashes his teeth in a not-unfriendly way, and Lin opens her new laptop and clicks on the files Clyde sent her years ago. There are 432 pages, including the court transcripts, the depositions, the therapists' reports, and the verdict.

She can't make her eyes focus, though. She can't make them cooperate. They roam the room, watching the nannies from the lofts of SoHo trying to corral their charges into the pillow-strewn Kidz Korner, away from the guy who can't stop scratching. She stares at the ceiling, the mottled fireproof tiles, the brown patches. She tries to find a pattern—

Abruptly, another part of her comes to her rescue.

"This isn't you," it says. *"This is just research."* The voice is calmly authoritative, a fourth-grade teacher, a beloved counselor, Justin.

"Okay," she answers.

And starts reading.

~

She takes pages of notes, distracting her brain by trying to map the contradictions. Of which there are many. Rodger didn't give straight answers, seeming to hold a counter-proceeding on the merit of the proceeding itself. He repeatedly earned, "Just answer the question," from the judge. Jayne was hysterical, her words funneling and swarming like bees. She had a paragraph, a diatribe, a syllogism for every yes/no. She also repeatedly earned, "Just answer the question."

But it's the questions themselves, the maddening questions, Lin can't believe. "Did you ever get into your daughter's bed in the middle of the night?"

"Of course I did."

"Come again?"

"She is six years old. She's had coughs, colds, scarlet fever—twice. Not to mention nightmares. My wife does not like to be woken."

Her eyes return to the ceiling, contemplating asbestos lurking in its recesses. *It could all be true. He may have done all those things and molested me.*

None of them were the right questions, none of it was the right answer.

Even when the prosecutor asked Rodger if he had ever touched Linden with the intent to arouse or gratify, and Rodger said, "No," what is it worth?

The psychiatrists' reports are no more helpful—when the uploaded scans of faded typed pages are even legible. Rodger was a narcissist. Rodger had an unhealthy preoccupation with Linden, versus his other three children. But in Rodger's mind, were the other three *his* children? Lin thinks of Brock, who probably collapsed on the tennis court unable to tell anyone what street Lin lived on, the name of her gallery, or that she has a faint scar by her left eye from a childhood leapfrog malfunction. So, was this proof? Rodger's indifference to people who looked nothing like him against his so-called obsession with the child who did?

Lin flings her pen to the tabletop, knowing that lastly, she must read her own account. She does not want to, because this is the part she knows. Her testimony is her memories. The divorce is fuzzy, mostly it is Jayne: Jayne smoking out the window; Jayne's hand holding hers as they walk to an appointment; Jayne dressing her, brushing her hair. Her childhood with Rodger is hazy, a stuffed animal, the light on a windowsill, dust particles suspended in air. But her testimony, she knows cold.

May 25, 1982, 11:00 a.m.
Present: Dr. Elizabeth Gerstein, Dr. Tobias Farber, Officers Terry Lombardo and Pete Scavoli, Jayne Donoghue, Linden Donoghue.

Dr. EG: Linden, I'm going to ask you a few questions about your father, okay?

(LD nods her head in assent.)

Dr. EG: Okay, Linden, do you know why you're here today?

(LD shakes head in dissent.)

JD: Yes, you do, honey. These nice people want to help you. You're safe, I promise.

Dr. EG: Linden, did your father ever do anything to make you uncomfortable?

(LD is unresponsive.)

JD: Honey, let go of Mommy's skirt. The nice lady here wants to hear what you have to say, you don't need to be scared.

Dr. EG: Has your daddy ever asked to touch you
in a way that you don't want to be touched?
(LD is unresponsive.)
Dr. EG: Has your daddy ever asked you to touch
him in a private place?
(LD is unresponsive.)

It goes on like this for what must have been excruciating minutes. Lin realizes she actually can't remember. What she does remember is getting dressed that morning, the gingham pinafore and blouse her mother picked out for her, with a pattern of tomatoes growing along the hem. It had a scratchy label, and for the first and only time, her mother allowed it to be cut out. That's what Lin remembers.

JD: I think she needs a break. Can I have a few
minutes with her? Could we have the room?
Dr. EG: I'm okay if—
TL: That's fine with us.

The record doesn't say how long they talked, but she's heard the story often enough from Jayne. How Lin thought she was in trouble and Jayne promised she wasn't—she just had to tell the doctor what she had already told Jayne—

But what had she already told Jayne? That's what stops Lin for the first time. She doesn't remember. She sighs in frustration, and the transgender woman across the way reading Nora Roberts gives her a shy smile.

LD: At the beach Daddy and I have our special
place. Daddy's office, where he makes his big books.
(LD pauses.)
JD: And?
LD: There is a bed.

Dr. EG: What happens in the bed, Linden?

LD: Daddy makes me come nap with him. But not in the bed. Hind.

Dr. EG: Behind?

JD: There's an alcove behind the daybed, it makes a kind of nook that isn't visible from the door. Behind the rocking horse.

Dr. EG: I see. You're on the floor?

(LD nods yes.)

LD: Hind.

Dr. EG: Behind it, yes?

(LD nods yes.)

Dr. EG: Linden, does your daddy touch you under your underwear?

JD: Go ahead, sweetie. Tell the nice doctor.

(LD nods yes.)

Dr. EG: Can you say yes for me? This nice lady with the typewriter needs to hear it.

(There is a long pause.)

LD: Y-yes.

Dr. EG: Thank you. You are a very brave girl. Linden, grown-ups are not allowed to do that. Is there anything else you'd like to tell me?

Lin slaps the laptop shut as if that would close a cyclone hatch in her brain. She wants to drop to the filthy floor and crawl on her stomach and elbows until she has sloughed off this skin, shed this entire layer of herself that has been here, read this.

She wants out of herself so desperately. For a moment, she looks around. If anyone could help her, it's her reading companions.

She texts, Andaz Hotel, 4pm, to a guy she knows who works on Wall Street. That will give her thirty minutes to down two martinis in the hotel's lobby, which she doesn't like and doesn't enjoy, before he arrives to take her upstairs, which she doesn't like and doesn't enjoy. But it's exactly what she needs, to be just numb enough, just outside herself enough, that nothing hurts. And to be hurt just enough, just inside herself enough, that everything does.

But then she thinks of Huck.

And turns her phone off.

And takes a breath.

~

Jayne startles when she turns on the light to find Lin sitting in her Hamptons kitchen, waiting for the sun to rise. "Oh my gosh, you scared me!" Her hand, freckled, fragile, betraying her age, anchors her sternum. "Why didn't you tell me you were coming?"

Lin's forearms rest on her closed laptop, her fingertips wrapping the edges, as though it were a shield she might have to raise.

"What time did you get in?"

"A little after midnight."

Jayne notices the bag at Lin's feet, the purse on the table. "Have you been sitting here all night?"

"I need to talk to you. Or with you. I need some answers."

"O . . . kay," Jayne says with a garnish of sarcasm. She raised five children; she's been confronted before. Allowances. Concert attendance. Piercings. "Can I at least have some coffee?"

Lin doesn't answer, and Jayne turns on the machine, filled and readied the night before. "You could have called, you know. This is a bit dramatic."

"I couldn't call."

"And why not?" Jayne asks as she sets out two mugs, two shell-patterned linen napkins, two coffee spoons and pulls the star-fish-patterned jug out of the fridge.

"Because," Lin explains, pointing to the items, "you need to be perfect."

"That's ridiculous," Jayne scoffs.

Lin pulls the ends of her black cotton sleeves over her palms. "For the record, Mom—and I hope you can hear this—none of us ever needed you to be. Maybe Clyde. But he's also a narcissist."

"Linden, are you okay?" Jayne asks in an infuriatingly measured tone, eyes on the percolating drips. "You don't sound like yourself."

"Well, we don't actually know what that means—"

"What?" Jayne cuts her off.

"—either of us. What I sound like. Because I'm always either pretending to be fine—or letting myself be so obviously not fine somebody actually does something about it."

Knowing there's no way out but through, Jayne pours one cup but stays standing at the counter, forgoing her morning view of the sun rising across the garden, turning the blades of grass and petals back to color. "Okay. What is this about?"

"I never said rocking horse."

"What?"

"I never said it. You did. And then you told me to tell them what I told you—but I don't remember what I told you. And I was six—"

Jayne flares and spins on her, slamming the mug down, coffee spilling. "Has he gotten to you?"

"No—"

"Is it Sage? Is she poisoning you against me?"

"Mom, no one is against anyone! I just want to understand what *really* happened. I want to remember it—for myself."

Jayne throws her hands up, her arms unusually silent without her jewelry. "Why? Why do you need to do that? It's all awful enough as it is. Isn't it a gift that you don't remember?"

"Do I seem gifted?"

Jayne bends at the waist, tucking her hands between her knees. "Oh, ha ha." She points. "That's your father right there. When you use words like that."

"You always do that. Whenever I say anything you don't like—that's Rodger."

Jayne crosses her arms. "Well, you're like him, you know." It's Jayne's last line of defense, saying something just nasty enough to remind her children she has much worse in reserve.

But Lin asks for the first time, "In what way?"

Jayne flinches. "What?"

"In what way am I like him? I want to know."

"Well . . . this. Ambushing me. That's a Rodger move. You're tenacious. And dark."

"Is that why you don't like me?"

An inhale—"What?" Jayne asks weakly.

"It's because I remind you of him? Because Sage is the beautiful one and she isn't yours?"

"Lindy, where is all this coming from?"

"Mom, I am thirty-seven years old. And I'm not happy. And I don't even think I'm particularly well. And I feel like the thing that has defined my whole life was decided for me before I even had a say, and I want to fully understand—"

"Oh, get in line," Jayne sneers.

"What?"

"*Your* life was decided for you? Whose wasn't? I have done everything, *everything*, I was supposed to. And I am still sitting here. Alone. Just hoping one of you ungrateful little shits gives me a call—"

"Mom, I'm sorry—"

"Of course you are, you all are. Brian might as well be dead. Did you know he's getting married? 'Just a small ceremony, Mom, no need to fly out.' No need for me to *trouble* myself. Clyde cares more about his own reflection than he does about me, and you—well, it's hard to look at you."

Lin slides her laptop in her tote, gathers her bag, heaves the whole mess onto her narrow shoulders.

"Where are you going?"

"You don't understand," she mutters, backing out of the room.

"What don't I understand? Huh? What don't I understand, Linden?"

"Your whole generation!" She raises her face to her mother's. "You treated us like fucking potted plants! Parenting only as much as you wanted in the ways that you wanted and ignoring any needs you didn't feel like meeting!" She trips backing onto the front-hall rug and catches herself on the console, knocking sunscreen and bug spray to the floor. "Leave it," she commands Jayne. "You know what, you can slag Sage off all you want, but twenty-four-seven, she does the things she doesn't want to do—she sits and does coloring and plays games and gives baths when she is literally trembling with fatigue from looking after Dad. *You* drag us through a heinous divorce and then need us to be totally fine. None of us could reflect your horrible life choices back at you. But guess what? We all do! We are exactly what you built us to be. And now you want this adoration, this bottomless suck of adoration? Well, Jayne Linden Donoghue Haniman, you can go fuck yourself."

~

She is halfway back to the city, taking the last hits on the memory of her mother's shocked face while they can still get her high, when she realizes: Jayne never actually answered a single question.

23

Like her mother before her, Lin rents a car to make a pilgrimage south. Though she bypasses Baltimore and the exit for Cherry Hill. It's so loud in this crappy car that it's hard for Lin to think, and she struggles to keep her eyes on the road, not to recede to the point that she forgets she's rocketing along at almost ninety miles an hour in an appliance, something fallible that comes with a warranty for small parts and labor.

Beside her sits Sage, eyes on the tract houses, and Lin knows she's wondering why she's come, if the home health aide is reliable, if Rodger truly has stabilized.

"Thank you," Lin whispers again, though Sage can't hear her.

The road veers left toward the coast, and suddenly the water is brilliant with the reflected sun, the air briny and benevolent. Both women roll their windows all the way down, letting the wind whip and braid their hair into a crosswalk down the middle of the car. But no sooner do their smiles surface than they are pulling up outside a house.

It is unmistakable.

But neither woman remembers it as sandwiched in a strip of mini mansions, once serviceable bathing cottages all torn down to accommodate every inch of luxury that can be crammed into their modest quarter-acres. Among this, their decrepit Victorian's second-floor windows look down, embarrassed.

They open the car doors and tentatively emerge. "I was here," Sage says softly. "Before you were born. The summer I turned five, maybe six."

"You were?"

"Mom was super pregnant with Brian, and I remember just running on the beach all day with Huck. Rodger got us a kite. And there were Triscuits. I thought it was magical."

"It sounds nice—"

"When we got back to where—I don't even remember, just that it was awful—all I talked about was how much I loved the beach. How much I loved Triscuits. I thought I gave her the idea to leave us."

Wordlessly, Lin puts her hand on Sage's shoulder, and the two women climb the porch, its paint weathered away. Lin withdraws the key from her bag.

"Where did you get it?" Sage asks.

"Hanging by the back door on Seventy-Ninth, labeled with a P-touch from the nineties."

"Of course," Sage answers, because both women understand the chiaroscuro of their family to be like this. Some critical details obscured, others left in a sunny spot.

"Ready?" she asks.

Lin nods.

The key turns, the bolt audibly shifts over, but the door has swollen and retracted so many times over the years Sage has to throw her weight into it.

"Sage—"

"I got it," she grunts, and it gives—swinging open into decades prior. Everything exactly as Jayne left it the last time—no idea it would be the last time. The chairs and tables covered with dustcloths, the mantel and carriage clock caked in a salinated crust. "It's so strange," Sage murmurs.

"Which part?"

"All of it. That she keeps it but doesn't refresh it or rent it out, like she can't bear to look at it but can't bear to let it go."

"But is she holding on to it as evidence?" Lin asks. "As proof? Or because this is where we were all happiest before it fell apart?"

Unable to answer, Sage can only look around at the warped floor, the abandoned nest on the ceiling beam from a family that made its way in long ago as Jayne's family made its way out. "Where do you want to start?"

"Up."

Leaving the door open, they cross to the listing, creaky staircase, both remembering at the same time how they had to pick a level and stay on it when Rodger was working.

On the second-floor landing, Lin rounds the corner to where narrow steps lead up to Rodger's study. At the top is another door. Sage hangs back because no matter how swollen or stuck—this one is Lin's to open.

Prepared to fight her way in, to prove she's worthy of whatever lies beyond, Lin puts her hand on the knob, flexes her forearm, but then her thumb rotates effortlessly to perpendicular, and just like that . . . there it is.

Rodger's summer office.

"What an odd space," Sage says quietly.

It's really two rooms, separated by an archway and what once might have been a pocket door.

"I think Mom said it was originally the nursery, so this was Bunny and Mom's."

Rodger's desk presides in front of the shuttered bay window, the leather blotter faded to pea green long ago. There is no whiskey bottle on the desk, no typewriter competing with the ocean. Yet it unmistakably is—and isn't—the place of Lin's memories.

"I don't understand," she says.

"What?" Sage asks gently.

But Lin is too focused on inventorying shadows, her head swiveling this way and that—if the rattan chairs were here and the filing cabinets were there, where was the daybed?

She drops to her knees. Maybe her height is skewing everything. Maybe if she's small, it will all lock into place. Her memories and this space where they happened will match.

Sage watches Lin crawl across the floor until she comes to rest, sitting on her heels, her defeated hands in her black-linen lap.

Finally: "Can I ask—you're eight years older. What do you remember?"

"Are you sure?"

Lin nods.

Sage takes a small breath, like the coil on a finely tuned instrument that requires the lightest tap to set in motion. "He never closed the door. He had to have it and all the windows open for a breeze."

"That doesn't mean I'm wrong."

"No, it doesn't."

"But that's what you've always thought."

"Lin, I don't know. Whenever it came up, Rodger would rant about how vindictive Jayne was, how preposterous the whole thing was. While you were steeped in one version, I was steeped in another."

Lin shakes her head, tears of frustration breaking. "I don't know, I don't know. I don't understand. I have memories—like the testimony, I have those memories. I'm on some kind of bed with him. But they're not here. They're not this. I don't know what this is."

They look and look, like the children they once were, heads bowed together over a *Highlights* magazine, searching for the hidden objects in the picture. But it's only walls and plaster and chair-rail molding, dust and one ceiling rosette.

At last, accepting that the room will not gather them at its feet and tell them a story, *the* story, the two women stumble slowly back down the steps, their faces swollen, blotchy versions of their faces.

~

They forgo camping on the beach, imagining when they planned this trip that they would find something, some clue they could Nancy Drew the night away over. Instead, they get back in the car, knowing they have come to the end of their search and possibly their nascent reconnection. They cannot answer anything for each other, merely reflect each other's wounds back and forth into infinity like those awful mirror walls in small bathrooms. Why would they continue to choose that?

On the drive, Lin knows only one thing: she won't drop Sage and return the car. She'll get on the BQE up to the 495 out to Long Island, and she won't ask about Bunny or why every interaction is always punctuated by some criticism. She will demand only this:

Why do my memories match your testimony and nothing else?

~

Around that same time, Jayne is doing her end-of-season gardening, deadheading the Angelonia, uprooting the patch of impatiens that didn't take. She's thinking about her children, she's thinking about fish for dinner, she's thinking about calls unreturned and calls she must return. She's thinking ahead to the fall. Trying to remember whether she decided it was better to get the mums and pumpkins out here and drive them back—or did she decide that was a waste of time and effort? She knows she wanted to remember. She knows she made a decision. She knows that a year ago she had a preference. But she cannot recall. She cannot recall what she wanted. What did she *want*?—when the sole of her ballet flat loses purchase on a patch of brickwork gone slimy with moss.

She slips. Simply slips.

24

This time Lin has fewer choices. Because each shoe on the shelf, each sweater—the cotton ones, the linen ones, the silk, wool, and cashmere—will need to be unfolded, evaluated, categorized. Useful? Could this be useful? Will anyone want to wear this? Clip-on earrings? Does anyone want clip-on earrings? Is this costume jewelry the kind of thing someone in Bushwick will think is fabulous? Can a woman today dress for success in these suits? A very slender woman.

She will have to make her way up—slowly—to the boxes on the high shelf.

But first there is the kitchen, with its cracked measuring cups and copper cookie forms, its charred baking sheets and blackened pot holders. The children hold each item their mother used to convey love the best she knew how, shocked to discover that, despite the daily irritations, the epic malfunctions, they are each deeply, almost inexplicably, in mourning for a woman who was quite marvelous in 1984. They grieve for her beauty, for the home they were raised in, for crêpes suzette and chocolate mousse, for everything she bought and was, for the world she endeavored to immerse them in. They spend hours telling stories of getting lost in Florence, the time she fell in mud at Glyndebourne, the toast she gave at Brian's graduation, laughing about coming home to find some new gadget she'd discovered on TV—a ThighMaster or spiralizer, ordered in triplicate and dropped off all over town like an elf with a drinking problem. And they mourn the end of an era, of glamour, of a Gershwin New York.

~

The funeral itself was so disorienting—standing room only at Frank E. Campbell's, over two hundred people needing to crush Lin's and Clyde's hands and impress upon them how much they loved Jayne. She accompanied them to every chemo appointment, never forgot a birthday, hand delivered a coat to a friend who had complimented it. She made the best leg of lamb, the best Grand Marnier chocolate mousse, the best walnut-cranberry muffins. Tearful person after tearful person, stunned by the loss, painted a picture of a Jayne so incongruous from the mother they thought they knew that it only refreshed the loss, like a child on a bicycle looking back to realize their parent has let go—*When did our lives diverge? When did you take Carol shopping for her first prosthetic breasts? Why didn't you tell us? We would have liked that.*

After the last guest left, Lin found Brian sitting at his old desk, palms splayed wide on its surface like a piano he was about to ravage. She dared to place a hand on his back and kiss the top of his head, newly shorn of his signature curls. They breathed like that for a moment before she took a seat on his old tartan bedspread.

"God, Jayne loved tartan."

"I miss her," he said softly, and Lin nodded.

"You were so close." It was the least she could do now—to reflect his memories back to him. "Growing up. She was always looking for things for you. A new sports coat or a book you wanted. She adored you—"

"She didn't want me to go to Howard," he said, implying this negated the adoration.

"She didn't?"

He shook his head, and she missed how the vibration of his emotions would travel up to the ends of his prodigious hair.

"When did you cut it?" she asked, gesturing to where his halo was.

"Yesterday." He ran a hand over his scalp and glanced at the ceiling as if awaiting Jayne's approval. "She wanted me to go to Brown. It was Brock who interceded."

"That was nice of him," Lin said gently, unsure. *Was* it nice of him?

"Actually, I think he just wanted—an expedient end to the question of me." Brian spun the chair to face her, his arms relaxing, like he would when she'd station herself on some earlier iteration of the tartan bedspread and he'd humor her for a few minutes before resuming his homework.

"The question of you?" Lin prompted.

"I was grown already when they started dating." He looked at the wall where his A Tribe Called Quest poster once hung. "He came into a household with a full-size Black man in it. You know he flinched sometimes? If he came upon me unexpectedly." Lin nodded. Although she remembered him flinching at all of them, each for different reasons. "And I could see that wasn't how he thought of himself." Brian rubbed his hands over his face, and Lin delighted in the sight of his thick wedding band. "So, to be fair, I don't think he wanted to get rid of the Black kid as much as he wanted to get rid of the suspicion that he might not have been who he'd decided he was." Lin took this in, embarrassed she'd never considered any of this before.

"So why *did* you choose Howard?" she asked. "I mean you're the only person from all our schools I've ever heard of going there—or Spelman."

He shrugged. "I was exhausted. In a way I couldn't even name and didn't fully understand until I met other people like me."

"Black kids?" she ventured.

"Only Black kids. The *only* Black kid in their prep school, or boarding school, or neighborhood. Yes, Mom single-handedly desegregated this building, but every time a new doorman started, he would try to send me to the service elevator."

Lin winced.

"The fact that nannies and whomever had to ride in the service elevator is a whole other thing I won't get into now, but still, I couldn't get a taxi to a friend's house unless one of them flagged it for me and then gave the driver a reassuring nod as I got in. Don't worry, he's not *really* Black."

Lin's embarrassment deepened to shame. "I'm so sorry. Where was I?"

He considered her for a moment. "You were a teenager. That is where you were." It was kind. It was generous. It was all the things Brian was and would be entitled not to be.

"But wait—why *didn't* she want you to go to Howard?" Lin asked, sensing she was still missing the point of this story.

He dropped his head, a fresh sadness visibly awash across his shoulders. "She was a really good mom to me. When I look at Lora with the baby, I think of her, and I think of being held and cuddled. I think of her defending me on the playground and opening the fridge and whatever I was into—it was always in there."

Lin nodded, quiet, attentive.

He raised his eyes to her. "When I told her that I wanted to accept Howard's offer, she said, 'But *why*, Brian? *Why* do you want to go there? That school is for Black kids. You've gone to the best schools, had the best of everything. You don't have to be Black.'"

Lin gasped. "Oh, Jayne," she whispered in dismay. And suddenly Lin understood that if Brian was the sandbag enabling the effusive floral arrangement, that the flowers were Jayne, that with his stalwart acceptance of the unacceptable, he was the ballast to their family. And now to a circus of creatives who needed him, his steadfastness. But that somewhere along the line he discovered that being the Good Thing Jayne had done was no longer his job. That he could leave.

"Brian?" she said.

He looked up.

"I love you like a spaceship."

His wet face smiled, and he squeezed her hand, and they went together in search of Kleenex.

~

Months have passed. Snow flurries outside the window again. Below, people scurry on the sidewalks, heads bowed against the wind, as they will next year—and the year after that. Somewhere in the building a girl is listening to music on headphones, awash in longing and desire and self-loathing—and hope.

Lin and Clyde and Sage each take mementos—recipes copied by hand from the *New York Times* and tucked into splattered cookbooks, a bowl that is the memory of making Duncan Hines brownies after school, a Raynaud holly-leaf-patterned platter that is nicer than anything any of them will ever buy for themselves.

"Tell me this is the last of it," Sage says, carrying another box to the pile in Jayne's front hall.

"Doubtful," Lin answers, caked in a level of filth that would have been impossible to imagine could be unearthed from Jayne Haniman's possessions. "You are a rock star for doing this, by the way."

"No, I'm just—here."

Lin sets down the silver teapot she is inexplicably polishing. "It never stops being weird, being here without her. I keep thinking she's in the next room, and any second, she's going to come in and tell me to get my feet off the coffee table."

"She is," Sage says, straightening and blowing her hair off her forehead so she doesn't have to touch her face. "Only the room is infinite."

Lin wonders.

She covers the dining table in crystal and china—elaborate gravy boats and salt dishes and wine coasters—and lets Clyde make off with the things he will use ironically. The rest she tags for the estate-sale lady.

It seems a desecration to dismantle this place Jayne invested so much of herself in, like burying her in a hot-pink animal-print dress. But the living room chairs are, in truth, uncomfortable. The mohair throw is itchy. No one wants a yellow silk couch. People don't write at secretaries anymore, nor do they have them tucked into corners of their living rooms. They want something from Room & Board fitted with a docking station.

"She lived," Lin says aloud, whether anyone is in the room with her or not, rubber duck–yellow gloves on her akimbo arms. "She lived and died, and her nutcracker collection got banged up, and now this guy only has one eye." Some things she has to throw in the trash behind her own back because otherwise she will keep all of it.

There is allotted time each day for holding some random item, like the reindeer-shaped cookie cutter, and just breaking down sobbing. There is also allotted time for day drinking (Clyde) and pot smoking on the fire escape to an old cassette single of Sting's "Russians" unearthed from the back of a closet (Sage).

Until, at last, the beds have been stripped, the cupboards emptied, the curtains taken off their pulleys, the antique rugs rolled up, the picture hooks extracted from the walls, and the furniture picked up by the auction house.

Only then does Lin climb to the top of the closet and get down the boxes.

"What are they?" Sage asks from where she sits on the floor, drinking whiskey in a take-out cup of hot chocolate.

"I don't know. The one with the carriage on the box is an old Easter dress, I think it was your mother's. You should take it—if you want it. The Tiffany one is her mother's photos and things, stuff Mom took from Baltimore. I haven't opened the other one."

"Don't," Sage says. "Take it with you, do it later."

But Lin shakes her head. She sits on the carpet in the emptied room, a pattern left on the sisal like crop circles, and takes off all three lids.

"Holy shit," Sage whispers, crouching next to her.

Staring up at them from the top of the third box is a snapshot of Rodger, all sideburns and confidence, holding Lin. He is glowing.

"How old do you think I am?" Lin whispers.

"The Christmas tree. You had to be almost one."

Lin gently tips the top layer toward herself, peeking below. It's image after image of the children with Rodger, on Seventy-Ninth Street and at Broadkill. Sage and Huck play near him while he reads the paper on the porch, or they are running in the sand while he barbecues just at the edge of the frame. But the photographs Jayne took of him and Lin are different. She is in his lap or holding on to his leg; they are lost in each other or laughing hysterically, Rodger in on Lin's joke.

"Oh, I love this one," Sage whispers. "You look just like Sarah and Adrian." Rodger is sitting in an aluminum folding chair on the beach, and Lin is in a sundress, lying atop him on her stomach. Her chin rests on her hand, her elbow balances on his chest; she is smiling brightly and looking adoringly into his eyes. She is maybe four.

Lin feels a deep sense of betrayal, but not *of* her; she is the one perpetrating the disloyalty, the violation. Because *these* are her memories, the forbidden ones, the contraband ones, the ones muled in by her brain in the slippery hours of sleep. The feel of his stubble against her face, the transfer of ink from his fingers to her skin, the feel of tweed against her cotton pajamas when he'd come home late to kiss her, the smell of cigarettes and whiskey and damp wool. Yet the betrayal is not the sensation but the emotion. Comfort. Safety. Love.

Sage slips her phone out of her back pocket and scrolls through her pictures. "See." She holds out a nearly identical composition from a summer a few years ago, Sarah gazing deeply into Adrian's eyes, a smile on her lips.

"I don't know how to see this," Lin says. "If he loved me and broke me, it only makes it worse. It means no one is trustworthy."

Sage reaches her hand into the middle box. The pictures are a muddle of color and black and white. There are a couple of leather-bound albums that audibly crack when Sage opens them. She turns the frail vellum, the pictures tearing as they're bent.

It's their grandmother's handiwork, carefully cataloging her new life with her new husband. Portraits of the boys, now young men, standing on the lawn, the house spit shined behind them, Margaret already eschewing the midcentury hourglass silhouette for her tent top and slim skirt.

Then a photograph of the entry hall, the double staircase, the parlor, and the dining room, their grandfather's smoking room, their grandmother's sunroom, then upstairs to the boys' room with its cowboy-and-Indian wallpaper, their grandmother's bedroom with its ornate canopy, and Joe's bedroom with its sedate tweed motif. Lin pries one of them off to read the back. "'Paulson and Sons Photographers, Cherry Hill.' Grandma paid to have these taken," Lin marvels, "to have this record of—"

"Her taste, her accomplishments?"

"Her choices. I'd never really thought about Mom's need for all of this"—Lin fans her arm at where "all of this" had been—"being about her mother. Look in the Tiffany box. Look what Margaret came from. Why did they need all this stuff? What was it guarding against?"

Sage turns to the last page of this tiny, crumbling black-and-white tour, and there is the nursery, mysteriously, the only picture in color. "That must have been taken later—what?" Sage asks, seeing Lin's abrupt strangulation. "What is it?"

Lin doesn't know if she can speak. She runs her tongue over her gums to wet her mouth. "A r-rocking horse."

Sage stares at the image, trying to see, trying to understand, to comprehend.

With trembling hands, Lin takes Sage's phone from her, pulls Rodger's letter up on the *Times* app, and hands it back.

"Oh. A rocking horse, I see. But this doesn't—"

Lin goes to the front door and gets her laptop from her tote.

Sage reads the transcript, her eyes darting from the words Jayne filled in for her six-year-old daughter—and back to the picture of a room with a daybed and an alcove behind it, a space invisible from the door.

"It's this," Lin says, the certainty that has been eluding her for decades filling her like rainwater in a trough. "*This* is the room. *This* is the place. It was never me. It was them."

They sit in stunned silence on the desecrated carpet, something that once arrived here with so much shine and polish and optimism that will leave cut and rolled and bagged.

"Oh my God, those poor girls," Sage whispers, running the film of her life rapidly backward, adding this detail like a colorizer, watching it all again. Now in order. Now making sense.

"What do I do?" Lin asks. "What do I do?"

She cannot yell. There is no one left to yell at.

She cannot break things. They've all been packed up.

"What do I do with this?" she asks Sage again.

"I don't know, Lin. I honestly don't know."

~

A week later she is waiting for the Viking repairman to fix the twenty-year-old stove the buyer is inexplicably insisting be serviced before it gets ripped out when the buzzer rings. Gloves on, because she has to clean the stove before they'll service it, she pushes her hair from her face with her forearm and opens the door, instantly stunned and its opposite, as always.

"Wow," she says. "Hi."

Justin stands in the doorway, in jeans and a brown leather jacket, leaning slightly on his hip like he did when she'd answer the door to him and no one else was home.

"I'm sorry I missed the funeral." He seems genuinely to mean it.

"I'm so sorry," she stammers. "I just assumed Mom gave you all your dad's stuff back when he passed—was there stuff you wanted? Was there stuff here of your mom's?"

Justin holds his hand up. "No. No, there's nothing. It's you. I came to see you."

Lin can feel twin forces, one pushing her into his arms, one pulling her back to—what, offer a drink? There are no glasses. A place to sit? There are no chairs. Lin Donoghue at last has nothing to give.

"Me?" she asks.

"You." There is snow on the shoulders of his jacket. "You okay?"

She looks at him for a moment, so many years tumbling through her head. "I think we're in a Phil Collins song."

He smiles.

"Oh, man, *no!*" she exclaims. "You got your tooth fixed! I'm so bummed."

"Yeah," he admits. "The root was dead, and bad things happened."

"You know, that could also be the answer to your question. 'The root was dead, and bad things happened.'"

He looks over her shoulder at the empty apartment. "Wow. How long have you been at this?"

"Weeks. Months. It was a treasure trove in your old room. Those high cupboards Mom built in? An actual Rubik's Cube. I mean, you know, you hope. You go through something like this, and you're like, *Please,* please *let there be a Rubik's Cube.* But—anyway, that was a good day. Oh, and we found your porn."

He blushes. "No!"

"Yep. She had boxed it up in a very Jayne way and put it with the Rubik's Cube."

He leans against the doorframe, and it is so hard to remember that she is newly thirty-eight, that the eyes he is smiling into are lined, that she hasn't bothered to color her hair since Jayne's death, that it is gradually turning brown, boring, unflattering brown. "You're amazing."

"I want to die."

"Can I come in?"

"Vampire rules?" she asks.

"Vampire rules."

The door shuts behind them, and Justin and Lin are alone at 141 East Seventy-Ninth Street, Apartment 6A. They have outlived Brock and Jayne, their tangential relation to each other. They have outlived adolescence and young adulthood, grunge and drugs, and knowing the city intimately at 3:00 a.m. They have outlived REM, Rumpelmayer's, Saint Vincent's, and second-wave feminism. They have outlived and outloved their own their-ness and them-ness and us-ness. Nearing forty, they have lived in what was once their someday and blown right past it. Now they are somewhere across their over.

Justin takes her hand and leads her down the hall to her old room, where the walls are stamped with the black shadows of tossed posters. He pulls her down to the bare floor with him and then atop his chest so that her ear is above his heart, and he strokes her hair.

She begins at the beginning. Two sisters, one of whom was sexually abused, one who wasn't, neither of whom left their childhoods unscathed. "And the crazy thing—okay, one of the *many* crazy things is that you remember how'd she always say Bunny was the favorite with so much jealousy—but she *knew*. She *knew* what being the so-called favorite had cost her. Or she didn't." Lin considers. "She wouldn't let herself. Couldn't let herself."

Lin pauses again, a new thought occurring, and Justin waits. "In my twenties I did a type of therapy for people with PTSD. Because I knew—I *knew*—something was wrong. Something didn't align. But that's all I could say clearly in my own head. I couldn't articulate the problem. I couldn't walk into therapy and say, 'My mom accused my dad of molesting me during an atomic divorce, and it's never felt totally right to me.' And I think that's like Mom. I think maybe we were having the same experience in our brains, but the inverse. She seemingly *never* articulated her sister's abuse to herself. Even though her whole life—both of their lives—were organized around it."

She pauses, takes in how good the expanse of his chest feels beneath her, how reassuring the sound of his heart is.

"It's like the experience—the trauma—leaves a hole, a shape in the middle of a maze. But while you're trying to find your way out of the maze, it's just a wall you keep running into over and over and over. You know this thing is there. But you have no idea *what* it is. Or your brain won't let you know. And then suddenly—suddenly your brain allows you to fly above the maze, and you see it. You see the shape. *My father abused my sister.* Or whatever your shape is."

Justin rubs her back as she speaks.

"I don't think she ever had that moment, that clarity; she just walked through the maze feeling the guilt—of not sharing the abuse, of being spared. I think it's why she took them in without protest. Mom felt she owed Bunny. And yet was still—*so* jealous of her. Like I said, crazy. There are so many things we'll only ever be able to guess at."

Justin gently sits them up, his forearm resting on his raised knee.

"Oh God, don't look at me," Lin says. "I'm a mess."

"Okay, first of all, messes are fine. Second, I never needed you to not be. That was something you put on yourself." He leans across the small space between them and kisses her on the mouth. "I love you."

"Really?" she can't help asking.

"At first, I was a little scared of you, and mostly you just gave me a raging hard-on, but then I loved you and have always loved you and will always love you. The you right now that has been cleaning for days and has eyes almost swollen shut. You are perfect."

Lin is amazed to find that even as he says these words, she knows they live here, in this room. Nowhere else. She is no longer a junkie crawling on the floor of a casino after a chip rolling away, something she can alchemize into a fix.

He is one of the great loves of her life. But he is not her husband. He is not her future.

But he is the one person she can ask.

"What do I do with this, Justin? I'm so angry I don't think I can ever forgive her. Even if I understand, which I think I do. She couldn't protect Bunny, so she protected me. She couldn't confront her father, so she confronted Rodger. I know she genuinely believed something had happened, genuinely believed that the way he loved me was—too much. But then I also just don't understand—why didn't he fight harder for me? He was so righteous, but he didn't think about me, he never came after me, even as a grown-up, just to say, 'Hey, you can hate me, but I love you. I just need you to know that I love you.'"

Justin sighs heavily. "Here's the thing, Lin: we were trying to put one foot in front of the other. Just get through it, get old enough, get out, get away. Think of all the fucked-up things you've done trying to outrun this. *We're* the fucked-up things they did. My point is, our parents might just have been fucked-up people who picked shit in the clutch. And then that shit became our lives."

Lin exhales, absorbing the raw truth of it. "She felt fear and thought she had pinpointed that fear, that she was protecting us from something—and here we are. Here I am."

"And you are awesome."

Lin smiles. "I smell like a barnyard. Oh, but I figured something out. I wanted to tell you when I read about it—I have synesthesia."

Justin nods in recognition. "Ah, yes. How you saw numbers as people."

"Right? It's a thing. I just have a thing. I love the twenty-first century. Live long enough, and it turns out all your issues were just things without names yet."

He takes her face in his hands and kisses her one last time.

"Justin?"

"Yes."

"Where do I go from here?"

"Wherever you want to."

25

Lin rings the bell, and after a few moments, Sage answers the door to Rodger's apartment. "Oh my gosh, Lin!" she says, surprised. "Hi."

"Hi." She doesn't move. She can't move.

"Do you want to come in?"

"I'm not supposed to be here."

Sage opens the door wider, its hinge audibly protesting, and extends her hand, guiding Lin gently into a time capsule of another New York. The cavernous vestibule is anchored by a long refectory table covered in books. Lin looks up at the ceiling coming down in strips.

"It hasn't been painted since they moved in," Sage explains, crossing her arms, grasping the edges of her fuzzy green cardigan. "In the kitchen, it even looks as though water came through at one point, but . . ."

"Barbara never painted it?"

"Turns out she had a finite amount of volition, and she exhausted the last bit of it crossing that threshold."

Lin walks left into the living room, which looks onto West End Avenue. One wall is floor-to-ceiling bookcases, heaving with titles, shelves warped. More books grow from the floor like stalagmites. The brown couch is partially hidden by them, and the kilim rugs and throw pillows hold up their hands like Tippi Hedren, waiting for the avalanche.

Lin exhales. "Oh," she says, now seeing what Sage has seen for decades. "They made no sense."

"No," Sage agrees, knowing she means Jayne and Rodger.

"Is any of this Barbara?"

Sage shakes her head. "After she moved in, she lived out of a purple hard-sided suitcase for over a year. It lay on the floor, and she dressed out of it every morning and folded and returned everything to it on wash days." Sage takes Lin's hand. "You ready?"

"No."

Sage leads her to the end of the vestibule and down the corridor. Lin can hear a machine making a *whoosh suck click, whoosh suck click.* She smells disinfectant. And under that, infection.

Carefully, she peeks her head around the doorframe. The bedroom is Spartan. A brass bed, wood floor, two dressers, a chair in the corner. The large windows face east and south and would fill the room with light on a sunny day. But today is not a sunny day.

And in the bed, under a white quilt, lies the man who was Rodger Donoghue.

"He needs help breathing now," Sage says. "So, perhaps, we may not give him that help and see what happens. Except every night I have nightmares that I can't breathe, so I think I'm having a hard time with it."

There is a tube taped into his mouth and another running into his nose. His gaunt face is flecked with white stubble. Hair sprouts defiantly from his ears and nostrils.

"He's so small," Lin says.

"You know, he always was. You probably remember him giant, but actually he and I were about the same height."

Lin sits gingerly on the bed, and Sage whispers, "I will leave you to it."

Lin looks around the room first, rendering it in miniature, then forcing herself to keep this end of a life life-size. So she searches the strange face on the bed, one half still limp from the strokes. She reaches out and takes his hand, covering it with hers. It feels papery and not quite warm enough.

"Daddy," she whispers, to the man and the memory, "I'm home."

She sits like that until cloudy is dusky, barging into chambers of her mind, snapping trunks open, extracting folded histories and opening them like maps. A father. Once she had a father.

~

A few weeks later, when she has been able to tell him everything, all of it, all of herself, the entirety, once she has helped bathe and feed him, taken his temperature and read to him, once she has stroked his hair and kissed his forehead and he, defying all medical expectations, has squeezed her hand, barely but distinctly, not a reflex, a gesture, the most he is able, Sage and Lin gather one afternoon to turn off the *whoosh suck click*. They make a pot of tea, and they sit. They sit until they are silhouettes in streetlamp. They sit until he is gone.

EPILOGUE

*S*he is walking through the East Village and passes an NYU student—
she goes rigid in her tracks, body frozen at an angle. She waits a
moment—two—three—

Oh, please.

This is silly—she can't—four—

Please.

"Wait!" *She turns and trots after the girl.* "I'm sorry," *she pants,* "where
did you get that coat?"

"Housing Works," *the girl says, taken aback, a little unsure.*

The words slosh out of her. "I think it was my mother's."

The girl smiles, confused.

"Does it have a silk scarf sewn into the lining?"

The girl nods.

I reach—I reach—I reach—

"She did that," *Lin explains, suddenly brightening with unexpected
pride,* "because it got this big tear when—anyway, it looks great on you.
I'm glad. Enjoy it."

I reach—*and she feels a tingle along her scalp and a flush down her
neck—then she shakes me off.*

*Still, I am with her as she boxes up her oversize black sweaters, as she
signs up for salsa classes on a whim, as she applies for a job teaching art to
kids with developmental delays. She has a real gift for it. I knew she would.*

And I do what I can—guiding her down a street on Mother's Day that dead-ends at a vintage-poster shop with a giant picture of Jayne Mansfield in the window and the words JAYNE CAN BE YOURS. INQUIRE INSIDE.

My recipes drop out of her books, along with cards she'd forgotten I'd sent her to celebrate her gallery openings. When she attempts to bake my Christmas cake, laughing with Clyde as they cover her tiny kitchen with flour-coated raisins, I press my mouth that isn't a mouth to her forehead, and she feels a warmth run over her face—for a moment.

~

She meets her husband at a fundraiser for the program. She is a wonderful stepmother, collapsing the universe back in reverse, gripping the hole shut until it is a new whole.

I sit beside her as she combs the internet until she finds an apartment in Brooklyn with a large tree in its yard, a linden.

She gets pregnant at forty-two.

She is a wonderful mother. So much better than I ever was. She is fun.

And now—now I can harness. I can harness and muster, channel and mobilize, swirling the death and the life around me in clenched hands that are not hands, managing to stay long enough for the child to speak, for the child to look into her mother's eyes after a nap, my lips at last in her ear, and lispingly whisper, "Rocking horse," words she has never heard. Then she places her tiny palm flat on my daughter's cheek, as I used to, and looks deeply, beseechingly into her eyes.

Lin is stunned for a moment, not sure she has heard what she's heard, or seen what she's seen. But then she whispers, "Thanks, Mom. I know." And then, "I love you, too."

She says that.

And it is worth everything.

ACKNOWLEDGMENTS

This book took eight years to complete, so I have many people to thank for their encouragement over that embarrassingly long period. This list is chronological.

First, Emma, who was passionate and emphatic that I tell this story, even when it was just an amorphous blob with a dark AF premise. My words are all for you. Always.

Stephan Block, I couldn't believe that a writer of your caliber was taking me seriously, and without your weekly thumbs-up and insightful feedback, I would never have completed the first draft.

Lucinda Halpern, your unwavering belief in me, even when I go off and do wildly unstrategic things (like write a not-funny novel with almost no dialogue in it) means the world to me. I am lucky to call you my friend.

Carrie Hannigan, I am still embarrassed that I foisted my novel on our nascent friendship and eternally grateful for your enthusiasm. There is no one I would rather get life-changing news with.

Soumeya Roberts, your steadfast faith that this story would eventually find a home kept me going draft after draft. I cannot thank you enough for your kindness, your sharp narrative insight, and your tenacity. You made my dreams come true.

Carmen Johnson, thank you for sharing my passion for this story. Your brilliant editorial support was invaluable, and every question you posed made the book better by far. I am so grateful for you.

Faith Black Ross, were we separated at birth? Thank you for putting your great brain and impeccable taste to this task. I look forward to many Sondheim-and-scones dates in the future.

Hannah Buehler, thank you for being my guardrails. Over eight years, several contradictions had crept in—I think you caught them all!

Patrick Nathan, thank you for your thoughtful feedback and suggestions, all deeply appreciated. And Ewoks!

My GLOBs, Allisyn, Jeni, Maia, Mary, Meg, Nora G., and Nora Z., you are the best book club a lady could ask for. I am blessed to have shared so many wonderful reads and belly laugh–filled evenings with you. And I have learned *so much* from sitting and listening to you, like even a Pulitzer winner can leave some readers cold. And no book will make *everyone* happy.

Thank you to Meg McQuillen, my Ideal Reader, and Nora Zelevansky, who wrote my favorite coming-of-age novel, for reading a primordial draft and encouraging me to keep going.

My brilliant, amazing, bighearted clients, you inspire me every day with your love of storytelling and your tenacity and determination to stay in the chair. Especially my Fiction Mavens, Susie Orman-Schnall, Samantha Woodruff, and Jackie Friedland.

The Laskow-Rosenbergs, Ian, Caroline, Alice, Leo, and Ringo. Books are your shared love language. Thank you for your friendship, your unflagging enthusiasm—and queso!

ME for "conversational stupid."

My family of origin—Xandy, Tony, Hilda, Jean, Berta, Irwin, and most of all Evelyn. I have felt love and support from each one of you on every step of this journey.

Mom and Dad, thank you for raising me to love the Muppets, Monty Python, Tom Lehrer, Peter Schickele, and *Your Show of Shows.* Thank you for always allowing me to swan around the house in a hamster ball of my own imagination. Thank you for strongly suggesting I quit acting and become a writer. I am so grateful for everything you exposed us to so young and your complete faith that, one way or another, I would entertain people professionally.

David, Sophie, and Duncan. Thank you for believing that I could do this. And feeding me. And cuddling me. And for allowing me to be so far away behind my eyes. Now you know where I've been! I'm so happy to be back.

ABOUT THE AUTHOR

Photo © 2022 Timothy Becker

Nicola Kraus has coauthored, with Emma McLaughlin, ten novels, including the international #1 bestseller *The Nanny Diaries*, plus *Citizen Girl*, *Dedication*, and *So Close*. Nicola has contributed to the *Times* (of London), the *New York Times*, *Redbook*, *Cosmopolitan*, *Glamour*, *Town & Country*, and *Maxim*, as well as two short story collections to benefit the War Child fund: *Big Night Out* and *Girls' Night Out*. In 2015 she cofounded the creative consulting firm the Finished Thought, which helps the next generation of aspiring authors find their voice and audience. Through her work there, she has collaborated on several *New York Times* nonfiction bestsellers. For more information, visit www.nicolakrausauthor.com.